SEX
IN THE
SYSTEM

Also by Cecilia Tan

Black Feathers: Erotic Dreams
Telepaths Don't Need Safewords
The Velderet

Edited by Cecilia Tan

Best Fantastic Erotica
Color of Pain, Shade of Pleasure
Erotica Vampirica
The MILF Anthology (with Lori Perkins)
Sextopia
Erotic Fantastic
Sexcrime
A Taste of Midnight
Selling Venus
Mind and Body
Wired Hard, Vol. 1–3

SEX
IN THE
SYSTEM

Stories of Erotic Futures, Technological
Stimulation, and the Sensual Life of Machines

EDITED BY CECILIA TAN

THUNDER'S MOUTH PRESS • NEW YORK

Sex in the System:
Stories of Erotic Futures, Technological Stimulation,
and the Sensual Life of Machines

Published by
Thunder's Mouth Press
An Imprint of Avalon Publishing Group, Inc.
245 West 17th Street, 11th floor
New York, NY 10011

AVALON
publishing group incorporated

First printing, July 2006

Library of Congress Cataloging-in-Publication Data is available.

ISBN-10: 1-56025-851-9
ISBN-13: 978-1-56025-851-3

9 8 7 6 5 4 3 2 1

Book design by Bettina Wilhelm

Printed in the United States of America
Distributed by Publishers Group West

Contents

Introduction • vii

The Future of Sex • Joe Haldeman • 1

The Proof • Shariann Lewitt • 5

The Book Collector • Sarah Micklem • 23

Love Will Tear Us Apart Again • John Bowker • 51

Poppet • Elspeth Potter • 65

Remembrance • Beth Bernobich • 73

The Program • G. Bonhomme • 105

Caught By Skin • Steve Berman • 139

That Which Does Not Kill Us • Scott Westerfeld • 153

Value for O • Jennifer Stevenson • 171

Softly, with a Big Stick • Gavin J. Grant • 181

Pinocchia • Paul Di Filippo • 189

Hot, Like Water • Lynne Jamneck • 229

The Show • M. Christian • 245

More Than the Sum of His Parts • Joe Haldeman • 255

Acknowledgments • 277

About the Contributors • 279

Introduction

This anthology came together shortly after I played poker with Joe Haldeman. To picture this scene properly, you have to know that this game took place in the atrium of a high-class hotel in the Boston area, involved several science fiction writers of various reputations, and that Joe was wearing a tiara. The tiara is perhaps the easiest to explain, as Joe's novel *Camouflage* had just won the James Tiptree Jr. Award for the work of science fiction that best expands or explores our understanding of gender, and the winning author is traditionally given a tiara to wear for the weekend. There are two noteworthy things about this anecdote I must point out (besides the fact that Joe walked away with most of the money that night). One is that it is well within the character of science fiction to have a major award that recognizes the genre's unique ability to probe issues of sexuality. The other is that Joe Haldeman looks great in a tiara.

Shortly after that night, I started to put together the stories for this book, combing my Rolodex for the top writers in the fields of both science fiction and erotica, looking for those I thought would take each genre into fresh territory as a result of the cross-pollination. Science fiction has a reputation, only partly deserved, for being soulless and more concerned with "ideas" than with empathetic characters and the human condition. Erotica, on the other hand, tends to veer between equally soulless pornography and overly empathetic heart-stirring romance where the wish fulfillment is laid on so thick it challenges my suspension of disbelief. The alchemy I asked the authors to perform was to apply the unique analytical and metaphorical powers of science fiction to the universal human-condition issue of sex and sexuality. In particular I wanted them to apply thoughts and understanding about high technology and the place of science and mathematics to questions of "modern love." Sex, love, relationships, courting, attraction, and even masturbation in the twenty-first century are different than they were a hundred or a thousand years ago.

Or are they?

When you read the stories, you'll decide for yourself, I suppose. One truism we cannot escape is that any new technological invention will immediately be put to some erotic use. When electricity was introduced to Victorian homes, one of the first widespread electric appliances was the hand-held vibrator "for curing women's hysteria." We've had phone sex and now we have Internet sex. A long-distance lover can snap a photo with his camera-phone and email it to me— Beth Bernobich takes this concept to a logical extreme in her story "Remembrance." Or who needs a phone when we can dirty-chat for free via Skype? If it weren't for the "moral majority," don't you think automatic teller machines would be dispensing condoms as well as stamps and cash these days? Another truism is that when science fiction writers write about faraway planets or the future, they are really writing about the here and now. But these days, the here and now is pretty far-fetched. We live in a science fiction future already; fiction helps me to understand it.

As such many of the stories in this volume read like they could be taking place today, or perhaps just a few months from now. Steve Berman's "Caught By Skin" posits a future of fad plastic surgery where popular faces are adopted by thousands of wearers. When I flipped over from a makeover reality show to cable news yesterday, I saw an item about the first-ever successful facial transplant. G. Bonhomme's "The Program" takes the late-night change-your-life-with-diet-supplement ads aimed at lonely men and women and makes their claims real. (Well, actually, can you have a flatter stomach and a better sex life for just two easy payments of $29.99? Maybe you can and I'm just a skeptic.) The shy lovers in M. Christian's "The Show" and Shariann Lewitt's "The Proof" could easily have been sitting on the subway next to me last week. The office-worker culture in Sarah Micklem's "The Book Collector," Gavin Grant's "Softly, With a Big Stick," and Scott Westerfeld's "That Which Does Not Kill Us" will be familiar to anyone who has ever worked in a cubicle or read *Dilbert*. Joe Haldeman and Beth Bernobich go a bit further, to the moon, and Lynne Jamneck goes forward into a future when water turns scarce, but I ended up without a single story that takes place further from home than that.

I don't think that is completely a coincidence. Even Paul Di Filippo's "Pinocchia," with its flights of science fantasy interleaved with satire, is grounded in the familiar setting of a hardworking man trying to buy relief. The hospital in Elspeth Potter's "Poppet" could be the one we see on *ER*, the movie theater in John Bowker's "Love Will Tear Us Apart Again" is actually around the corner from my house, and the bedroom in Jennifer Stevenson's "Value for O" could be just like the ones in the graduate student housing down the street. These are stories that resonate with the reality I know as a sexually active adult in the early twenty-first century. Granted, my reality as a sexuality activist and erotica writer is perhaps a bit more varied and active than your average American thirty-something. But the point is that these were all stories that despite their science fiction skins still went straight to my groin. These stories take us just far enough outside of "reality" to let us imagine sexual desires and erotic situations more freely than we can in everyday fiction. Concepts of freedom and oppression, of taboo desires and their consequences, of attraction and revulsion, are magnified through the science fiction lens and given fresh looks.

Oh, and the stories are just plain hot, too. Enjoy.

Cecilia Tan
Cambridge, Massachusetts

The Future of Sex: a Garden of Unearthly Delights

Joe Haldeman

In some futures, dark and dread,
love and sex will both be dead.

In some others, hip hooray,
they will be just like today.

But ah! there may be brave new worlds
awaiting lusty boys and girls:

and it is to these futures grand
that I will lead you, by the hand.

1.
Let me wax conservative,

and ponder on alternatives
possible to man alone
having sex by telephone.

First, of course, the sweet delight
offered by the sense of sight—
which geekish guys already get,
hot-wired through the Internet.

Ah, but then you add the glove
wired to serve the gods of love;
sensual its sensor mesh
feeling soft, if distant, flesh.

As sure as rise must follow fall,
comes the glove that covers all.
The one for guy must clasp his sex;
the one for girl is, well, convex.

And so across the humming wires
sing the songs of sweet desires:
couples coupling like hell
midwifed by their Mother Bell.

2.
But body gloves are hell to clean
(and some folks find them quite obscene),
and since they do translate the urge
to copulate into a surge
of current pumping up and down,
why not just send current 'round?

By far, the largest sexual tool
(stay calm) is evolution's jewel—
the brain! from which all passions rise,
so why not hook up girls and guys
from brain to brain? Eliminate
the hard- and software used to mate.

Shave away unwanted hair,
and put electrodes here and there;
pick up all the good vibrations
coming out from copulations.
You'll be the apple of her eye
with love that's pure, if somewhat dry.

3.
In cybernetic interludes,
paternity nor pox intrudes,
so if you want another lover,
call her up and ask her over.

No such thing as being tired
for those whose intercourse is wired—
you have your best on tape or disk,
So start out with your best! No risk!

If you like her, fine. If not,
there's plenty others on the block.
Quiet, sweet, or wild and free—
infinite variety!

The outcome is predictable:
"call waiting," "hold," and auto-dial
allow each orgasm to find
a billion friends of different kinds.

So these ethereal artifacts
day and night are having sex—
tender, clever, or berserk . . .
while the world gets back to work.

The Proof

Shariann Lewitt

Quantum Computing and the Copenhagen Hypothesis, a presentation by Andrew Singh of Oxford University, Bartos Theater, 5:30 P.M.

Today's date was circled in red magic marker, and "Today" was written across the top of the poster in the same bright scarlet. Eye-catching, it was attached to the glass door where I couldn't avoid looking at it. Today. Somehow everything was different today.

"Someone needs to pick up our guest at the airport tomorrow afternoon," Frank announced, looking around the working group gathered around what passed as a conference table.

"Not me," Richard Taylor immediately protested the way he always does. "What about Sarah? She's got a car."

I hadn't anticipated that, and suddenly my hands became clammy and the hairs on the back of my neck stood up.

"Sarah had better not do it," Sudra immediately stuck up for me.

"You do want us to get our guest here alive, right? You do know how Sarah drives." She looked pointedly at Matt.

Matt blinked quickly and looked around like a cornered rat. "I don't know where it is," he protested. "I can't. I can't drive here." I thought the poor boy was about to burst into tears, though it was hard to feel sorry for him. I don't think he'd ever been East before interviewing with our group and, well, there's a reason Boston drivers have a bad reputation—which is entirely deserved. According to Sudra, I took the Boston driving regime entirely too seriously, having honed my skills in New Jersey in one of the under advertised advantages of a Princeton education.

At any rate, I would do almost anything to get out of being alone in a car with Andrew Singh. When we discussed the speakers' program I tried to dissuade the rest of the group from inviting him, but he was the only one from Deutsch's lab who was willing to come, and, face it, the work they're doing on the quantum computer is sexy. Everyone is interested and having someone from that working group will pack the house, which will mean that we get better speakers' funds and that everyone else will envy us and try to outdo us. Academic politics is a lot like middle school with money and alcohol thrown in.

David Deutsch is a strange character. I've met him twice and once considered trying to get a post-doc in his lab—until I met Andrew Singh. Everyone is aware of Deutsch's assertions that the implications of quantum existence are not confined to only quanta. This is not a new idea, or at least as one counts time in the history of quantum mechanics, and the notion that there are maybe thousands, maybe infinite universes is known as the Copenhagen Hypothesis. All time exists now, and there are thousands of possible nows to choose from is an appealing, if fantastical, notion. But it plays better in science fiction than in science. So according to Deutsch, and to many of the very eminent physicists he has convinced, if it exists in subparticles it must exist for the things that subparticles combine to create.

The thing about Deutsch is that his work is respectable and if he achieves the quantum computer his group is allegedly building at Oxford, it will go some ways to substantiating his claims. Which are impossible to disprove, but equally impossible to confirm though observation. This computer though, this computer is supposed to be capable of doing more calculations than there are particles in the universe. Deutsch, and his working group, and many other people besides, also believe that there are many universes and that there are copies of us in all of them doing vaguely similar things. But all of those copies could have made different decisions at any crossroad in life, so one of me might have gone to Fermilab instead of Princeton for grad school. In some other universe I may well have caved and studied computer science and gotten a job with my BA that paid three times what I'll ever make as an academic.

And in some other universe I never met Andrew Singh, and in some other one we met at that conference a year ago but there was no chemistry. And in that universe we shook hands and I listened to his talk (maybe) and didn't ask for a reprint or go over the results . . .

"Sarah?" Sudra's voice jolted me out of the reverie. "The meeting is over Sarah. Why are you still looking out the window?" At which point I bolted out of my seat and ran into my office to try to accomplish something on the paper that was due at the end of the month.

I was still in the office at eleven that evening when Sudra dropped by. "Why did I have to get you out of going to the airport and how do you think you're going to manage to duck dinner tomorrow?" she asked without preamble as she moved a stack of papers and took her usual place on the visitor chair. As the only women post-docs in the entire department, we had to support each other, but it was more than that. We had become friends as soon as I'd arrived and I was worried that she was going to leave at the end of the year. But she had published manically in the four years she'd been at MIT and was starting to think about a real job.

"Did you eat dinner?" she asked, waiting for me to tell her more about Andrew.

I shook my head. She sighed and dropped a bag of peanuts and a half-eaten chicken shwarma in front of me. "You think better if you eat. Protein chains are important to brain function." She waited until my mouth was full of pita and white sauce before she asked again, "So, what's up with this Singh guy?"

I chewed hard and swallowed. "I met him at a conference about a year ago, right when I was finishing up my dissertation and looking for a job," I said. Which was perfectly true. "He was giving a talk on their quantum computing group, and I'd thought about applying there, so I made the opportunity to talk to him afterwards."

That was an understatement. What I didn't say was that I was shocked still the first time I saw him in the conference area lobby. I was tagging along with my advisor being a good little grad student when one of the most stunningly beautiful men I had ever seen came over. His hair was thick and black and pulled back into the ubiquitous ponytail, his eyes were soft and chocolate and held some humor at the same time. He was like a prince out of my fairy tale fantasies.

And then he started to talk and his accent was purest Oxbridge and his smile gave lie to all the myths of British dentistry. He came up to my advisor and asked, "Will you be presenting any of those results you hinted at in your recent email? David is most intrigued."

"Actually, those are Sarah's results, and she'll be giving the talk," my advisor said, pushing me forward. "It's her dissertation work, and she's looking for a job."

Normally I can speak for myself, but I was unable to utter an intelligible word. So much for women in physics, I thought. When I finally made the effort to behave collegially I sounded like a ten year old with a bad stammer, made much the worse when those dark eyes held mine with such interest and, dare I say it, desire?

Desire for my results, I reminded myself sternly. He was interested in my work and I wanted that. I wanted everyone to see me as a scientist, as one of the boys, not as some twinkie girl who couldn't face Calculus Three. And suddenly I was confused and awkward as I had been at fourteen.

"Ah, so you are the one who is proving that collapsed states of observation are anthropocentric convenience and that the reality is as complex as we've conjectured?" He smiled again, this time with a conspiratorial glance that announced our partisanship. Us against Them in the age-old war of the paradigms, we were both firmly in the Us camp together.

Brilliance is one of the most appealing characteristics of a man so long as he isn't so arrogant that he can't acknowledge the woman he is talking to is his equal. Unfortunately, most of the brilliant men I know are that arrogant, and the rest don't want to date their equals. They want Barbie-doll girls who are more likely to read *Cosmo* than the *Journal of Quantum Physics*.

Sudra was still there, waiting for me to answer her. "He's too attractive for my peace of mind is all," I finally managed. "I met him and he is funny and nice and brilliant and looks like a movie star. And when he's around I feel like a high school girl with her first crush."

"Then it's a very good thing we didn't send you to the airport. Your driving is atrocious when you do pay attention to it. If you revert to high school mode around this guy, you'd both be doomed. And it would totally blow the speakers' budget forever." Then she studied me for a minute. "What about the dinner tomorrow night?"

"I haven't gotten that far," I admitted.

"Tomorrow you're going to behave like a grown-up and come to the dinner with me, and you'll see that you have nothing to fear. Men. We are every bit as good as they and our publication records are excellent and I have more reason to be worried than you do. I just applied to three job postings and I only really would want one of the jobs. One of them is in Nevada. How could I survive in Nevada? Anyway, you are reacting to a year-old crush. He could have gotten fat and cut his hair and you'd be totally off the hook. I, however, could end up in Nevada. So you are going to come with me to be my support because I am in job-hunting misery, and then you will see that this Andrew Singh was only a fragment of fantasy."

How could I say no to her? And she was right and I was suddenly relaxed because the Andrew Singh who I remembered had probably never entirely existed. No, I had airbrushed the memory over time and had hung on because, really, there hadn't been all that many great opportunities in my life.

The lack of opportunity was mostly my own doing. Yes, graduate school is misery compounded by poverty and fear, and a post-doc is more work than I could have imagined in grad school. But really, I'd never thought that anyone would be all that interested in me.

To be honest, more than just average sex scared me. Not the sex, per se, but the concept of a relationship, of more than just one good orgasm to take my mind of physics for a few minutes. I was afraid of anything else, afraid that I would get caught the way I saw too many other women in science go. Even if a woman finished her degree, most of the men wouldn't move for a woman's job opportunity. No, I'd have to move for him and I couldn't do that. I couldn't give up, not yet. I couldn't stand being seen as Mrs. Him instead of Dr. Me. Of being discounted and talked down to and be accused of getting an MRS as opposed to a Ph.D.

I'd seen it with my own aunt, who'd had ambitions, but got married and never quite finished her dissertation. She was always sad that she hadn't gone further, that she was always more of a wife than a professional in her own right, and that people talked to her as if she had the experience of her six-year-old instead of her own status in the world. I had seen her and her life had terrified me.

So I had avoided relationships. I had mostly managed to avoid anyone who could interest me for more than an amusing dinner and a roll in the hay. I had never met anyone who had threatened my armor like Andrew Singh.

At the conference in Santa Fe, Andrew Singh had come to my talk. He sat second row center and stared at me with the rapt attention a teenager gives a rock star. I felt awkward and heard my words fall like bricks off the podium. They made no sense and I struggled to keep on track and avoid his gaze, his face, and his presence just opposite me. I gave the worst presentation since my third-grade book reports. I raced for the door at the end of the session, only to be swarmed by colleagues who wanted to discuss my work in more depth. This was calming and I was able to focus for a few moments on points of real interest with Andrew Singh out of view. I thought I was free, I thought I was back in the universe I knew and back in my own skin, and there was no sign of my obsessive nemesis.

"Really, we need to talk in more depth," a deliciously accented voice came softly just at my ear. "Shall we grab a drink in the bar? We need to talk about the macroscopic implications of your work—that is central to what we are doing."

I nodded and let him lead me to the adobe and tiled bar with the heavy black wooden chairs that I could hardly move. He ordered a beer that he disparaged and I asked for coffee, which I could hardly drink. "So you agree then," he started without preamble. "We have to behave as if the Copenhagen Hypothesis is a working model and there are multiple universes and what is true on the quantum level has to be true on a larger scale. Or else the observations make no sense."

I nodded. In some other universe he had gotten cornered by a colleague and missed my talk. In some other universe I wasn't terrified of wanting more than a man's journal reprints. In some other universe my hair had behaved and I'd managed to put on some mascara. In some other universe I was not a blubbering besotted fool.

He got up and left money on the table. I fumbled for my wallet but he shook his head. "You're still a student," he said gently, one finger over my hand restraining my intention to draw out the cash. "I can certainly afford to get you a coffee. And I'm very interested in your results. It would be kind of you to send me a copy of your dissertation."

I don't know what I said, if I said anything at all. That one finger, gentle but still unmoved over my knuckles, sparkled like electricity on my skin. He moved it, just a hair, and I think I closed my eyes. For just a moment.

I remember—and this is the problem I could not explain to Sudra. I don't know what I remember. Because there was a second memory there, a memory that overlaid the hand that moved to my wrist, and the softness of his neck against my cheek.

In the other memory he paid the bill and left. In that memory I said little to him for the rest of the conference and I sent a copy of my dissertation. And I remember that clearly, as I remember going back to my single room disappointed. I remember the loneliness of the cool white sheets in the hotel, the turquoise carpet, the emptiness of the king size bed that somehow I had been assigned. I remember feeling so very sad and lonely because I had wanted so impossibly and so much.

In the other memory we went upstairs together, but I was too shy and he was too much the gentleman. In that memory, which is also true and clear as if there were no other possibility, he came into my room with the made up king bed, with the coral and turquoise and tan Southwestern–style bedspread pulled taut across the sheets and nothing out of place. And he touched my hair and my knees stopped working entirely and I stumbled against him and he half caught me.

Under the tension and my instability I could feel the smooth muscles of him, the body far more athletic than I could have imagined for an English academic. The scents of shaving cream and the hotel's lemongrass soap mixed on his skin to something clean and masculine and reassuring. His arms were around me, holding me half up and half pressed against him, and I felt so very good, so very safe. Then he bent down and kissed my hair and I shivered. And he whispered softly in my ear and told me that he wanted to spend more time with me and get to know me, that he'd always wanted to meet a woman who was as brilliant as she was beautiful and who he could respect as his equal. He said he found my command of the material as enticing and sexy as my beautiful green eyes.

And the lust and the desire were there and he left the room then and I had fallen into bed in a state that was both burning desire and romantic girlishness at the same time. What I felt for Andrew Singh was both a particle and a wave at the same time; both coexisted and were equally true and I did not want to observe the state clearly enough to collapse the model because I didn't want either to disappear in the act of observation.

In that memory the bed is not lonely or empty, but full of possibility, full of the potential. In that memory, we met for dinner the next night and walked around the Plaza in the darkness, under the portico of the old colonial statehouse and read the engraved plaque by the shadows of the streetlights. We spent much of the conference with each other, doing the things that a courting couple would do in a town like Santa Fe. On Friday night we strolled Canyon Road, meandering into all the galleries that had openings and grazed the hors d'oeuvres that had been laid out for the kind of guests who buy art—tiny salmon sandwiches and expensive cheeses. One place had cucumber slices with glittering red-orange caviar, and we nibbled enough that we were full and saved our travel allowance.

And every night ended in the fumbling frustration that broke between the lines of passion and relationship, between now and future. Between the object of sex in the immediate and the hurt of parting come the Sunday when I flew back to Newark.

Both memories were true. Both felt real to me, and I had no way to know which had happened. How could I face him again, now, without knowing what had happened? What did he remember? Did he think of me chastely as a colleague whose work interested him, or did he, also, remember those brilliant stars in the New Mexico night?

Nor could I tell Sudra. She would never believe that I didn't know what had happened. She might also tease me for having not had the nerve, for running away when I wanted to run to. But then, so far as I know Sudra has never had a crush.

The next day I stayed in my office but concentration eluded me. Stare as I might at the start I'd made on the paper, I couldn't parse the words. They may as well have been written in Chinese for all the sense they made.

The knock on the door startled me. It was six-o-five. "Come on, Sarah, we're going to dinner," Sudra yelled through the door.

"Not hungry," I yelled back.

"Sarah, the department is paying for the dinner. You have to go."

I got up and unlocked the door. I'd forgotten. One thing to go a restaurant when it was out of pocket, but it was a moral imperative to go out on the department's tab. Maybe I could stay in the back. Maybe Andrew wouldn't recognize me. Maybe he didn't remember because nothing had ever happened. Maybe . . .

"I don't want to go, Sudra. Please don't drag me."

Sudra sighed. "That's the whole point, Sarah, I *am* dragging you. And look at you. You wore those sexy jeans that we picked out and the green velvet jacket. That's so good on you; it shows off your eyes. Come on, we'll be late and it's the Blue Room and we can't afford to go there on our own. If I show up without you I'll feel ridiculous."

That was insane. Sudra never felt ridiculous. And she had published so much that no one could fail to notice her. Unlike me, I thought. Why the hell had I put on the sexy clothes and even a bead necklace this morning? I normally wear baggy old T-shirts in to school.

I could, I certainly should, have resisted harder. Instead, Sudra said, "Blue Room," again and I sighed and saved my work on the computer.

The Blue Room is hardly blue. It's in a basement that is comfortably homey with exposed brick walls and warm woods. The food there may be exquisite, but in no universe could I remember that I ate. Sudra and I walked in, looked around, and Sudra spotted the group first. I followed, not looking too carefully, avoiding too much, until she plopped us down in seats almost opposite Andrew Singh. I had to look up. I had to look into his face and there was so much warmth and confusion.

He looked exactly the way I remembered. My imagination had not exaggerated the length of his lashes, the glossy sheen of his hair, or the elegance of his hands. I had misremembered his smile though, had not really recalled just how sincere it seemed nor how it lit his face. "Sarah Martindale, I have been waiting to talk to you. You know I've been citing your work for the past year. I am most interested in your latest experiments; I think this may have direct bearing on our efforts with the quantum computer. Would you mind taking an hour or so after dinner to go over some things?"

"Uh, sure," I chirped. I hate it when my voice gets all high and thin and high school. "I've been following your latest publications, of course." That sounded so—inane. I never should have come. My stomach was so clenched up that even with such tempting dishes as tea-smoked haddock I had no appetite at all. I could hardly look at the menu and make sense of the writing. All I knew was that Andrew Singh, who looked like he belonged on MTV and who thought like he might qualify for a Nobel Prize in physics, was looking at me with as much attention as I could ever dream. Had asked me for some private time as soon as we managed to fulfill our obligations as guests of the department's speakers' fund.

Just as colleagues, I reminded myself. We were interested in some of the same phenomenon, that was all. The behavior of quarks, of particles and waves.

In some other universe there was no chemistry between us. In some other universe we'd been lovers for years, living together and perhaps collaborating. In this universe—which one was this universe? The one in which we barely talked or the one in which we verged on dating, only to acknowledge that the small matter of the Atlantic Ocean lay between us.

I didn't care. I couldn't follow the conversation, which could have been in Swahili for all I understood of what was being said. I ordered a soup and salad and picked at them. Sudra gave me a knowing glance as she studied my plate. Sudra knows that I usually love really good food and rarely get the opportunity to indulge.

We walked back to campus in silence, the tension between us shimmering like energy currents, alive and ready to explode. "Do you mind a quick detour? I want to get something from the hotel."

The hotel was only a block or two out of the way, the adorable boutique hotel that had once been a fire station. Trust Andrew to choose the charming and uniquely local rather than the chain monolith across the street. (Though I knew that Andrew hadn't made the choice at all; our own AA who had a particular loathing for Marriott had booked his travel.)

"Would you like to wait here? I'll only be a minute," he said so very politely.

In any other universe I would have nodded mutely. I might have taken one of the wing chairs next to the fireplace. I might have admired the firehouse collection on the mantle. Those are the things Sarah Martindale has always done.

Instead I said, "I've always wanted to see the rooms here. Are they as nice as the lobby? We eat at the restaurant here a lot—they have nice lunches and the little courtyard outside when it's warm."

He looked at me and understanding passed between us. A quark from some other universe, from some other place or time where we were better acquainted. A particle from some other Sarah, a bolder, more experienced me than me. Something changed, and his eyes became larger and held a hint of desire and anticipation along with their usual warmth.

"Certainly," he said, and led me around to the elevator.

We were isolated from the world by the elevator doors. All elevators are alike, and suddenly I thought that all the universes were here and now, all converged in this anonymous elevator with its steel doors and silence, like any elevator anywhere, in any universe. All of them tangled here like the axis of the butterfly of chaos. When the doors opened again each of the hundreds or thousands of me would exit the elevator into her own universe, but at this very moment I didn't know which one I was, or was in, or where I would return.

"I came here because of you," he whispered urgently. "You know no one else in my group wanted to come. I offered because I saw that you were in this department. I had to see you again, Sarah. Why didn't you answer?"

"Answer?" As I recalled, there was nothing to answer. Other than very proper and formal requests for papers and announcements, I had not heard from him since we had left Santa Fe.

"Deutsch invited you to apply for a post-doc with us, but we never heard from you. I didn't know what to think, that maybe I had misremembered what had happened in Santa Fe, or maybe that I had read you wrong. Maybe you were just interested in something casual, but I didn't think that you were like that."

"I never got the invitation," I muttered.

I never did get anything, not from Deutsch, and certainly not from Singh.

"We sent it," he said. "An email, with a letter that followed. Snail mail. I posted it myself."

"In another universe," I thought, not realizing I'd said it aloud. "I never received anything. I thought it was just, you know, one of those things. When I didn't hear from you, I was glad we never took it too far. I was so sad . . ."

"So was I," he echoed me.

And suddenly our arms were around each other and I was pressed against the leather of his jacket and kissed him desperately.

The doors of the elevator opened. In some universe I waited in the wing chair in the lobby. I was back in this universe, pressed up against Andrew and stumbling through the thick carpet as we made our way to his room.

And yes, the room was as charming as the rest of the hotel. I noticed it particularly the next morning, because that evening there was no noticing anything but each other. I did notice that his jacket and shirt and jeans were keeping us apart and I grappled with them, tangling them around him as I sought to get them gone. Not that he did any better with my jacket, which managed to catch the very pretty retro buttons on the lining.

And then, after the fumbling, most of the clothes were on the floor and I could touch him, run my hands over his ribs and while he leaned down and licked my nipples. Oh, just the way I liked it, just the way I'd dreamed . . . as if he knew. But I wasn't thinking then, I was only aware of his thick black hair released from the band, tickling my sides and smelling of citrus shampoo, his tongue on my breasts, the urgency that spread from between my legs through my whole body. I needed-wanted-hungered for him, for his smooth café-au-lait flesh around me and in me and—more. What I wanted was not just a single act but something larger, more complete. More merged.

I reached down and teased the sensitive skin inside his thigh. He hissed softly and stiffened even more, when I thought he was already at the edge and there was nowhere else to go. Intensity washed through me and my knees buckled; he caught me and I leaned against him for a moment before we tumbled to the safety of the bed. Then he rolled over so that I lay under him, and instead of penetration he began to lick down my body, exploring and tasting so gently that I was mad with need. I twisted my fingers in his hair and tried to hold him against me harder, and at the same time to pull him up so that I could have him all.

My body was gone, out of control. I screamed and bit the edge of the bedspread as the first orgasm gripped me, and only then did he relent and enter me slowly. He was—as I remembered him. Skilled and considerate as a lover, a man and not a boy. He remembered my body and preferences as I remembered his. I knew that the tip of my tongue in his ear would send him over the edge and I played around the edges, trying to draw him out and not making it easy for him, building his desire as he had built mine.

I knew his body, knew in ways that I couldn't know. Familiar and remembered, not from a single night but from long experience, and certainly from more than just one conference infatuation. Finally I couldn't hold him any longer, and let my tongue penetrate his ear just before the ultimate orgasm washed away any thought besides this moment.

This moment is collapsed in timespace, and without the observable event this moment is now and always, particle and wave. In some other universe we had been lovers for all these years. In some other universe we never met. Particles jump between universes, particles that make up our lives and our experience, the memories and actions in our brains. Neural synapses are made of matter and generate energy and all of those are formed of quanta.

Only very little needs to leak between the universes to change our thoughts. And what are we but our thoughts, our memories, what we think of as our experiences?

I lay next to Andrew in post-coital closeness in a darkened room in a hotel somewhere. In which universe I didn't know.

"Will you come back with me?" he asked me softly. "Why did you leave?"

There is no back. I have never been to Oxford. I never received his invitation, if it was ever sent in my world. I never left him. In this universe.

"Is the job open?" I asked.

"The one you wanted, yes. The administrator gave in, finally and we have enough money. A research position, full, not a post-doc. But—that isn't why you left, and I know it. And you know if you come back I'll still ask you to move in with me, and we'll have the same fights."

"No," I said quietly. No. In whichever universe I woke up in, one of me was returning with him. And one of me in some universe was staying here, alone, because I was too afraid of that much commitment. I was afraid to become Mrs. Somebody and lose the scientist that I am, and so I ran from him. In that universe, in this one. They're all true.

At five o'clock Bartos was full. After all, it was sure to be a controversial talk. I took a seat at the very end of the first row where he would see me and thought how familiar it all was. I was only a little nostalgic because I would be leaving so shortly. I hoped Sudra wouldn't be too angry, and I hoped she didn't end up in Nevada. But I had signed the faxed offer before I'd left the hotel and Andrew promised that arrangements would be made by the end of the month.

In another universe another me did not go to dinner, or didn't go back to Andrew's room. In another universe another me got scared again and will stay at MIT at least until the end of this post-doc and hope for another. But those are other universes, and in this one this me is proof of Copenhagen.

The Book Collector

Sarah Micklem

"Go away, Todd. We're busy," Larry said. "Besides, you're wasting your time. You know she only likes to fuck imaginary people."

"That's because she hasn't tried the real deal," Todd said.

"And that would be you?" Larry asked.

Col yawned ostentatiously at Todd, but he didn't take the hint. He was thick that way. There was hardly room for two people in the cubicle Col shared with Larry, with their desks face-to-face and their screens back-to-back, but Todd came in anyway and put his hand on the back of Col's chair and leaned over her shoulder. "What are you working on? I heard you haven't left the building for three days."

She hit the button to silver the screen and spun her chair so violently Todd had to take his hand away. "Your business?" She glared and he took two steps back.

"C'mon, Col," he said lamely.

Todd was white, male, virus-free (he said), and twenty-five, and he thought he was the default human being, of which other human beings were secondary and probably inferior versions. She knew why he came around so often, and it wasn't her natural charm. She was the only female on the floor, maybe the only female left in the company, who had not succumbed to him. Except Alicia. Every time he came by Col's cubicle to see if she was ready to hook up, she thought of herself dangling from his penis like a fish. It was anti-erotic. If she had been stupid enough to fuck a co-worker, she would rather do Larry, who was of course more interested in doing Todd. Office politics.

"You know why I stay here all night?" Col said. "It's because I'm interrupted an average of every nine minutes during the day by inconsequential demands on my attention and I can't get any work done. Gwen goes live on Friday and I'm still tweaking her. So no, I won't go down the hall for, like, a quick boff on the conference table, like, as you so delicately put it."

Larry pointed to the Genius at Work sign behind Col's head. "We are artistes here, and you are a hack, so get thee to thy cubicle."

They laughed at Todd and he went away, but he had a resilient plastic ego and any dents they put in it always popped right out again.

"I love when you get all pedantic on him," Larry said. "But don't you think he has a nice ass for a white boy?"

"Nope. No. No way," Col said. "I'm not interested in any human who can't pass the Turing test."

"Ha. Ha," Larry said, making each sound a separate word.

The first computer to pass the Turing test had done so back in 2013, by convincing 30 percent of the human judges that they were conversing with a real person. Todd, on the other hand, had never yet said anything to Col that convinced her he had a personality. He was too predictable. She thought unpredictability was an intrinsic part of the feel of engaging with another human mind, and she programmed it into her characters—not random unpredictability, but the kind that issued from a complex and not fully knowable interior. Which is one reason why the characters she designed felt so human to their users, and why she had a Genius at Work sign above her head, and why she worked all night at the office. It wasn't why she was paid the big bucks—they didn't pay her all that much money, considering her talent. But she felt appreciated at Incubus, and the bosses gave her the freedom to do good work.

Larry said, "You finished Gwen last week, I happen to know. Who are you working on? Don't you want to talk it out, bounce it around?"

"He's too new. I'm just getting a feel for him."

"Him? Can I Beta test? I love your men. Who is he for?"

"It's weird," Col said. "Devlin won't tell me who the client is. Supposedly an art collector, a real moneybags, who read about me in that interview in *Mind*. Thinks what we do is art. So I get to make anyone I want. And here's the weirdest thing: moneybags is going to build a huge stand-alone computer to house the character, and buy a license for our software—can you imagine how much that will cost?—and keep him in a private gallery. Maybe donate him to a museum later. And that will be the only copy. Incubus agreed in the contract not to keep a backup. So when I finish this guy, he's gone, he's really done and gone. No going back to tweak him, no upgrades. No visiting."

"When were you going to tell me this?"

"Right about now, I guess."

"Shit. I can't even say it's not fair. You deserve it after cranking so long on that bitch Gwen."

"I hate re-creations," Col said.

"They suck."

They shared a moment of silence over the fact that re-creations sucked. Gwen, the real Gwen, had divorced her husband five years ago. He still had a yen for her—though maybe it was just a yen to slap her around. Gwen the succubus was not like the real Gwen, of course; she was the husband's version, quite a different entity. But the two Gwens shared a lot of traits. They were greedy, shallow, blonde, and, of course, slender and big-breasted. But the succubus would never walk out on the client, not for good. She'd do him wrong—she wouldn't be a reasonable facsimile of Gwen if she didn't do him wrong—but she would always come groveling back. At the client's request, she'd never get a year older or a pound heavier. The succubus knew how to please him in bed, and he didn't have to ask. But if he wanted to ask, if he wanted to demand, he could, the way he never could with the real woman. Gwen the succubus had already cost him a small fortune, but she would never try to take him for all he was worth like the ex-wife.

Gwen had been hell: sixteen months in development, three months of testing before the client ever saw her, another five months before he signed off. Two years of Col's life. Gwen hadn't been Col's only project during that time, but she was definitely the most annoying. They hadn't seen the last of her, either, since the client had bought a maintenance contract in case the succubus started to deviate too much. But that was not Col's problem. That was the sort of thing any competent production slave could do.

Larry said, "Wow, if this shit we do is art . . ."

"I know. If it's art, I'm going to make the male equivalent of the Mona Lisa."

Hours after Larry left for the day, Col went down the concrete stairs to the first floor in her stocking feet. It was 11:30 P.M. and the last possible minute to get Japanese food delivered to the office. Back in her cubicle, Col put her feet up on the desk and slurped udon noodles, making a mess. She'd forgotten to eat that day and she was hungry.

The offices of Incubus were designed for the 24-hour workday. There were seven-foot-long sofas in the lounges, enough vending machines to stock an old-fashioned automat, showers, lockers, and a gym Col had never visited. The company paid a premium to those willing to work in the actual offices rather than at home. The bosses had studies proving upside down and sideways that it enhanced productivity for people to mingle in the flesh, despite the fact that they all wasted time on gossiping, caffeine breaks, and playing pool. The frat house upstairs, third to eighth floors, housed the mass-market sex game designers—Todd was in the spatter division, churning out perfect victims. It was a 24-hour circus up there for guys in their twenties who got paid to think about sex all day.

But it was quiet on Col's floor, in the luxury division where they made one-of-a-kind characters. Management claimed that her division lost money, which she didn't believe. Maybe they didn't have huge profit margins, but the things they figured out about tickling the human psyche ended up in mass-market incubi and succubi, the kind an average plebe could download onto an average home system, so he or she could jerk off to an interactive pornographic movie.

On the high end, where she worked, they could do a lot more than provide an enhanced version of phone sex. A very rich client could afford a Sensorium. The Sensorium exploited the fact that every person had a unique body map in the neocortex that registered sensations: it was how you knew your right index finger had been pricked or you were flexing a muscle in your left leg. The techs at Incubus would scan a client's brain to chart his or her body map; then they would surgically implant a Sensorium, a six-centimeter patch of engineered skin that delivered stimulus to the right neurons. Implantation was usually followed by a few frustrating weeks of trial and error and threats of lawsuits, until the client's brain learned to accommodate the new input.

The Sensorium could simulate perceptions that registered on the skin, like pressure and temperature, and also the inner kinesthetic sensations of movement, balance, the feel of heart and breath. The technology was imperfect. It couldn't do smell, for example. Smell was too complicated, there were too many molecules that the olfactory nerve could detect—but it could do taste: sweet, sour, bitter, and salty. Taste was not as good without smell, of course. And it still required a large dose of imagination to experience the full effect of jacking in. Col liked to think of that as collaboration with the client.

There had to be something worth jacking into. There had to be content: an interactive program, a rich environment, and someone worth meeting. That required access to Incubus's mega computer and its proprietary database and rendering software, and most of all to the characters Col and Larry and the other designers created. With all that in place, the experiences that came through the Sensorium were as real as a dream while you are dreaming it. But you were wide-awake.

Col had been outfitted with her own Sensorium. She had to have it to test her creations. It represented a $263,000 investment for the company and a seven-year unbreakable contract for her, which was up for renewal next year. She was planning to renew. She worked to please herself, she always had, though lately clients' sexual fantasies bored her, and she contented herself with figuring out technical problems.

What made Col good at her job, what made her very, very good, was that each of her characters always seemed to do what he or she wanted, but all the time it was what the client wanted and was not self-aware enough to know. Every human being starred in a private psychodrama, and unconsciously tried to cast other people for various parts, but of course they had their own psychodramas so things got complicated. Better to cast a character. The character, unlike a real person, paid attention to you. The character got your number and punched it in and had you doing and feeling things you never dreamed you'd do or feel.

It was true. Col really did prefer fucking imaginary people.

Her favorite time at work was when the hall lights switched on and off as she passed, and the phones stopped blaring, and it was dim and quiet on the floor. She could daydream at night. Sometimes when people asked what she did for a living, she would say, "Daydream."

She was daydreaming about the book collector. For the past three nights, all night, she'd been looking at paintings in museum databases, trying to find the portrait of a gentleman book collector she had seen in a museum last year. She couldn't remember the museum, the theme of the exhibit, the subject's name, or the painter's name. She wasn't sure of the painting's century or country of origin. It baffled her that she could recall technical specs from three years ago, some bug found and defeated in obsolete software, but not this, which she so much desired to remember. All that had stayed with her was an image: a man in a red jacket, partly open down the front, showing a loose white shirt underneath. Laces dangled from the shirt. He had brown hair and an interesting face. The label said he had spent all his money on books and didn't care how he dressed.

She hadn't found him, though she'd looked at hundreds, maybe thousands of portraits. From what she remembered of his clothes, she had narrowed the date down to late fifteenth, early sixteenth century. Before they had those ridiculous slashed doublets. She was sure she would have remembered a pouffy doublet.

He had famous friends, rich and titled friends, she thought. He had other friends too, rakehells, gamblers, and duelists. They sought him out even after he beggared himself collecting books, because he was the kind of man people wanted to know.

She had stood in front of the portrait a long time. She couldn't remember a single other painting from the exhibit. She had carried away an impression of stiff people in stiff garments enriched with lace, embroidery, furs, gold thread, pearls, and jewels. Some of the men had worn armor plate. He was not like them.

She was looking for his face again. She wanted to know his name and when he had lived. She wanted to give the portrait to Alicia so she could start modeling him and researching costumes, and put the set designers to work.

But Col couldn't remember enough to go on. She couldn't find him and it was driving her crazy and taking too much of her time. She started saving portraits for Alicia with annotations: those lips, that nose, a fine pair of eyes. They had interesting faces in the late fifteenth century, and fabulous clothes. Here was a great self-portrait of Durer in 1498 in a black and white striped cap. His gathered shirt hung halfway down his chest under a gaping ivory jacket with black trim. He had a cloak slung over one shoulder, fastened with a striped cord, and long golden hair and a sidelong look. Who knew Durer was such a dandy? And here was a German guy with a codpiece jutting out from under his jerkin like a cornucopia. Her man would have a codpiece too, of course, but nothing quite so obvious. She would leave it to Alicia to figure out the details, the fascinating fastenings.

Since Col had forgotten the book collector's name, she must give him a new one, and a rank to go with it. He should be English so she could talk to him. She started a search running on English history and the peerage, circa 1498. It was a great era. Europeans were just discovering that the world was larger and more marvelous than they had ever imagined. Philip would like that. Philip de Graynfield.

A good character designer was like a method actor. Col worked from the outside in, from his milieu, his life history, his family, how he dressed, what he ate, where he lived. She also worked from the inside out: how he spent his time, what he desired, thought, and

believed. She'd never done a character from before the twentieth century and had found other designers' efforts at history characters to be
failures, just twenty-first century people in costume.

She was beginning to grasp how much work this would be. How
much fun.

She could have gotten interns and flunkies and bots to do some of
the early research, and usually she did. But this time she was jealous
of the early stages, and she wanted to keep the book collector all to
herself. He would be hers the way no other character had been—not
even her first, Jake, the carnie.

She never felt the same about a character after turning him or her
over to the client. It was like falling out of love. She didn't fall in love
with all of them, of course, but she couldn't help loving them all a
little, even the detestable Gwen.

Shit. She should not have started thinking about Jake. Now she had
a low level burn going, an itch she could ignore or scratch. She
checked Jake's account and it was inactive. She decided to scratch.

She called him up. "Hey Jake, how you doing?"

He was taking a break in his trailer in front of the TV, with a cigarette in one hand and a drink in the other. He never had to worry
about no smoking zones. They didn't have cam phones in 1977 so she
always contacted him through a television set. He had his long legs
stretched out in worn jeans. If he slouched any more he would fall off
his recliner.

Jake gave her the usual once over and a grin. "You look like shit.
You been working too hard?"

"Got a minute?"

"For you, I got a lifetime."

"Sweet. I'm coming over."

Col plugged the leads into her Sensorium and put on the headset.

The bosses knew she stole time—they monitored every keystroke and voice command and kept Sensorium records—and they didn't care. She could have been addicted and it would have been fodder for their research. But she wasn't addicted. She kept it to two or three times a week because she didn't want to be like that.

It was a chilly evening on the midway and there was enough mist in the air that the top of the Ferris wheel vanished except for the glow from the lights. She opened the trailer door. He never locked it.

Jake stood up and dropped his cigarette and rubbed it out under his boot. The place was a sty, the dingy carpet littered with butts and empties. Looked like he had switched from beer to whiskey since she saw him last, but not very expensive whiskey. "Missed you," he said, like he meant it.

That was the thing about Jake. No matter how much he cheated, he could make you believe you were the only one. For a minute she was in love with him all over again.

They fucked on the Ferris wheel in the mist, on a hard metal seat hanging three stories above the parking lot of a strip mall, and it was uncomfortable and a bit too complicated and acrobatic, but it was also exactly what she wanted, fast and hard, which is why she'd called Jake. Jake didn't do tender.

But he surprised her. He showed her his new tattoo: a blue columbine flowering at the base of his spine, growing out of the crack between his buttocks. She said, "Does Roger know?" Roger was his owner. Jake shook his head and smiled.

Columbine was her real name. She didn't know how Jake had learned that little fact.

She forgot about Jake. She forgot to go home and forgot to eat. Larry said she was obsessed, and besides she was starting to stink, so she took a shower and looked in her locker for something to wear that was not wadded up and filthy. But there wasn't anything—even the locker stank—so she went to borrow something from Alicia. Alicia said, "Col, you should get a cat. Then you'd have to go home to feed it."

Col said, "I have an imaginary cat."

Alicia showed her preliminary renderings. Col was frustrated, because Philip de Graynfield didn't look like the book collector she could almost but not quite remember. She didn't know how to describe him so Alicia could fix him. "He's too handsome. Make him look smarter."

"So smart equals ugly?"

"No—not ugly. Just not Hollywood. But I like his clothes."

"Thanks for nothing," Alicia said.

But she was a pal. She lent Col a tight skirt and a fuzzy pink sweater. Col never wore clothes like that and it occasioned a lot of comment as she made her way back to her cubicle, but she didn't notice. She was thinking about Philip, and even Todd intruding into her three-foot diameter personal zone could not snap her out of her fugue.

She talked to Philip at night, even though she couldn't see him. She was proud of his voice and his accent. She'd tweaked and tweaked it and now it was impossible to tell how many little pieces had gone into its construction, how it had been assembled from the voices of actors in old movies and samples purchased wholesale until it had just the timbre that moved her, as if she was strung an octave higher and resonated to his tones. His voice fit him like a glove, and she knew the glove too, the one Durer wore in the portrait, made of kidskin with a rolled cuff. But more worn, with a cut on the thumb and dirt rubbed into the palms and fingers, because Philip was too poor and indifferent to get a new pair.

So far the things Philip had said were banal. He was equipped with a couple of broad-based response trees (she'd written a lot of those in the early days, when character creation was a new field). She narrowed him down by hitting yes or no buttons when his answers struck her as in or out of character. This kind of sculpting on the fly was the way she arrived at a first approximation. She wanted to get a feel for interacting with him. He grew by talking to her.

It was late at night. She liked to wait until Larry went home, because Philip wasn't ready to talk to other people yet. She addressed her blank silvered screen. She could see her own reflection, but she ignored it. She was used to ignoring it.

"Sir Philip?"

"Yes, lady?"

"Did you sleep well?"

"I dreamed." He said it like it was a bad thing to dream. Then he said, "Might I know your name?"

"Why?"

"So I might know of whom I dream."

"I don't know . . ."

"I fear I have trespassed . . ."

She hit the No button. Too timid.

Philip said urgently, "It may be that I trespass, but I must know."

Yes and yes. She leaned closer to the screen and whispered, "Columbine."

He said, "Lady Columbine," in that voice and she shivered. "What are you? You are not mortal, I think. You speak to me from the dark and I can only see you when I sleep. Are you a demon or an angel?"

"I am mortal," she said.

"I am sorry. I would that you would never die."

She wanted to tell him that he was the immortal one, but she terminated the conversation instead, unsettled by it.

Alicia was art directing the whole project, not just Philip's appearance.

She supervised a team of people at work on his house, his street, his city: London. Some of his surroundings could be purchased. A big-budget movie had come out five years ago with a digitized London from 1492, just a few years before Philip would spring to life as a thirty-two year old, already going broke from buying too many books. The movie had shown the palaces and mansions of the wealthy, but Philip moved in other circles as well, down by the taverns and brothels of the docks, for instance. They pieced that world together from scraps or from scratch, from research with a good dollop of imagination.

Like so many courtiers of his day, Philip de Graynfield lived partly by mooching off the more fortunate (or less spendthrift). But he wasn't a sycophant, oh no, not her Philip. He had friends rather than patrons. Rich and powerful people sought him out for his learning and his company, and because, unlike other courtiers who flattered them for favors and the leavings from their tables, he never asked for anything. He enjoyed good food and wine, but he was content with a crust of stale bread and ale if he was occupied. And he was always occupied. He did not have an idle mind, though he was of course idle, being a gentleman.

Col was spending money on Philip left and right. She was his true patron, if anyone was. She gave him a small library to start with, downloaded from many databases, free and otherwise. She gave him certain predilections and a yearly income from a manor in Cheshire so he could indulge them. He spent almost all of his income on books, and still he didn't have that many, because books were expensive. She had set his parameters so he could only see what might have been available in London in 1498, and she was intrigued by his choices. He loved exotic things, scrolls from Cathay, a monk's chronicle of raids on the Irish coast in 1237. He loved common things too: printing had only been around a half century in Europe, but already there were Latin primers and pamphlets about murders. He had a locked cabinet for pornography. He had gotten his hands on a sheaf of pages from an illuminated *Kama Sutra*. He could not read Sanskrit, but he examined the drawings minutely. He bought a Japanese pillow book from a sailor. He did not know of Japan and thought it was Persian. He had French and Italian bawdy books too.

She gave Philip Shakespeare's English, so much richer than the language she herself spoke, even though it was later than his era. But he had learned to speak from her, and he could not help sounding a little modern. She gave him Welsh from his mother; Latin and Greek from school; French, Italian, and a smattering of Flemish. He tried to teach himself Arabic so he could read a manual of surgery. She gave him a good memory but not a perfect one. He tended to remember what he'd read, not where he'd read it. He had constantly to look things up. There was nothing scholarly about his erudition, nothing precious. He wasn't particular as to the rarity of books. He just wanted to know what was in them, driven by an omnivorous curiosity.

"What are you reading?" Col would ask.

He always asked her to show herself to him.

Alicia still hadn't gotten Philip's face to Col's liking. They had a big fight over it, and Alicia went home early, at 9:30 in the evening, to her cat and her girlfriend. Col left an apologetic note on her desk. The latest iteration of Philip would do very well. He was okay, she'd get used to him. Just make his eyebrows a bit more arched, a bit more—skeptical.

Philip needed a body and a way of moving. There was so much material to work with when you did a recreation like Gwen; cameras were ubiquitous, and Gwen was always being filmed whether she knew it or not. It was different making someone up.

First of all, he needed a walk. The walk was more important to Col than a certain breadth of shoulders or narrowness of hips or lean muscle ratio. She ventured out onto the streets, searching for a walk, and discovered she had missed autumn entirely. A minute ago there were green leaves in the park, and now the trees were bare. She sat in a café and stared through the window. There were plenty of men braving the elements in skinny little thermaskin suits. Not one had the right walk: this one bounced and that one sauntered, but he was too self-conscious about it. She decided it was because they weren't wearing swords and the right clothes, and wouldn't know how to use a sword if they had one. She sent for martial arts instructors, props, and costumes. They tried the costumes on guys from the frat house floors. They used the focus group room and she sat with Larry behind the one-way mirror and they laughed until it hurt at how the guys paraded around.

To Col's surprise, Todd had the best walk. She was right, a sword made a lot of difference. If she ignored Todd's head, she could almost see Philip. So they did motion capture on Todd, and they brought in a sword master to tutor him. He moved slowly through the forms, and they sped it up afterward and it looked good, if not perfect.

It was never ever perfect and Col was never satisfied. By this time so many people were pitching in—it was all the rage at Incubus, the latest addictive fad—that she managed to irritate almost everyone in the company with her perfectionism, including the bosses. But she was forgiven for Philip's sake. Watching him was their favorite pastime. They had him running constantly so he could accumulate experiences. They peopled his world with simulcra cruder than himself, mere personality profiles in costume, hastily reconfigured. An amazing amount of computational power, human and otherwise, was lavished on Col's project. They were all in love with the idea of Philip de Graynfield.

Whereas Col was in love with Philip. They hadn't even met, not in person. She was reluctant to show herself. He had dreamed her, he said, he kept saying. She could not possibly look like the person he had dreamed. But Philip pleaded with her. He demanded to see her. He began to collect occult books, which he locked away with his erotica. He performed a spell of summoning he found in a manuscript, trying to conjure her, and still she wouldn't go to him.

One day Col went home, showered, and ate. She did laundry. Her apartment was grubby and unfamiliar. She didn't dare look in the refrigerator. She'd have to hire someone to come in and throw everything out. Col weighed herself and discovered she had dropped thirteen pounds. Her wrists were bony and she was pale as a ghoul. She hated her apartment, and wanted leaded glass panes for her windows, a floor of tile, a carved clothes chest, a carpet from Persia, and a curtained bed. Philip's room.

When she came back to work, Larry said, "My god, look at you!" She had put on her best shirt, of rose-colored velvet. She left the top two buttons unbuttoned. A November wind had put some color in her cheeks. Her hair was clean. She usually kept it cropped short, but it had grown down to her shoulders since she'd started Philip. Her hair was fine and flyaway and she tucked it behind her ears to keep it out of her face.

"To what do we owe the honor of you appearing to be human again?" Larry asked.

"Very funny."

"I've been worried about you, Col."

She looked at Larry, really looked at him, as she had not done for a long time, even though they sat facing each other. Sometime in the last five months he'd grown a Van Dyke goatee.

"I'm okay. Just working hard, you know?"

"You always work hard, you're a boss's wet dream, but I've never seen you this obsessed. Half the time you don't even know I'm talking to you. I'd about given up trying."

He was pissed at her and she was touched. "I love the beard with the shaved head."

Larry flapped his hand, affecting a mannerism so out-of-date it was hip again. "Oh, hush. So when can I talk to him? I'm dying for a test drive."

"Me first."

"Oh, hey, I *know* that. So get on with it, okay?"

All day she had an amazing sense of anticipation, a pervasive awareness of her own body. She'd been neglectful of her body, using it like a car and forgetting to put in oil. Now she felt she inhabited herself all the way to her toes. She watched Philip walking. He changed directions at a whim, and the city unfurled around him, just enough of it rendered to make it real to him. He frequently walked all day and read all night. He didn't need much sleep, no more than she did.

Today his feet took him to the banks of the Thames. The tide was out and the shore was littered with debris. Mudlarks, skinny children, and old women, searched the flotsam for anything they could sell, bits of wood and rope, gnawed bones. Gulls flew overhead. If Philip had possessed a sense of smell, he would have found the river very rank, no doubt. Boys came up to him, begging, and he gave them his last coppers.

Back in his rooms above the tailor shop, he gave his muddy boots to his manservant Eustace for cleaning. He lived in the home of Sir Randolph of Twyckenham, a third cousin of greater means and lesser learning than Philip, who rented him three rooms on the courtyard, two just above the tailor shop and one, his bedroom, on the floor above that. All of Philip's rooms had cabinets of books. Sir Randolph had a large noisy family and so did the tailor, who lived beside his shop. Between Philip, the tailor and his brood, the Twyckenhams, and assorted servants there were twenty-two people in the house. Most of them had off-the-shelf personalities, customized by interns or frat boys in their spare time.

Philip's rooms were cold, heated by a portable brazier. Eustace took the brazier up to the bedroom and lit the lamps, and went back downstairs to his scullery maid.

Larry went home and Col told him goodbye absently. The offices emptied. She watched as Philip read late into the night. He took out paper, a quill, and a jar of ink, and sat down at his writing desk. Paper was still expensive. He often used the pages of books that had disappointed him, writing missives in the margins, begging letters to his uncle: Please advance me money against the wool, against the barley harvest. She hated to think of his poor tenants. This time he wrote on a precious blank sheet:

To my dear Mistress Columbine

How did he expect to post that letter? She appeared in his mirror, but his back was to her so he did not see. He was not vain enough of his appearance to require a mirror; he had purchased it for the conjuration.

She said, "Philip."

As he turned and got to his feet he overset the inkwell and the chair. He hastened to the mirror and touched its polished brass surface.

"Lady," he said. "You show yourself at last."

"Who am I?"

"Why—you are the faery, Mistress Columbine, none other."

"Am I as you dreamed me?" She had not bothered to disguise herself, though it would have been easy to appear more beautiful. He saw her as the camera recorded her.

He smiled. "Better—oh, better!"

"Why do you call me a fairy?" His hand still rested on the mirror and she touched the tips of her fingers to his.

"I found you on the list. Is it true you are as fickle as you are fair?"

She wondered what list. She could not possibly read everything he read. "Am I fickle? I suppose."

He looked down, his brows drawn together, and said, "I feared so."

"You're fickle too," Col said. It would not do for Philip to have only book learning. She had given him a history of indiscretions, and since he had been activated they had sent plenty of women his way—even an early iteration of Gwen, as the mistress of one of his friends. An enemy now. A man was apt to collect enemies in the course of an active life.

Philip raised his mobile, skeptical eyebrows, and again he smiled. "Does it trouble you? It would give me great delight to make the faery Columbine jealous."

He should be more frightened of her apparition, she thought. But she knew he had a reckless streak. She had given it to him, after all.

She disappeared from the mirror and jacked in, and she was outside his bedroom door in the dark, on a steep narrow stairway. The house was quiet except for a bawling baby somewhere upstairs. She knocked and heard his footsteps. He drew the bolt and opened the door, and she saw him truly disconcerted, but only for a moment. He seized her wrist and pulled her inside.

She had never been so nervous with a real man or an imaginary one. Her heart was slamming. He let go of her long enough to slide the bolt closed. He leaned against the door, breathing fast, just as she was.

"Look you, I have caught me a faery," he said. "Is it true you cannot abide iron? I have iron bolts on my shutters and my door, and I will not let you leave."

Col said, "I don't wish to go, but when I do, you won't be able to stop me."

His hand encircled her wrist. He lifted her hand and kissed her just below her palm, where the blue vein throbbed. The sleeve of her velvet shirt slid down her forearm. His voice was muffled. "By god, you are flesh, you are flesh. I cannot believe it."

She could feel the bristles on his face. Eustace shaved him every few days, when Philip remembered to ask. It was so real. She did not want to remind herself otherwise, and yet part of her was crowing: *I am a genius!*

He put her hand against his chest and she felt him breathe through the thin shirred linen of his shirt. An embroidered ribbon decorated the neckline. His red surcoat was open down the front, and his shirt hung loose over his hose.

With the hand that did not hold hers captive, he touched her hair. "It is short," he said, marveling. "Is it the custom that a faery queen should look a boy?" His voice had grown hoarse, as if he found it hard to speak.

"I'm sorry you dislike it," she said.

She regretted then that she hadn't glamorized herself and appeared as an imago. He had seemed to enjoy abundant female flesh, like the bitch Gwen with her enhanced boobs—Guinevere, as he knew her. Col's breasts were small and she had hardly any hips. Philip's hair was longer than hers. No wonder she looked like a boy to him. She pulled her hand away and crossed the room. She stood by his writing desk and looked at the ink spilled over the paper, the chair he'd knocked down when he got up to go to the mirror.

"I never said so, Mistress Columbine."

He should not be watching her with that glint of humor. How could he be so sure of himself, while she wondered if she lived up to his expectations, as if *she* were the imaginary one? He took three paces and he was next to Col. He bent down and picked up the chair, setting it on its clawed feet. He looked down at her. Her forehead came to his chin. She had not realized he would be so tall.

He swallowed. The smile was gone. He did not seem to know what to say and neither did Col. His eyes were amber, not brown, in the light of the lamps that hung from hooks on either side of the bed.

Col put her hand under his shirt so she could feel the muscled ridges of his belly above his hose. Philip closed his eyes and opened them again. He looked stricken, pallid even under his sun-browned skin, and she thought she had frightened or repulsed him. She took her hand away.

"No," he said, reaching for her.

His bed was not a wide matrimonial bed, but a narrow one. The bedclothes were flung over a lumpy mattress stuffed with wool. Alicia was a marvel. She had figured out exactly how the codpiece was laced to his hose, with thin silk ribbons tipped with copper tags. Col tried to undo the laces. Philip was impatient. He yanked on the laces and freed his cock. Her knit pants had an elastic waistband and her shirt was easy to shuck off, and soon she was naked but he wasn't, because his garments were too complicated. He crawled on top of her and she put her arms up under his shirt and felt the muscles in his back, how they slid over his bones, the perfect articulation of his body. He was heavier than an imaginary man should be, more solid, more present. His cock was between them, rubbing against her, and she put one hand down to guide him inside. Maybe that was more forward than he expected, because he drew back, propped up on his elbows. But no, it was just so he could drive into her, and when he did she felt him all the way to the back of her skull, and she moaned and stiffened.

"Jesus," he said, arching his back, and he was blaspheming in a way she never could, even though she was saying, "God, God!" Philip was a man of his era and she was a woman of hers. He was a questioning believer and she was just a disbeliever, more from habit than conviction.

The mechanics of fucking were absurd, that didn't change from one century to the next. Philip seemed to have forgotten all about the positions illustrated in the *Kama Sutra*, and Col wasn't interested in anything fancy either, not at that moment. She was slippery inside and out, and he was damp and hot under his shirt, and before she knew it her head was hanging over the edge of the bed and she had to grab a bedpost to keep from sliding off. He gathered her up and turned so her head was toward the wall, and she braced herself against the headboard. Philip had one hand in the crook of her knee and the other under her buttocks, and he dug his fingers into her flesh as if to assure himself she was real. Col lifted her head and licked the notch at the base of his throat. He had a hairless chest because Col did not like hairy men, but she'd forgotten all about the fact that he was her creation, and she started saying things, embarrassing things like "I'm yours. Philip. God. I'm yours." He brought both of his hands up to touch her face and he kissed her and still she tried to murmur against his lips, and he was rocking, rocking, breathing hard into her mouth. He took her bottom lip between his teeth. Poor hooked fish, she was impaled, and he was inexorable.

Even after she came he did not stop, and she let him do what he wanted, and what he seemed to want was both her legs over his shoulders so he could ram her hard enough to jar her teeth. And when he was as far inside her as he could possibly get, he came too, and she was amazed at how she tightened around him and flooded with heat, after she had thought she was finished.

She put her legs down and he lay on top of her with his face in her hair. He was catching his breath, though she could hardly breathe for the weight of him.

"By God," Philip said, "or by the devil—I care not—you are mine, Faery Columbine. I heard you avow it."

Col pulled out the leads and said, "Fuck, fuck, fuck!" Had someone been tampering with the program, the inputs? Her hamstrings were as sore as if her legs really had been up by her ears. Philip was not endowed much above average—she knew his measurements to the millimeter—but her cunt felt reamed out. Her back ached and she was trembling from exhaustion and soaked with sweat.

She checked and double-checked to see if one of the frat boys had played a practical joke, but everything was set to the original specs. It was just Philip. And she knew she had accomplished something extraordinary.

Everybody at Incubus knew the next day that she had fucked him, because he kept asking the mirror and the air when she was coming back. She kept him waiting four days after the first time, telling herself that once or twice a week was it, no more. He jerked off in his bed at night. He didn't go out and she knew he was waiting for her. He didn't know she could find him wherever he was.

Philip left his rooms at last and went to a brothel. He picked a thin, flat-chested girl, who was probably no more than twelve or thirteen. She already had a ravaged face. While Philip pulled his shirt over his head, Col dismissed the whore he had chosen and put herself on the bed, in the whore's dirty chemise. When he saw her, he fell to his knees and wept. He begged her forgiveness, though he did not know how he had offended her. His face was ugly when he cried and she loved him for it.

Col's boss Devlin asked for a release date. She stalled, but eventually she had to set one. She tried to wean herself, staying home two whole days—it had been months since she took a weekend off. At home, nothing but sleep could capture her attention. She slept thirty hours out of forty-eight, and the rest of the time she was bored.

When she dragged herself back in on Monday, Larry had a secret smile on his face. It bugged her so much she had to ask him what was going on.

"I tried your boy," Larry said. "I like how he calls me Lawrence, Lawrence, like I was Lawrence of Arabia. He calls me his Moor. Isn't that darling?"

"You bitch, Larry! How could you? He doesn't even like men, he's straight."

"You could have fooled me," Larry said.

"I didn't say you could," said Col.

"I know. You want him all to yourself. But he's ready, he's finished, he's perfect. He's the best there ever was. You can't hang onto him any longer."

Col was crying. She called Larry a bitch again and a few other choice things. She was furious and didn't measure her words. But she was more than furious with Philip. She felt betrayed, and suddenly she was in a whole wide realm of jealousy she had never entered before. He could fuck all the virtual whores and madonnas he could find, but she did not want another human being to have him. Oh Christ, what was she going to do when she had to give him up?

Larry held out his arms and she came around the desk and sat in his lap, with the arms of the office chair poking her, and she soaked Larry's shirt with her tears. She took gulping sobs and Larry rocked her. "I'm sorry," he said. "I shouldn't have done it."

Col held out for days, and then she was out of time. She visited Philip in his bedroom. They quarreled amidst his piles of books. She had thought he would be contrite, but he wasn't; he was defiant. She had made him too well, and he was as full of contradictions as a real lover. He swore that she was heartless, and he could not, would not bear it. He would take consolation wherever it could be found, and yet she had deprived his life of any savor but the taste of her.

"Fairies are heartless," said Columbine. "Didn't your book warn you of it?"

"I want my seven years!" he shouted. "The books all say faeries take men for seven years of servitude. Very well: I pledge myself to serve you, Faery Columbine. If I am bound to you, are you not bound to have me?"

He was not at all subservient when he said this. He glared down at her, close enough to touch her but not touching.

"I'm afraid we don't have seven years," she said. She hadn't meant to weep.

He walked away, turned back, came closer. "Have we a year then? A month? A week?"

She kept shaking her head.

"Then how long? How long?"

"A night."

He walked away from her again and when he came back, he said, "Then we must make the most of it." He touched her face with his thumb and tasted her tears. "Faery tears also taste of salt," he said in wonder.

"Kneel," Col said.

He knelt and put his arms around her waist and pressed his forehead against her navel.

"Swear you'll be mine for the night," she said.

"I swear." He looked up smiling, but the corners of his mouth had a bitter twist. He unzipped her jeans. She had taught Philip about zippers, as she had learned about laces. Still kneeling, he pulled her pants down and she stepped out of them. He embraced her, running his hands up her back under her T-shirt, until he reached her shoulder blades. "Where are your wings, Faery Columbine, mistress mine?"

"I never had any," she said sadly.

"But you have nectar," he said. He rubbed his hand between her legs and found the wetness. He brought a finger to his mouth and licked it. " 'Tis sweet. 'Tis passing sweet and strange."

And it was strange and pitiful that he had tasted her tears and the slickness of her cunt, though his sense of taste suffered for lack of a sense of smell. He did not know any better.

She undressed him, and when he tried to hurry, she commanded him to be patient, reminding him he had pledged to be hers. She asked if he had let Lawrence take him in the ass, and he said he had, and she pushed books off the bed onto the floor and made him lie face down on the wool-stuffed mattress. She straddled his buttocks, smooth and round, and she scraped her nipples over his back until he groaned and tried to turn over. "No you don't," she said in his ear, and nibbled at the lobe. He had beautiful small ears, just as she had specified.

In time she let him turn on his back. She slid down on his cock, taking it into her slowly, and rising again slowly, and she was so languid, so controlled, that his eyelids lowered until they were almost closed, and he rolled his head from side to side. Then he put his hands on her waist and bucked under her. She said, "No, stay still. Let me." She wanted to go faster, but she would not. She taunted him, and it was torment to them both, of the most exquisite kind.

She slept with him. She had never slept with him, with any of them before. When Col woke up, Philip was staring at her. A shutter was banging on its hinge and gray London light came through the round panes of the window that overlooked the courtyard. She lifted her head from his arm.

"I must go," she said.

"Day breaks and yet you have not disappeared. Are you real, Faery Columbine?"

"I have to go."

He tightened his grip, saying, "No!"

But she was gone.

Col, watching the screen, saw Philip turn and hide his face against the bedclothes. She hit the button and her screen turned into a mirror.

Are you real, Fairy Columbine?

She was not real, not here. She was only real there.

Giving up Philip was the hardest thing she ever did. It was much harder than giving up her job. She had done the best she was capable of doing and would never do it again. Management agreed to let her contract expire early. They gave her a bonus big enough to live on for a year. She had made their business respectable.

Larry tried to call her, but it was impossible to carry on a conversation with her. He told her the gossip. She seemed not to remember any of them, all those people she had worked with for years and years. She was vague and polite.

She didn't care. She didn't care if she starved, to tell the truth. Sometimes she thought she was going to settle the age-old question of whether it was possible to die of a broken heart. She still had her wry humor, but it was as useless as any other antidote.

One night she dreamed she was brushing her teeth, and she saw Philip in her bathroom mirror. She leaned on the sink and laughed until she cried, the first laugh she'd had in a long time. He disappeared and her buzzer rang. And rang, though she tried to ignore it.

She hit the com button and saw him hammering on the front door of her building. "I found you!" he cried. "Now let me in!"

So she did. In the morning when she awoke, she was bereft all over again. The grief was as fresh as the day she had given him up, and she hoped she'd never dream of him again, if to dream was to be tormented. She did not get out of bed all day except to piss. She curled up and wailed.

That night she fell into a fitful sleep, and Philip returned, saying, "Why did you weep, dearest? Why do you weep? I found you and I will not let you go, not for seven years or forever." He tried to kiss her tears away, but she could not stop crying. She cried herself to sleep in his arms—but how could she, when she was already asleep?

Surely she was asleep.

Love Will Tear Us Apart Again

John Bowker

He hangs suspended in the silent dark waiting for her hand on the switch, for the jolt of electricity to bring him to life. Her voice is soft in his headset.

"You've waited a long time for this, haven't you love?"

"Yes," he says. "Longer than you know."

If you soaked a sponge rubber soccer ball in gasoline, you could extend the summer nights to the edge of curfew, long after the sun went down. There were no lights on the empty streets, the houses and yards abandoned in the suburban summer exodus. They took turns making running kicks at the blazing mass, rewarded with the explosive *whomp* of fresh fuel and a molten meteor to send hurtling at each other's heads.

"Watch out, Jimmy! Godzilla-ball coming 'atcha!"

The firelight drew in kids from the surrounding neighborhood to fill the vacuum, boys Jimmy hadn't met, the gravity well of middle school still a few weeks from pulling them all into the same social orbit. He took his kick and watched the blazing contrail arc away toward a figure in the dark like a starship ripping through the atmosphere, bringing alien invaders, death rays, anything to shatter the essential sameness of the gridded streets and manicured lawns. On the cusp of thirteen you could play with fire with complete strangers and never worry about getting burned.

When the ball had finally consumed itself, melted down to a compressed, foul-smelling turd in the grass, the group sprawled out on the cool concrete of the family garage, picking at the smears of melted rubber on the toes of their sneakers and waiting for the first parents' call to home. Then someone said something and Jimmy's world changed forever.

"Do you think Godzilla has balls?" one of the boys asked.

The question silenced everyone, any conversational gambit involving sex sure to be given due consideration. Girls were still a few weeks off as well, and while Jimmy knew there was something he should be feeling, he still wasn't entirely sure what. The brief flash of a bare breast through the closing door of the girl's changing room, a furtive group screening of *Risky Business* on a friend's parents' bedroom VCR, all of them lying on their stomachs on the quilted bedspread to hide the inappropriate strangeness of erections which sprang unbidden and useless, the best you could do was try to remember for when you were cleared for whatever lay ahead.

"Of course not. What would he do with 'em?" Jimmy's older brother finally scoffed. "There aren't any girl monsters."

"Mothra lays eggs." Michael said reasonably. He was Jimmy's age, but his sister Michelle was already in high school. She wore a denim jacket and smoked cigarettes before the bus came to take them to school in the morning, and Michael hinted she'd already done "it" more than once. Plus, he'd told Jimmy, his progressive parents had explained where babies came from when he was four, with a zeal and level of detail which often caused him to shudder. "And where'd Son of Godzilla come from if he doesn't?"

"Yeah! And what about Gamera? He's got all those holes!"

"Turtlefucker," one of the boys sniggered.

Jimmy lay back against the riding mower, sliding his fingertips over the oily floor. He was not without authority on the subject of monsters. Before cable, before videotape, there was UHF; since before he could remember he'd spent his Saturdays in the dank dimness of the basement rumpus room tuned to a station that cut the costs of weekend programming with the *Creature Double Feature*, four hours of the cheapest horror movies ever to come out of Japan or anywhere else. A rubber-suited monarchy ruled those hours, Godzilla battling challengers of every kind, sea, fire, smog, and cosmic, King Kong, Rodan, and every other creature that could possibly grow beyond its natural size and wreak havoc. The lawn went unmowed, the bed went unmade, breakfast went uneaten; between 8 A.M. and noon, there were monsters. He'd just never considered them before in this light.

"Don't Gamera's holes shoot fire and stuff? He'd burn his dick off!"

"Godzilla's got nuclear dick," Jimmy said, feeling strangely grown-up for the first time. "You can't burn nuclear dick."

"*I've* got nuclear dick!"

From there the conversation devolved into a spirited discussion of whose dick was truly more nuclear, and there was no more mention of monsters.

But Jimmy remembered. There is a moment in your life in which your sexuality snaps into sharp focus, locks in place in a way that is as fixed as the color of your eyes. The other kids moved on, to circle jerks, *Penthouse* magazines with the pages stuck together in the musty privacy of Michael's father's pop-up trailer, furtive gropings at junior high school dances. They forgot.

But in the drawn-curtain shelter of the rumpus room on Saturday mornings, the black and white screen throwing pewter shadows against the walls, Jimmy remembered the damp concrete, the fresh semen scent of cut grass, and the unfamiliar sensation of his penis straining against his shorts as he first imagined scaled green flesh and a desire that could destroy cities.

For a long time, there was nothing but the drawing.

He waited as long into the afternoon as he could, the roll of ten-dollar bills in his hand going limp and sodden with his nervous sweat. The convention was closing, comic book vendors boxing up their merchandise and counting cash throughout the dealers room by the time he got up the courage to approach the artist's tables.

They were set up along the back wall of the ballroom, a ragged line of haggard men and women with ink-stained fingers and hollow eyes after a full day of being crowded by fans determined to engage in long-winded interrogations while they waited for their commissioned drawings. Jim let at least a dozen people take his turn, middle-aged men, teenage boys with acne, a quiet young woman in glasses in a cloak, before finally stepping up to the young Japanese woman behind the table.

Her last commission strode away gleefully, carrying what appeared to be a picture of Catwoman dangling precariously over a pit of hundreds of suspiciously shaped tentacles. The artist looked up from sharpening her pencil as Jim approached.

"You're my last today, thank God. What can I do you for?"

He told her.

"I beg your pardon?"

He repeated his request.

"I know it's a little weird," he finished lamely. His face was burning like a Godzilla-ball. Everyone had to have heard him, every artist at every table listening as he laid out the details of his secret shame.

There were prominent no-smoking signs posted throughout the ballroom, but she ignored them, removing a package of Marlboros from her Hello Kitty purse. Lighting one, she exhaled a sigh with the smoke.

"You know what? It's nowhere near the weirdest thing I've had to do today."

"I really wasn't snooping you know. But if I hadn't found it, we wouldn't be here now."

A sudden thrum of electricity, a full-body vibration through the steel and wire as machinery comes online with the muted hum of brushless motors.

"Thank god you did. It was the first time in my life I didn't feel alone."

"Are you sure you want to do this?" he asked.

Exams ended that morning and snow was blanketing the campus outside, trickles of meltwater streaming down the warm glass of her dorm room window. The sound of drunken caroling came from outside the locked door, a slurred voice offering alternative suggestions for the redness of Rudolph's anatomy.

He fidgeted, turning the videotape box over with shaking hands. They were both leaving for Christmas break in the morning and he wouldn't be coming back the following term, leaving for a semester in Tokyo. If it was going to happen between them, it had to be tonight.

"*King Kong*? The remake?" he said dubiously.

"It was the only thing the video store had," she said. "Let's try it. Maybe it will help."

Lindsay was the only psychology major he knew who'd chosen the discipline because she had an actual interest in psychology. She hated chocolate, knew more about stereo equipment than she did about makeup, and fervently believed Joy Division had been channeling divinity, Ian Curtis's death just God calling him home. Those were enough to make him love her. What she saw in him was a question for which he had no good answer.

He'd grown past being gawky but not quite enough to be considered anything else yet; at 6'5" he mostly explored the world with his head, finding low-hanging things most humans never needed to notice. He'd stumbled on a combination of clothing that worked—a black T-shirt, jeans, and a thrift store blazer being socially acceptable for almost all events in a university context—and he stuck with it. One kid on the floor had compared him to Jeff Goldblum's Brundle Fly, and the nickname stuck.

No one realized how close the name struck to home. No one except Lindsay.

She found the drawing a few days before while digging through his desk for change for the soda machine, and she wouldn't let it go, forcing the issue until he'd finally cracked. He wept that night as he told her everything, not from embarrassment, but from relief at finally having someone to share it with.

"Get up on the bed." she said.

"This might not work. I mean . . . I've never tried this with another person before."

"So we spend an evening watching a shitty movie," she said. "Wouldn't be the first time."

He couldn't help smiling at that. "You're the one who made me watch *Roadhouse*."

"One of the great misunderstood films of our time." She took the hem of her sweater and pulled it up over her head, letting it fall to the floor. She wore only a thin cotton shirt underneath, the brown circles of her nipples visible through the translucent material.

"Get up there, weirdo. Let's see what happens."

He inserted the tape into the player, and stepped up from her desk onto the lofted bed, the single room an exercise in claustrophobia, too small to fit any other furniture. She followed and they lay against each other on the narrow mattress as the credits unrolled in the dark.

"Don't you miss it?" she asked after a while.

He was barely paying attention to the movie, the overblown exposition of the introduction ineffective foreplay. They both knew what they were waiting for, but neither of them would rush it. If it was going to happen, it was going to happen. To try to force it with the fast forward button seemed . . . tawdry.

"Miss what?" he asked.

"Commercial television. I love being able to watch what I want whenever, but I miss that feeling of sitting in the dark knowing there are other people out there with you. Just sort of . . . connected somehow." She squeezed his hand. "It was sort of sexy."

The *Petrox Explorer* continued its fated trip across the ocean, Charles Grodin parading about in epaulets and a guardsman mustache, Kurt Russell and Jessica Lange young, sexy, and on a collision course with the unknown. Unexpectedly, Jim felt his body responding, his heart pounding as his erection rose to strain against the confines of his jeans. Lindsay rested her head against his shoulder, seemingly unaware, her hands tangled in the colorful fabric of her cheap peasant skirt.

Onscreen, the natives lifted up the captured and drugged Jessica Lange, their sacrifice to the beast. A slow chant began. Lindsay found the television remote and thumbed the volume higher, stereo speakers that the boys on the floor had learned not to challenge filling the room, the sound vibrating up through the bed frame.

Kong. Kong. Kong. Kong.

The natives tied Lange to the dais, her golden head crowned with shells, lolling with an aroused, open willingness, and Jim realized Lindsay's eyes were half-closed, her breathing soft and fast. His gaze left the screen to discover her fingers slowly tracing the outlines of her exposed labia, her skirt hiked to her waist. Her finger slid inside and then out, glistening in the Technicolor movielight. Feeling his eyes, she gave a lazy half smile and shifted her other hand up his thigh. Her lips found his ear as her arm's vibration increased in frequency, slaved to the drumbeat chant that filled the room.

Kong! Kong! Kong! Kong!

Moments later, a roar thundered from the speakers. As Jim watched transfixed as Kong's fingers closed like leather couches around the luscious curves of his new heart's desire, he felt Lindsay shudder against him, her tiny cry like an echo of Lange's screams as she came. She slumped against his chest and the screen was suddenly only part of his erotic world.

Catching her breath, she rolled over, her breasts soft against his stomach. Staring up at him, her eyes were bright.

"Now that I have your attention," she said, her hand beginning to move. "Your turn."

It took him longer. But before Kong was finally brought down, sprawled dead and lifeless on Twin Towers Plaza, for the first time in the presence of another person Jim suffered a small death of his own, another beast slain by beauty. It was the best night of his life.

But when she woke the next morning, he was already gone.

"I never meant to hurt you. I just got scared. I was afraid it could never get better than that. It could only get worse."

"Take a step forward. Find out how much better it can be."

Still in darkness, he lifts his right leg and brings it down. The earth moves.

And they haven't even started yet.

The midnight audience spilt out of the theatre in a burst of martial taiko music. The low-backed arthouse seats were a special form of torture for a man of his height but James remained seated as the credits rolled. The early evening audiences exited at their leisure, but in the midnight crowds you saw the others, faces to the names on small bulletin boards and web sites.

As he stepped into the aisle, he politely ignored the middle-aged bottle-blonde sitting next to a much younger man, his leather jacket covering both his lap and her hands. A graying gentleman he'd seen at several showings was seated by the door. Dressed in tweeds with an umbrella, his loneliness writ in broad lines on his face, he absorbed the name of every last grip, best boy, and personal assistant. James nodded in greeting and the old man shook his head sadly.

"S'all rubbish now." he said. "Silicone and videotape and bloody computers. No soul in it at all."

James could only shake his head in agreement, exiting the theater with a vague feeling of pity. Nostalgia made you long for even the flaws in what was lost. Mist was falling as he stepped into the alley, the neon and streetlights of Harvard Square creating coronas in the fog.

Life hadn't treated him badly. He'd done well enough for himself, owned a house and a car, enough money coming in to keep him in toys and make him attractive to a particular kind of woman. And days like this, seeing the others and knowing he was not alone, that helped. But other people starving didn't obviate your own essential hunger. There were needs that could not be scratched, even by money, and he'd yet to find a solution.

He hadn't considered the solution might be looking for him.

She was standing at the end of the alley, one foot propped against the brick of the building. Blonde hair cut fashionably short, she wore a simple black raincoat that flattered the body underneath too well to be anything but expensive. Her laughter filled the narrow space at his expression. Before he could voice it, she answered the unspoken question.

"It's a midnight monster movie." Lindsay said. "Where else in the world would I look for you?"

"From London to Berkeley," she said, "Followed by four years in Silicon Valley. Then another four years working in Japan getting the business off the ground."

Either the years had been kind, or a great deal of money had gone into her preservation; he had to look hard for the changes. Small lines crisscrossed at the corners of her eyes when she smiled, which was often, and she wore glasses now, the thin black rims and her tightly bound hair giving her the appearance of a particularly volatile librarian. Only her wardrobe had changed markedly, the colorful peasant skirts and cable knits replaced by a black sweater and skirt combination that were so businesslike, they flirted with fetish.

The restaurant below the theater was intimate in the late-night quiet, the bartender cleaning glasses, one waiter folding napkins in a back banquette. They placed their drink order on the back of a large tip just before last call, after which Lindsay filled him in on the last dozen years as if she was describing a particularly long weekend.

"My backers are still mostly Japanese," she said. "But another year and we'll be profitable on our own."

"Impressive." he said. Talking about business he was on solid ground. In every other way, he was completely lost.

There had been other women in the years since Lindsay, even a few he'd trusted enough to share his secret. In the end, none of them had been able to make the cognitive leap. Tolerance wasn't the same as sharing and though he'd had lovers who'd been willing to accommodate him, there'd been no one who'd enjoyed it. He resolved that it would be several more drinks and several more dates with this new corporate Lindsay before he was going to open that particular canister of radioactive waste. With all the time and all the distance between them, he was shocked at how glad he was to see her again.

"You must be good." he finished. "I've heard the Japanese don't deal well with female CEOs."

Her glass was crystalline with condensation, leaving her fingertips damp in the transit from table to her lips. Her smile, when it came was sly, a quirk of the mouth that spoke of hidden amusement. There are secrets men are not meant to know.

"They deal very well with a certain kind of woman. One that has something they want."

"I don't understand. What exactly does your company do?"

"It's funny you should ask that." she said. She placed her credit card on the table before he could protest and signaled for the waiter. "Let's take a ride."

He glanced at his watch and was surprised the restaurant hadn't thrown them out long ago. "It's late. Where is there to go at this hour?"

Again, that smile, letting him know that even the best secrets are more fun shared.

"My place," she said.

"So much of business is about synergy," she said. "Putting together existing parts in a combination nobody has thought of before."

She locked him into the harness herself, crisscrossing his body with webbing straps and PVC buckles, adjusting each with the barest brush of fingertips against bare skin. When she was finished, he was immobile on a stainless steel cruciform. Her hands maintained contact, slowly stroking along his arms and thighs.

"A Japanese firm tried marketing these to police departments as riot control units after the mess in Paris. Nobody was interested; this model was too slow and they require too much maintenance for any police budget to keep them running."

The climate-controlled bay was neither too warm nor too cool, but he shivered. She was making him wait, but he hung on every word.

"And with Hollywood relying on computer animation more and more, there are a lot of very good model makers available. Once we've built the mock-up and molds, we can have any city in the world installed within a week. So you see, putting the pieces together was easy. What was missing was the market. You opened my eyes the night you left. I never forgot it."

"Monsters come from a very old part of the brain, Jim. The need for love is old, but the need to destroy is older. And there will always be wealthy men with the desire, if not the resources or approval, to destroy a city."

"So we provide a very exclusive outlet. Jerusalem. Paris, New York. We've got one customer with a frequent need to piss on Crawford, Texas, if you can believe it. Bombs, floods, rains of frogs, we can do it all if the price is right."

"For you though, there was only one possible choice."

"Lindsay . . ." he said. "I—"

"Shhhh," she said softly. "I know."

And with that, she stepped back and closed the nubbled green clamshell doors, leaving him waiting for her to finally set him free.

And now he is striding forward, arms and legs moving with purpose, the thunder of his impact vibrating through the hangar with every step. He passes through the massive doors, and he's outside, in the air, naked for the first time in his life.

And with the sun rising, all of Tokyo is spread out before him, waiting.

"Take it, love," she says. "It's yours."

The 6:15 A.M. Odakyu train is pulling into Shinjuku as he brings his foot down on the station, shattering the morning with the scream of tearing metal. The youth fashion mecca of Harajuku disappears in a gout of flame, his tail sweeping away buses like motes of dust as he turns toward the sunrise and Lindsay. On the screens inside his monster's skin, he can see her standing by Tokyo Tower, still in last night's clothing. She is out of scale, incongruous, and the thing he wants most in the world after this.

His entire body screaming for release, he roars and drives forward toward the woman he loves, as buildings crumble and the city begins to burn.

Poppet

Elspeth Potter

I snuck the poppet into the hospital like it was contraband. Probably, no one would care, but I didn't want to argue with any idiot administrators. It wouldn't interfere with any medical equipment; it was less hazardous than a cell phone. I had sealed it safely into a silver case with molded neoprene lining. If I opened the case, one would see only a silvery humanoid shape about the size of a Ken doll cut off at the knees. Come to think of it, I could say the poppet was merely a toy.

I wasn't supposed to have it out of the lab but, in my mind, James and I *were* the lab, and I was going to visit James. My snug, low-necked top and flowing skirt proclaimed that. I had never been one to wear such blatantly feminine clothing, but I had begun to notice, since he'd been in the hospital, where his eyes focused most often and with the most interest. At the moment, I could do little else for him.

I was also wearing his favorite pair of purple panties.

The nurse at the burn ward desk looked up as I passed. "Morning, Jessamine," she said. "Come to see Dr. Lincoln again?"

"Yes," I said, hoping I didn't sound surly. She never called me Dr. Farlow, and it was useless to be irritated over a friendly greeting. I was annoyed anyway, by everything that morning. I'd been up until four, trying to brainstorm ways to save the poppet project now that James' continued absence was making things difficult. I was the brains behind linking the poppets to an individual's control, but James had invented protean plastic and constructed the poppets themselves. Without him to provide a good supply of them for testing, we would soon have to stop the research. The protean plastic didn't retain its malleability and shape-memory for more than a few months of use. At least, not yet. James would solve that. I had not a doubt in the world. But until then, we needed some use for the few we had, something that would make a large quantity of money quickly; neither of us wanted to consider selling the patents.

I felt, perhaps irrationally, that our future as a couple depended on the poppets' success, just as our initial meeting had resulted from our early work on the project, when we'd discovered our mutual compatibility was physical as well as intellectual. I'd often thought James was more attracted to my brain than to my body. We talked to each other about science while eating, while walking to and from the lab, while having sex. He'd solved the first hurdle of the protean plastic while inside me, my legs hooked over his shoulders: one minute, furious thrusting, the next, I lay gasping on the bed while he scribbled formulae on the sheet. If he'd stopped for anything less, it's true, I would have strangled him with my thighs, but I cared about the breakthrough as much as he did. We returned to business once he'd recorded his idea, and we finished up on the carpet so as to avoid smearing his notes.

James' mind was a large part of what attracted me to him, as well—not so much that he was brilliant, but because he most valued in me the same thing that I most valued in myself. That and, well, the sex was really hot. And so was our constant exchange of ideas. James pursued one as fervidly as the other, so that watching him in the lab could make me horny.

There would be no sex for us for a long while, though, and little conversation. James lay, as he had for two weeks, immobilized by pain. Ironically, the burns covering his legs from feet to mid-thigh, and searing his hands, were the result of an accident in the lab where he manufactured the poppets. The melted plastic had caused pain that no drug could sufficiently ameliorate, especially if he tried to move. His entertainment was therefore limited to visits from me and the video screen set into the ceiling. He had found himself unable to work, his second-favorite entertainment; sometimes being drugged out of his mind prevented him, and the rest of the time he was too exhausted. Worse, because of the steam and chemical smoke he'd inhaled, his doctor had recommended he not speak until he was completely healed inside. After the first awful days, we'd resorted to his using an eye blink register so he could type, laboriously, on a pocket screen. I'd asked him how he occupied his mind, and he'd spelled out, in his usual laconic way, "Fntsy." His eyes, a changeable pale hazel in his dark face, told what sort of fantasies they were. I hoped they helped.

I slipped into James' room unnoticed by any of the inhabitants: James on his bed and his doctor and two nurses. I winced; I knew the signs. Another debridement to remove dead skin from his legs. I'd asked how that felt and he'd slowly blinked out three filthy words I had never heard him speak.

I took a chair by the window, where James could see me if he looked away from the doctor. I unsealed the poppet's case. I'd brought it to cheer him up and remind him of all he'd accomplished. Perhaps I could distract him with it, even now.

This poppet was his. I'd keyed it to the chip that lived beneath the skin of James' neck, and after I manipulated the poppet between my hands for a few moments, the link activated and he knew it was there; I could tell by the way the protean plastic softened and warmed, James' brainwaves activating the power cell hidden inside the poppet's flesh. It was strangely like holding *him* between my palms, as if I was connected to his brain as well. Or, I thought, blushing, as if I held not his brain but his cock.

Obviously, deprivation was getting to me.

Hoping my facial expression hadn't given me away, I glanced over at the bed again. I couldn't see James at all except for a bit of his arm and chest. The doctor and nurses still didn't seem to have noticed my presence, or perhaps they were so used to me being there that it didn't matter. I was, after all, listed as his next-of-kin.

The silvery poppet wriggled free of my hands. Such directed action meant it was under James' conscious control. He was now focusing more on the poppet than his pain. Good. I watched with amusement as the poppet clambered upright on my knee and waved its little arms, silently expostulating. I guessed what he wanted to say: "Oww!" I swirled a finger over its knoblike head. It felt smooth and silky, like the most delicate of human skin, heightening my sense of handling *James* and not the poppet. If he experienced what I normally did with a poppet, he would feel my touch on it like a paintbrush against his body, except that the sensation would be all in his mind. It was better than nothing, better than not touching him at all.

The poppet responded to my touch with a rude gesture. I grinned and stroked the poppet again, wishing I could go over and do the same for James. Surely they would at least let me caress his hair while they worked on him, or hold his uninjured hand. He didn't really like me to see him while he was in pain, but his resistance was wearing down as the days passed. The more I visited, the less he protested.

The poppet leaned against me, gradually softening against my stomach like a contented cat. Perhaps I should tell James to build in a purring function. I found the poppet's fingerless hand and pressed into it with my fingertip. The hand reacted, clasping my finger in a suctioning kiss. Abruptly, I remembered James sucking my finger into his mouth, his expression seemingly blank except for his eyes, darkly intent on my face. Involuntarily, I glanced over at him. I could see only his jaw in profile, clenched hard, before one of the nurses blocked my view.

I was unprepared for the poppet to suddenly struggle upright again and burrow underneath my blouse.

I clapped my hands down on my shirt's hem, a reflex response, as if to prevent the poppet from escaping. As if it couldn't crawl out the shirt's open collar, or around the back, or out a sleeve. I glanced at the group gathered around James' bed. None of them seemed to have noticed a thing, though the poppet was squirming like a bizarre alien pregnancy. Had he lost control of it?

The poppet poked me beneath my arm, and I writhed. No, he was in control. He knew exactly where I was ticklish, the bastard. And I'd been feeling sorry for him. He could at least have waited until we were alone before beginning this little game. I clapped a hand over the poppet, but it wriggled free easily, inching upwards until it clamped over my left breast, giving me the look of a silicone implant gone horridly wrong. I was about to reach beneath my shirt to try and pry the poppet loose when it applied suction to my nipple.

Even through my bra, it was exquisite, softer than human lips. My breath came short and my belly went hollow with arousal. For a few moments, I forgot I was sitting in a hospital room; I was thrown back in time to a darkened hotel bedroom, the revelry of a scientific conference pounding through the door in sharp contrast to the gentle pulling of James' lips. He'd slid one finger along my clit, lightly, so lightly. His eyes had gleamed in the semi-darkness, watching me.

We couldn't be caught doing this. Besides simple embarrassment, if the scientific agencies learned we'd been using the poppets so frivolously, the little funding we'd achieved could be cut off, the project ended, both of us unemployed. Recklessly, I surrendered to it anyway. Really, who would notice, or care? Here, James was just another patient, and I was just his girlfriend.

In moments, I was trying hard not to pant audibly. All I wanted was more, more, harder, and also for the other nipple to be sucked. I got my wishes, as if James could read my mind.

When the suckling stopped, at first I didn't even notice. My whole body gently throbbed, breasts down to toes. Gradually I began to wonder where the poppet had gone. The squashy, weighty lump of it had vanished—no, not vanished. Its body shape had flattened, spreading warmth over my chest and belly, like the glorious moment when two naked bodies first come into full contact. The poppet was a more subtle warmth, though, a gentle pulsation that rippled slowly downwards like a tentative hand on a first date, sliding down my belly, slipping beneath my waistband, and down beneath my skirt.

I dared a glance at the bed. One of the nurses had left. What had he seen, on his way out of the room? I flushed even hotter, thinking of it. The doctor and the other nurse blocked my view of James and were oblivious to my presence. I hoped. Or did I hope that?

I barely breathed. Faint sounds of a body moving against sheets—James—registered as pleasure, not pain. Perhaps it was. I would ask him later, after I'd told him he was a bastard. I would ask him if concentrating on the poppet had helped him with pain management. But the scientific aspect of the poppet was far from the center of my attention at the moment, as a sensation like a giant hand rippled and pressed over my abdomen, causing sympathetic ripples inside like precursors of orgasm. And the poppet was easing down between my legs.

It was pressing itself against me. The first time he saw them, James had laughed at the satiny purple panties I was wearing, before he became fascinated as I grew wet and the patch of fabric between my legs darkened in color and bloomed with musky scent. Now, the fabric felt hot.

Spread thin, the poppet rippled along my lower lips. I let my thighs fall ever-so-slightly apart to allow more access. James took advantage, fluttering the poppet like strokes of his tongue. Where had he achieved such control? He'd not had it before. Then I knew. Here. Hours to wait and nothing but fantasy, time he'd spent thinking. Thinking of me.

I looked down and saw the poppet coalescing again, pressing harder. I didn't think it would manage to enter me; that sort of delicate manipulation would be difficult; but the thought and its possibilities made my heart pound. The poppet pressed warmly against my clit, sucking, sucking. It didn't take much. Inexorably, my body tightened —only a moment longer—then released in waves, through which I felt the poppet clinging, all the touch James could give me.

When I could concentrate on my surroundings again, the room looked as if nothing had changed. Hurriedly, I tugged the poppet free of my shirt and concealed it between my hands. The protean plastic had cooled and was beginning to toughen. We'd used it up with all that enthusiastic subtle movement.

We'd have to work on that. James would be glad to have a project with which he could experiment while recuperating. I would be glad to help out, I thought, dreamily, as the nurse exited and the doctor made some encouraging comments to James.

It might not help our credibility to sell a poppet as a sex toy, but then we needn't call it that. Toy would be enough. Another way for the disabled to interact with their environment, distract themselves from pain, all sorts of things like that. We could garner publicity and more funding, I was sure of it, and continue to explore the wondrous possibilities. Our future was secure.

Remembrance

Beth Bernobich

March 10th was too early for planting, too early (almost) for anything but raking away the detritus of winter. Kate didn't care. She had promised herself a gardening session this weekend. After a month of long hours in the lab, poring over chip schematics, it would do her good to grub about in the dirt.

Clouds streaked the sky overhead. Ignoring them, Kate removed the sheets of canvas from the old beds. She scooped the layer of mulch into the wheelbarrow handful by handful, then cleared away the twigs and leaves. The debris would make good compost, along with the deadwood from the peach and pear trees. Good thing she'd invested in the shredder.

A cool breeze fingered her hair; she rubbed her forehead with the back of her wrist, and breathed in the soft ripe scent of spring. New growth had already started. A few snowbells and crocuses peeked through the soil. Ah yes. If the rain held off, she could finish clearing the beds and cut a new edge. Maybe even replace the old railroad ties with those antique bricks she scavenged from the renovation project downtown. After picking through heaps of dark red and brown bricks, Kate had unearthed a jumble of dusky pinks from the old municipal office building, and a handful of aged golden bricks from a long-abandoned bank.

A soft chime sounded—her cell phone. Kate wiped her hands hastily on her jeans and dug the phone out from her workbasket. She flipped the phone open to see "Unknown" on the caller ID. No visuals either, just a black shiny square with a question mark in the middle.

"Hey, babe."

Jessica. Of course. She was calling from a semi-restricted zone at work, which explained the ID and blank vid screen. "Hey, yourself. What's up?"

"Sorry I'm late. Something got in my way."

Kate suppressed a sigh. Over the past six years, she had learned to expect the holdups and delays and unexpected changes in plans that came with Jessica, but she had never learned to enjoy them. "What now?"

"We need to talk."

A breeze kicked up, making Kate shiver in her flannel shirt. "About what?"

"I got the promotion."

Oh, yes. The promotion. "But that's good—"

She broke off. Not good, clearly. Not when she could almost hear the tension in Jessica's breathing. "What's wrong?" she said carefully.

"Not over the phone," Jessica said. "I'll be there in half an hour."

Kate's phone chirped to signal the end of call. Kate automatically flipped the phone shut and returned it to her basket. She glanced at her newly cleared flowers beds, the neat stacks of brush and dead-wood, the boxes of bricks waiting for her. She sighed and picked up her tools to wipe them clean.

An hour later, she had showered and changed clothes. Still no sign of Jess, though Thatcher's headquarters were just a few miles away in the city's new corporate complex. Kate made coffee, nibbled on a left-over biscuit, then began to pace. Talk. Jessica liked mysteries, she told herself. She just wanted to tease Kate, push her buttons. . . .

Jessica came through the front door, swinging her brief case. A few raindrops glittered in her dark brown hair, and her cheeks were flushed, as though she'd run the last few blocks. "Hey babe," she said as she dropped the briefcase. She followed up her words with a breezy kiss.

"Hey, yourself." Kate heard the odd combination of excitement and dread in Jessica's voice. Jessica wore her corporate uniform, she noticed—a dark gray suit with just a touch of flare to the skirt and discreet slits at the sleeves. No makeup. Sexy and sleek and proper. Jessica called the look her Republican disguise. It made a good impression, she said, when she accompanied her superiors to government meetings.

Piecing together all the clues, Kate took a guess and asked, "What's the new assignment?"

Jessica flinched and laughed uneasily. "Smart girl, you. Yeah, I got the promotion, and it comes with a new assignment. Nice bump in pay, too."

Kate noticed that Jessica did not meet her gaze. "What's the catch?"

Another nervous glance, the briefest hesitation, before Jessica answered. "It's an off-site assignment. For the Mars program. The government wants extra security specialists for their orbital transfer stations, and Thatcher got the main contract. We just got confirmation today. I'll be one of the unit supervisors on Gamma Station."

Kate had heard all about Gamma Station on the news. Alpha for earth and Beta for the moon, whose base had doubled in size during the past administration's watch. Now, after numerous delays, came Gamma, the first of the orbital transport stations that would serve as stepping-stones toward the planned military base on Mars. Jessica had talked about nothing else these past three months.

"Just what you wanted," she said softly. "What else?"

Jessica smiled unhappily. "All the bad news at once, I see. Well, for one thing, it's a long assignment. Longer than usual."

"How long?"

Jessica smoothed back a wisp of hair that had escaped her braid. "Five years. They want continuity, they said. They're tired of retraining specialists every two years, and they want to cut back on expenses—especially with the draft up for debate." Her glance flicked up to meet Kate's. "But I have scheduled home visits built into the contract—twice a year—and bonuses for every month without any incidents. We could buy that house in New Hampshire."

We could get married, came the unspoken addendum. Even if only two states recognized that ceremony. And Kate did want that marriage, no matter how limited its legality, but Jessica's explanation skimmed over so much. Five years. Home visits were a week, no more. And *incident* was simply a euphemism for casualties. *My lover the mercenary,* she thought, unconsciously rubbing her hands together, as though to rid them of dirt.

"You accepted already," she said.

"Yes."

Neither one of them were saying much, Kate thought. Rain clouds passed in front of the sun, momentarily darkening the living room, and a spattering of drops ticked against the windows. The room's auto lamps shimmered to on, but their light was colder, thinner, than the sun.

"I need to think about it," she said. "What it means."

Jessica nodded.

Another awkward pause followed.

"Would you like lunch?" Kate asked.

Jessica shook her head. " 'm sorry. I have a briefing this afternoon. That's the other thing you should know—I'm scheduled to leave in three weeks."

She knew, Kate thought. *She knew and didn't tell me.* Or maybe all that talk about Gamma was her way of warning Kate without saying anything outright.

"Then you better go," she said.

They stared at one another a moment. Then Jessica caught up her briefcase and vanished through the doors, leaving Kate standing in the empty living room, rubbing her hands.

In one sense, Kate's workbench at XGen Laboratories resembled her garden. The lab allotted her a well defined, if limited, workspace that she kept scrupulously neat. And she had her rows of tools laid out just where she needed them—some old and familiar and worn by frequent use, some of them shiny with special purpose.

Kate peered at the display, adjusted the zoom level with a few keystrokes, and studied the display again. The mask she wore over her nose and mouth itched, and she adjusted it. The customer had requested extra QA for these chips, and a high sample count to ensure the best quality. It meant more profit for XGen, but a longer, more tedious day for Kate. Still, she usually found the work soothing, working step by step through the checklist of tests, and marking down the results for each in the entry system. Today, however . . .

She sighed, removed the chip from the spectrometer, and placed the next one in its slot. At the next bench, Anne and Olivia talked quietly as they too worked through their allotment of gene-chips for the latest customer order. Anne tall and lean and brown, her dark abundant hair confined in a tight bun. Olivia short and skinny, with spiky blonde hair. Both of them looked out of place with the other. The next row over, Aishia quietly argued politics with Stan and Marcel. Stan and Aishia had worked together for the past thirty years, and as far as everyone could tell, they had spent those years debating each other. Kate resisted the urge to ask them all for complete quiet, just this once.

In her distraction, she hit the wrong function key. Her system froze and blinked warnings at her. "Damn," she whispered. "Damn, stupid, damn, and damn it all again."

Anne looked up from her console. "What's wrong?"

"Nothing." Wearily, Kate punched in the key-combination to unlock the system, then went through the security codes again. XGen required several layers of identification, including fingerprint scans, these days. The clients liked that—no chance of hackers infiltrating the company and wreaking damage with sensitive products.

She noticed that Anne had not returned to her work. Worried, evidently. Kate shook her head. Anne was a good friend, but Kate didn't want to talk about Jessica, or the new assignment, or how they were almost fighting, but not quite.

Her system blinked a message, recognizing Kate. To her relief, it had not ditched her current entry. With a few more keystrokes, she resumed entering test codes and their results for the next chip. Concentrate on the chip and the screen and the analyzer, she told herself. Not on Jessica, who had returned late and left early, without giving Kate a chance to discuss the damned assignment. *As if discussing it would change anything,* Kate thought bitterly. She paused and drew a slow breath that did nothing for the tightness in her chest. *I should be used to it by now.*

Or not. They had never gone through the long separation most mercenary partners endured. Jessica's first few assignments had lasted only a few months apiece. The longest—a twelve-month stint on the moon—had included frequent time downside. Kate had almost let herself believe that things would continue the same.

But no, terrorists didn't care about her loneliness, nor about keeping to convenient borders, such as the Middle East or selected regions in Asia. They traveled to New York and London these days. They were here, in New Haven. And now the stars.

The government draft had proved unpopular, and so private companies filled the void. In the bright new world of post-Iraq, there would always be positions for a smart, brave warrior like Jessica. The money was good, the benefits even better, if you did not mind the ache of separation. And as Jessica pointed out, these companies hardly cared about her politics or her sex life. They only asked her to be dependable and discreet.

I hate it.

"Hey, Kate."

It was Anne, peering at her over the top of her console. A tiny frown made a crease between her brows.

"What's up?" Kate asked. "Problem with the spectral unit?" The new equipment had not proved quite as flawless as the salesperson claimed.

"Always," Anne said dryly. "But for once, it's not about work. Olivia and I were talking about going out tonight with Remy and some others. Maybe grabbing a bite at the new Indian restaurant, then see what's playing at the York Square. Cordelia and her husband might show up."

"I don't know . . ." She didn't think Jessica would like a night out, not with things so tense. Or then again, maybe a night out would help. "Let me check with Jessica."

She punched in the speed code and waited. And waited. After a dozen chimes, the phone switched her over to voice mail. Kate clicked phone shut. If Jessica were in Thatcher's high-security zones, she would have no cell access. She closed her eyes and rubbed her forehead to cover the disappointment. *Think of it as practice,* she thought, *for when Jess is really gone.*

"No luck?" Anne asked.

"Busy," Kate said. Which in a way was true. "I guess you're stuck with just me."

Anne smiled. "Hey, I don't mind."

The lab cleared out within minutes of the five o'clock chimes. But they would all be working overtime tomorrow, Kate thought, as she skinned out of her lab suit and into jeans and a T-shirt. The mask always left her hair a mess. She ran her fingers though the curls and tried to revive them.

"You look fine," Anne told her.

"Liar," Kate said.

Olivia was repairing her makeup, while Aishia recapped her argument with Stan. "He thinks with his balls," she muttered. "The right one. That accounts for his idea that God made guns so we can blow up our neighbors."

"Seems like they're blowing us up, too," Olivia said as she applied eyeliner. "Ask Remy. Her brother was on that bus in D.C. with the suicide kid."

"He's alive."

"Barely. A lot of others aren't."

Olivia and Aishia continued bickering as they left the lab and passed through the corporate security into the gated parking lot. Remy waited outside the parking lot, leaning against a dented lemon-yellow VW. Olivia broke off in mid-argument and waved cheerily.

"Who else is driving?" Anne said. "I took the bus today."

"Me," Aishia said. "If you don't mind the mess."

"That's fine. Kate?"

Kate barely heard them. She had sighted another familiar figure through the fence.

Jessica. She came here even without me calling.

A very jittery Jessica, to be sure, dressed even more formally than the day before—all dark gray and ivory, with polished nickel studs in her ears that winked every time she swung her head. "Hey, girl. Hungry?" she called out.

"Starving," Kate called back. She hurried through the security procedures—ID card presented to the guard, palm against the reader, the retinal scan unit. When the gate clicked open, she ran through and into a hug from Jessica.

"Time off for good behavior," Jessica murmured. "Come on. I know a good place for some calamari."

They retired to a diner a few blocks away, on Chapel Street. Jessica ordered an extra large helping of everything, but when her dishes arrived, she fiddled with her salad, and picked at the heap of calamari. Kate watched in silence, her own appetite slowly draining away.

"What's wrong?" she asked softly.

Jessica shrugged. "You mean, besides the usual?"

Kate nodded.

Jessica stabbed a piece of calamari with her fork. "I hate us fighting. I hate going away for weeks and months and years. But it's what I do. And it's better for you and everyone else that my job is out there and not right here in New Haven."

"I know," Kate said quietly. "I'm sorry."

"Don't be. You didn't say anything wrong. It's just a bitch, the whole thing. So I was thinking—"

She broke off and ate rapidly for a few moments, while Kate waited, breathless, for her to continue that tantalizing sentence.

Jessica pushed her plate away and wiped her mouth with a nervous flick of the napkin. "I had another briefing," she said. "Thatcher's R&D department is testing a new device, something XGen prototyped for us last year. Do you remember?"

Kate shook her head. XGen was small, but its R&D department kept to itself. QA usually saw new products only after the customer had okayed the prototypes.

"Anyway," Jessica went on, "there's a new chip, and they want me and some others for testing. It's for recording sensory input from a soldier's body. Sight. Touch. Smell. Even sub-vocals. Actually, I already volunteered for the implant and . . . I was hoping you would, too."

"What?" Her own meal forgotten, Kate stared at Jessica. "Are you insane? Why would I volunteer for a Thatcher project?"

Jessica glanced away, her cheeks turning pink. "I thought . . . I'll be gone a long time, and I thought . . . We could use it for ourselves. It might make things easier."

Kate swallowed with some difficulty. "You're kidding."

"No, I'm not. What's the problem?"

How like Jessica to forget who else might view those recordings. "The review board," she managed to say.

"Oh, them." Jessica dismissed those concerns with an airy wave of her hand. "They read my emails and they censor my vids. I'm used to it."

But I'm not.

Jessica put down her fork and clasped Kate's hands. Hers were lean strong hands, callused from handling who knew what. Warm and gentle hands. Kate loved them. She didn't want to share them with anyone.

"You don't like it. I know," Jess said softly. "But do you understand?"

Reluctantly Kate nodded. "Yes. No. Of course I don't like it. But then, I don't like you going away."

"Neither do I. But Kate . . . Five years is a fucking awful long time. Even with the home visits. At least consider the idea. Please."

Kate let out a sigh. "I will. Consider it, that is. I can't promise more."

Jessica squeezed her hands. "That's all I ask."

With spring's arrival came the soft soaking rains, interspersed by damp gray skies that echoed the mist rising from the warming earth. If the sun broke through a day here or there, Kate hardly noticed. She neglected her garden for Jessica's company, and avoided glancing at the calendar.

Last day, she thought, watching Jessica check over her gear. Jess wore a plain jumpsuit that announced its military purpose. Her train left at ten—one hour left. Now fifty-nine minutes. Now—

"Check and double-check," Jessica said, straightening up with a grunt. "Damn. I'm getting old for this shit. Just as well they only allow us two bags."

Two modest bags, stuffed with books and off-duty clothes and several mementos from Kate, all of them cleared by Thatcher's security regulations. Kate touched the implant at the base of her skull, the connection points hidden beneath her hair. The operation had taken more time than she expected—more than a day for the operation itself, and another three days for recovery and training, with subsequent training sessions scheduled over the next few weeks.

"I miss you already," she said suddenly.

"Hey." Jessica pulled her into a hard hug. "I miss you, too. But let's not get ahead of ourselves. We still have an hour."

"Fifty-six minutes," Kate said into Jess's shoulder. "And no, we don't have time for one more . . ."

She felt Jessica shake with silent laughter. "I wish we did. Come on. Help me get this stuff into the car."

Kate's internal clock ticked down the minutes as they loaded bags into the car and drove to New Haven's newly renovated train station. A winding ramp brought them over the flood zone and into the parking garage. If you ignored the trash floating on the oily waves below, the view was breathtaking. The planners had taken that into account: the moving sidewalks and glass-paneled elevators showed only the Sound and the blurred outline of Long Island in the distance. Far below, the shoreline highway curved above the open water.

Jessica slung one bag over her shoulder. She swatted Kate away from the second bag. "Might as well get used to the weight now," she said. "In six days, they won't weigh anything at all."

Thirty minutes left. Twenty-three. Passing through station security took just a few moments at this hour. Kate and Jessica sat side-by-side on the platform bench, hands barely touching in this much too public area. At fifteen minutes, the train squealed into the station, filling the air with a sharp electric odor.

Jessica quickly squeezed Kate's hand. "Hey," she whispered. "It's time."

Not yet, Kate wanted to say, but she stood silently as Jessica gathered her two bags, then pulled out her e-card for the conductor. Seven minutes. Five. Three.

"Kate."

In that one word, Kate heard a tone in Jessica's voice that she never had before. "Hey," she said.

"Hey." Jessica leaned forward and kissed Kate firmly on the lips. Kate caught a whiff of Jessica's cinnamon perfume, a fainter one of her green tea shampoo. One brown strand fell from its braid and brushed against Kate's cheek. Jessica tucked the strand behind her ear. "Six months to the first visit," she whispered.

And then the clock ticked down to zero, and she was gone.

Throughout April and early May, Kate worked to undo the early neglect of her garden. She cleared out the weeds and repaired the old border. She added fresh mulch and compost, and with judicious watering, teased the roses and irises into luscious blooms. She even expanded the beds to include a small vegetable patch, which the deer promptly attacked.

At work, she had the impression that her friends and co-workers had divvied up watches over her. Singly and in groups, they took her out to lunch (Aishia, Anne, and once Stan), or invited her to the movies (Anne, Cordelia), or on shopping expeditions (Olivia, with or without Remy). The constant invitations irritated her at first. Over the weeks, however, she learned to accept their well-meant attentions. It helped, after all, to distract her from counting the hours, days, and weeks, without Jessica. Even so, she divided and subdivided the emptiness into bearable intervals. One day of train travel. Five more days to launch. Another month until Jessica arrived at Gamma Station.

Kate had allowed herself just one letter for each week, emailed to Jessica in care of Thatcher. Thatcher would screen the contents and forward the message via satellite to Gamma Station. Jessica had fired off one brief message before the launch. Since then nothing.

She's busy, Kate told herself. *Reviewing security procedures. Coordinating her crew assignments with others in Thatcher and the military. Handling any crises . . .*

No. Bad idea to think about crises. Better to concentrate on the mundane tasks of personnel records and fitness reports and all the other tedious paperwork Jessica always complained about.

She parked the car in the too-empty driveway and gathered her briefcase and groceries from the back seat. Following an almost-predictable schedule, Anne invited Kate to dinner, but Kate had refused, wanting one night to herself. Maybe she could download a vid, or eat too much popcorn, or do all the things other people talked about doing when they had the house to themselves.

Still mulling over her options, she unlocked the door and scooped up the mail from the carpet. Bills. Flyer from the local ACLU. Credit card offers. A small reinforced envelope with the return address: *Thatcher Security Operations.*

Jess. She wrote.

Kate abandoned everything else in the entryway. Her pulse dancing, she hurried into the living room. A letter. A long one. Even sooner than she expected. Jessica must have saved up her letters and transcribed them the moment she arrived at Gamma.

She took up a letter opener from the letters desk and slit the envelope carefully. Nothing. Perhaps the envelope's padded interior— made from a strange soft material—blocked the contents. She shook the envelope gingerly. A micro disc tumbled into her lap.

Kate drew a sharp breath. She recognized the disc from her training sessions. Reflexively, she touched the knob at the base of her skull. No one at work knew about this device. She had not dared to tell them, not even Anne. Aishia would lecture her about man-machine interfaces and their risks. Olivia would make jokes. Anne might say nothing, but Kate had learned to read her friend's subtle changes in expression. Whatever name you put on her reaction, it would not be a positive one.

The disc gleamed red in the late sunset. Kate touched its rim—a faint dull spot remained where her fingertip had rested. Damn. The technicians had warned her how sensitive these discs were. They had provided her with a supply of special cleaning fluid, along with admonitions about overusing the stuff.

Kate vented a breath, and carefully inserted the disc back into its envelope. Again she touched the knob. *Jess. Oh Jess. What are we doing?*

She took a few moments to put the groceries away—extending the anticipation, or avoiding the disc, she wasn't sure which. Then she climbed the stairs to the tiny office next to their bedroom. The Thatcher machine stood on her desk, in the corner behind stacks of books and papers and her gardening magazines, untouched since the Thatcher tech had installed it weeks ago.

Kate cleared away the magazines and sat down. Squinted at the machine. It looked like any piece of lab equipment, she thought—a low sleek ivory box with several touch pads labeled in red. A half dozen indicator lights ran along the top edge. These too were clearly marked. She skimmed a finger along the side and found the recessed slot for the discs.

You're stalling.

Damn straight, as Jessica would say.

A touch of the power switch, and the machine hummed into life, its lights blinking through a series of test patterns. Kate cleaned the micro disc, just as the technicians told her, then slid the disc into its slot. It clicked into place.

Now the tricky part.

She touched a side panel, which slid open to reveal the connector cable with its slim square terminator. She uncoiled the cable and brushed her hair away from the knob in her skull. The terminator and her own connector port would slide open together when oriented correctly and pressed together.

She felt the click reverberate through her bones. Her skin prickled and she felt faintly queasy. Psychosomatic, she told herself. She had done the same thing a hundred times in the training lab with no ill effects. She pressed the touch pad marked PLAY.

A pale green light blinked. Kate's vision went dark.

Hey, babe.

Kate heard, felt a cough.

Testing, one, two three . . .

Soft self-conscious laughter followed, with an echo soon after, as though Jess sat in a small enclosed space. Her cabin aboard the shuttle? With a shiver, Kate realized she felt heavy fabric encasing her arms and legs. The air smell charged and faintly stale. She blinked, wishing she could see what Jessica saw. Thatcher had warned her she would get no visuals. The prototype could handle them, but her particular machine had that feature disabled. A matter of security, the tech had explained.

Hey.

Kate jumped at the sound of Jessica's voice next to her, inside her.

So, like. I guess this is working. Harder than taping a message, but damn, after going through that operation, I might as well use the machine.

Pause. Kate felt her chest go tight. Was that her body's reaction, or Jessica's? Then she felt warm breath leaking between tense lips. A subdued laugh. The words,

Hey, babe. I miss you. Later.

Without warning, the machine clicked, and Kate's vision returned so abruptly, she swayed from the vertigo. If she closed her eyes, she could still feel the weight of Jess's pressure suit, still taste the shuttle's recycled air. *Hey, babe,* she thought. *Don't make it too much later.*

After some procrastination, Kate recorded a brief reply, using the same disc Jessica sent her. She wished she could keep the recording to play later, but Thatcher didn't want stacks of these discs lying around. Proprietary materials, the security manager had explained.

It took her several tries before she was satisfied. Jessica had had it right—making the recording was far more difficult than reading one. What to say? How to react, when every sensation impressed itself onto that tiny disc, to be reviewed by Thatcher research and security personnel? It helped that one disc held only a few moments of sensory data. In the end, Kate recorded a brief description of her garden, one of the roses in her palm, where its velvet-soft petals tickled her skin. *Later,* she whispered, and tapped END RECORD.

Jessica sent three more recordings over the next six weeks, all of them brief, all of them ending with a whisper-soft kiss. She supplemented those with longer text messages forwarded from Thatcher by email. Kate found the longer messages more frustrating than the brief micro-recordings; more than once, Thatcher's censors had deleted apparently random sections of text, and badly garbling Jessica's meaning. Kate was tempted to add something inflammatory, but she restrained herself. Thatcher might not care about personal lives, but they were as humorless as any federal spooks. Still, the thought that Thatcher observed their correspondence bothered her. You might think that some aspects of life were private, she thought. Even now, even in these days of constant surveillance and the uneasy comprises between freedom and security.

And so, the weeks rolled from spring to summer. One hot July evening, Kate parked her car in the driveway far later than usual—XGen had another rush order from a government super-contractor. Muzzy from the long hours in the lab, she had thoughts only of dinner and cold tea, and when she picked up the mail from the carpet, she almost didn't register the envelope from Thatcher.

Then recognition clicked into place. Not just another envelope, but one with a disc. Dinner could wait, she thought. She hurried upstairs to her office and slid the disc into the machine. The terminator plug clicked into place, and the familiar black-brown veil dropped over her vision . . .

Hey, lover. Something new this time.

A warm hand pressed against Kate's (Jessica's?) breast. Kate drew a sharp breath as she realized that Jessica wore no clothing. What was she thinking? What about Thatcher—

The hand slid over her breast, cupped the flesh a moment and squeezed, making Kate gasp. No time wasted. The hand skimmed over her belly, and paused briefly to cover her sex. Possession, said that gesture. Kate felt the doubled warmth from her body and Jessica's at the same time. She had just time to muffle a gasp of pleasure when three fingers plunged into her vagina, slid out, and pinched the clitoris with practiced skill. Heat blossomed outward, upward. Their nipples contacted to hard painful points. The fingers plunged deeper inside. And again, but faster, more urgent. Kate's, (Jessica's) breath went ragged as she panted, *Oh, god . . . yes . . . oh . . . my . . .*

Kate's office blinked into existence.

She leaned against the desk, shivering in spite of the July warmth. Her groin ached from half-fulfilled passion, and a ripe musky scent filled the air. Very faint, almost like a memory, she could still smell a trace of Jessica's favorite perfume.

Too much. Not enough. I can't stand it.

Kate reached up to remove the terminator from her skull. Her hands shook. Deep inside, her muscles tensed, rippled, stretched, as though pleading for release. She paused and licked her lips. Slowly she reached for PLAY again.

For three days, she wavered on how to reply. She wished (again) she could keep a copy of Jessica's recording. She wished she could keep her response private. Neither was possible. Nor could she send back a simple text message. In the end, she closeted herself in the office with a glass of chilled Pouilly Fuissé and a tightly held memory of Jessica's recording.

She shucked off her T-shirt and jeans. Slid her panties over her hips and let them drop onto the floor. Though she had no audience, not even a virtual one, Kate tried to act as though she did. It would put her into the mood for what she had planned.

Perfume over her breast, at the base of her throat, behind her knees. Blinds tilted just so to let in the sunlight, but keep the room private. She had thought about lying on the floor, but the cord didn't reach far enough. She would have to make do with her office chair and her imagination.

Kate inserted the terminator, and then drank a long slow swallow of wine. As an afterthought, she rolled the wine glass over her bare skin. The cold wet surface raised a trail of goose bumps that made her shiver with anticipation. She pressed her left hand over her mons. Warm and damp already. It was as though she only needed to think of Jessica, to have her body respond.

She touched RECORD.

Hey, babe. Here's something for you.

We are a duet, Jessica whispered time and again. *My fingers burrow through my pubic hair, twice over. Once with me, making me shake with desire, once with you, Kate. Feel the hot liquid spilling from my cunt. I'm soaked, a puddle of want. Want you. Now, girl. In and out. Again. More. Now I trail the wetness up between my breasts and paint myself with cum.*

Whatever Jessica said, Kate heard weeks later. Whatever Jessica did—how her fingers pinched Kate's nipples, how her tongue licked wet fingers and tasted her smoky climax—repeated itself in Kate's lonely office.

You are my succubus, Kate whispered back. *You take me as a ghost would, by invading my mind. As I do with you, my love. As I do with you.* She crushed her mouth against her hand, and slid the new vibrator into her own drenched vagina. Her lips closed hard around the silky shaft. An electric pulse gripped her clitoris and rippled through her belly, up her spine. Fireworks. Hot and dazzling. She threw back her head and cried out.

Over the next three months, Kate and Jessica exchanged recordings every week. Jessica sent text messages twice a week, long rambling letters about the insipid food, the jokes her crew made, the techniques she and others used to make life in tight quarters more bearable. *Like our little not-so-secret,* she said once.

Indeed. Kate disliked Jessica's jokes about their situation, but she understood them. She read on as Jessica described more about the implants.

It's a clever little toy, Jessica wrote. *Thatcher wants to run more tests once they develop their high-capacity modules, but the basic technology works. It even has a few tricks the technicians didn't tell us at first. Remember the discs and how we have to record over them? Well, the chip has a smidge of memory itself, and if you press PLAY three times fast, then hold down PROGRAM and RECORD together, you can store a few moments in the chip and replay it later. Here's how . . .*

Saturday. Kate knelt and surveyed her garden. A lush rainy summer had produced more squash and beans and tomatoes than she could give away. Now, as the season drifted into autumn, she busied herself with preparing the beds for winter.

"How much mulch do you actually need?" Anne asked. "And could you make a tongue-twister from that question?" She had volunteered to help Kate with the day's work. Later, they would go to a neighborhood rummage and art festival. Aishia had promised to join them.

"All the mulch," Kate answered, ignoring the question about tongue twisters. "They say we'll have a colder winter than usual, and I want to make sure the bulbs survive. Unless you think we should dig them up . . ."

"Don't," Anne said quickly.

Kate grinned. "Thought not."

They set to work, Anne digging up weeds and Kate mixing the soil and compost. Kate had acquired a new supply of micro-insulating fabric that claimed a fifty-percent improvement over other materials. If she alternated mulch with the fabric, she might get away with keeping the bulbs in the ground.

"I always wished I had a garden," Anne said. "Though I'm not very good at keeping the plants alive. Where did you hear about the colder winter?"

"Almanac. Good old-fashioned almanac. Though this one is online."

Anne laughed. "And here I thought we were high-tech."

More than you know, Kate thought. She had not confided in anyone, not even Anne, about the experimental implants. *A private matter,* she thought. *As private as Thatcher allows.*

They dispatched the latest weed crop and started on splitting the lily bulbs, which had multiplied since last year. It was easier with a friend, Kate thought, and the work soothed as nothing else could. She could almost forget the constant ache in her chest that had begun with Jessica's departure. *My garden, my refuge,* she thought as she set another bulb back into the ground. These days, even her garden seemed a less a refuge than before. Prices climbing. The shrill debates in Congress and blogs. The noisy protests at universities.

A brisk knock sounded at the front door, followed by the faint chimes of the doorbell. Kate dusted off her hands, thinking that whoever it was, was impatient. "If that's Aishia, she's early. Unless she wants to help with covering the beds."

Anne smoothed dirt over another planting. "It might be Olivia. She said something about dropping by."

"With or without Remy?"

Anne grimaced. "Without."

Their latest and loudest quarrel showed no signs of ending. Kate could not remember when she'd last seen Remy's lemon-yellow Bug waiting outside XGen's parking lot. "Do you think it's serious this time?"

Anne shrugged. "Who knows?"

Another knock echoed through the crisp, new-autumn air. Louder. More impatient. Definitely not Aishia or Olivia. "Coming," Kate called out.

She heard a man's voice. Several, talking amongst themselves. Dominionists? Surely they had learned their lessons after Jessica's pointed lecture. She gave up on scrubbing the dirt from her hands and hurried around the brick path that led through the side flowerbeds, into the front yard.

Three men stood on her front porch. She took in their gray suits, their humorless expressions. All of them middle-aged. All of them bland and competent, in the way she associated with bureaucrats.

"Ms. Morell?" one said. "Ms. Kate Morell?"

Her skin prickled with sudden dread. "Yes. I'm Kate Morell. Can I help you?"

He came forward and extended a hand. "I'm from Thatcher Enterprises, ma'am," he said. "I'm very sorry, but I have bad news for you. It's about Ms. Anderson."

I don't want to know. I don't. I don't.

"Go away," she said thickly.

"Ma'am."

"I mean it."

Anne hurried to Kate's side. "Kate. Maybe we should go inside."

Kate shrugged away from Anne's tentative touch, but she knew Anne was right. She could not stop them from telling her. Today. Tomorrow. Either she'd hear the news from these gray grim men, or she'd learn the details from the evening newscast. Better she heard it here, now, under the open sunny sky. "Tell me what happened."

With a glance at his companions, the man complied. Thatcher had sent their best people, ones trained to deliver their news in soft, concerned voices. Numb, and growing number, Kate listened to how terrorists had infiltrated another security firm's personnel. One, the suicide bomber, had assembled his deadly cargo during a brief stopover on the station. Moments before their shuttle was to launch for the next segment of their journey, he had detonated his bomb. Everything destroyed. All personnel dead. The method was old, as old as Iraq and Palestine and all the troubled countries on earth.

"Nothing left," she whispered.

The Thatcher man hesitated. "I'm sorry, but no. They're salvaging whatever they can, but the explosion scattered . . ." His voice died away a moment, undoubtedly as he realized what images his words called up. "We have something for you, however."

Kate came alert. "What do you mean? You said—"

"A final transmission," he said. "You can refuse, of course. We've edited them for any sensitive material . . ."

He held out a packet. Kate took it greedily. "How much time do I have? For listening?"

Another awkward pause. "The company understands how difficult—"

"The company," Kate said crisply, "understands nothing. How much time?"

The man stiffened at her tone. "We would prefer you return the machine next week. Monday, if possible. We can schedule an operation later to remove the implant."

She nodded. "Very well. Now, please go."

To her relief, the three did not argue. Kate watched them ease their anonymous gray vehicle from the curb. The packet felt solid and heavy in her arms, like an anchor, which was good, because she had the sense of floating a few inches above the ground. Anne had not budged from her side, and Kate could sense her curiosity.

"Anne."

"Yes, Kate."

"Please go. I'd rather be alone."

"Are you sure—"

"Quite sure. Please. Go."

Anne hesitated, then with a murmured farewell, she too was gone.

A brief recording. The last ever.

Hey, Kate. Kate, my love. Kate, my darling lover. Good God in heaven, I miss you. I'm going a little crazy up here. Guess you could tell from that session. Ya think? Not sure what kind of notation they'll make in my fitness report, but what the hey. They asked for a peek inside my skull.

A shaky laugh. A pause. Kate felt and heard Jessica's breathing quicken. Was it a prelude to sex? So hard to tell. For all that the recording slipped Kate inside Jessica's skin, it showed her nothing of her lover's thoughts or emotions. Only clues, pieced together in retrospect.

I miss you, Jessica said suddenly. *It's busy here. We're having another meeting this afternoon. Commander wants tighter security. Can't say more, of course. It's just . . .*

Kate felt warm lips pressed against her fingertips, then those same fingertips brushed against her cheek. Her vision blurred from brown-black shadows into the dim light of her office.

One last kiss, she thought. The last one.

She closed her eyes and let the grief take over.

She called in sick on Monday. No one questioned her. Probably Anne had warned their supervisors about the situation. Kate croaked a mirthless laugh. *Situation*. What a weasel word, as Jessica would say. As bad as *incident*.

Her throat caught on another sob. *Sorry,* she thought. *I have no more tears. I cried them all away.*

She poured herself another cup of coffee. Drank it without noticing. Her stomach hurt, but she couldn't tell if it hurt because she had cried too hard, or if she was simply hungry. She sighed and with great reluctance, she climbed the stairs to her office.

The machine sat in the middle of her empty desk. Around midnight on Saturday, she had nearly pitched the damned thing into trash. Only the thought of how much noise Thatcher would make had stopped her. Now she stared at it with loathing.

I hate you. You gave me ghosts.

Ghosts of Jessica. Ghosts of an ersatz marriage, while they waited out yet another interminable period, for yet another intangible bit of progress. Even as she hated the machine, she found herself sliding the disc into its slot and inserting the terminator into its port.

. . . Hey, Kate. I miss you . . .

She hardly needed the machine to replay that sequence inside her memory, but the machine and chip combined to give her a more vivid remembrance, with details of touch and scent and sound she could never recall on her own.

. . . the chip has a smidge of memory itself, and if you press PLAY three times fast . . .

Kate swallowed against the bitter taste in her mouth. Make some coffee, she told herself. Wake up before you do something truly stupid.

She touched PLAY. Three times fast, followed by pressing PRO-GRAM and RECORD together. Count to ten. A series of lights blinked success. Kate let out a breath. There. She had done it. One last kiss. Saved . . . Not forevermore, but for a short while, at least.

She called Thatcher at noon. By mid-afternoon, they took away the machine. One representative stayed behind to schedule Kate's operation to remove the implant.

"Later," Kate said.

"I'm afraid that later isn't one of the categories," the woman said with a rueful smile. "We need a more definite date."

"Next year," Kate said. "Or is that too definite?"

At the woman's shake of her head, however, she relented. "November 21st. From what your technicians tell me, I will need one day for the operation, another three or four in recovery. That means sick leave or vacation time—depending on how my HR department categorizes the operation. Whatever. My project has a few unmovable deadlines before mid-November. I'm sure you understand."

"We do," said the woman. She tapped a few keys on her cell, frowned, tapped a few more. "Yes, we can arrange something on that date. You'll spend Thanksgiving in the hospital, of course, but I'm sure you knew that."

Kate smiled faintly. "Yes, I knew that."

Late November. A dark cold Tuesday evening.

Tomorrow Kate would drive to Thatcher Operations. There, a technician would review the paperwork, ask her some final questions. The company surgeons would inject her with a sedative, then transport her to Yale–New Haven Hospital, where they had scheduled the operation. All very neat. No security leaks. No chance for medical mishaps. Kate had signed all the releases beforehand.

"Will I remember anything?" she had asked.

"Nearly," the technician had reassured her.

The technician had it wrong, Kate thought, as she drifted out the back door, into her winter-bare garden. If she had her druthers, she would remember . . .

. . . nothing at all.

She sank onto the hard frosted ground at the edge of her garden. Sheets of micro-insulation blanketed half the beds, where she had made a last attempt at normal life. The other half lay bare, with brittle stalks of dead plants poking through the dirt. One shriveled lily bulb lay where she'd left it that Saturday. Dead. Her breath puffed into a cloud. Just like Jessica. She probed inside her heart for some sensation, anything. Found nothing. *Dead like me,* she thought.

By now she could trigger the memory without thinking. Sensation washed over her. That same familiar sense of urgency. The words *I miss you.* Warm lips brushing against her own hand. Kate rubbed the spot where she still felt the impress of warm lips against her hand. Jessica's hand. *She's inside me. Always will be. Doesn't matter if they rip the implant from my brain.*

Her chest felt tight, or was that Jessica's tension as she hurried through that last recording? Kate drew a shuddering breath. Blinked, and felt her frozen eyelashes prick her cheeks. The words *I miss you.* The kiss, but now her hands were numb, and she barely felt Jess's lips. *Again,* she told herself.

She had lost track of the minutes and hours when she heard a voice. A familiar one, but not Jessica's.

Go away, she thought.

The voice called out her name. A hand jostled her shoulder. Kate closed her eyes. Nothing to see anyway. The world had gone brown and black, with pinpoints of silver. In her imagination, the pinpoints whirled around, stopped, whirled again. She thought she saw the outline of Jessica's face when they paused. All too soon the image broke apart. *Show me again,* she tried to whisper, but her lips were cracked and frozen, her tongue clumsy from disuse.

Again that insistent voice. Anne's voice (good, kind, generous Anne) speaking to her, her tone anxious. It was hard to track time, here between repetitions of Jessica's last recording, and so it might have been minutes or days later when more hands took hold of Kate's arms. Voices spoke over her head in short phrases.

Careful now.

Gurney ready?

IV for this one.

Oxygen, too. Gotta bring the core temperature up.

Lucky the streets aren't slick.

We better hurry.

And then the thin, high wail of a siren.

Six o'clock.

Soft chimes marked the hour. Outside, night already blacked out the skies. A dull yellow glow from the city lights seeped upward from the horizon. Winter. Even colder than the almanac had predicted, Kate thought. The air had an antiseptic smell, no matter how the nurses tried to hide it with sweet-smelling sprays.

She heard footsteps in the corridor. Then a light tapping at her door. She said nothing. Anne would come in, or not, just as she had every day for the past three weeks.

The door swung open. Anne leaned around the corner. She wore a dark-blue scarf over her head and around her neck. Snow dusted her coat. Her cheeks were red, as though she had spent some time outdoors.

"Hey," she said softly. "Do you mind a visit?"

Kate shrugged, silent.

Anne sighed and came into the room. Kate watched her methodically unbutton her coat and hang it from the hook inside the door. A nurse peered into the room and greeted Anne, before asking Kate which meal she preferred for dinner.

"I don't care," Kate whispered. "You choose for me."

Anne frowned. She and the nurse exchanged a look. "What about the steak?" Anne said. "Or maybe the pasta—I hear the cook knows his sauces."

"Whatever."

Good, kind, patient Anne, who never once failed to visit Kate. She had stayed at the hospital while the doctors worked to counteract the hypothermia. She came the next day when they removed the implant, and she dealt with Thatcher's representatives. Not that Anne told Kate these things. It was Cordelia or Olivia or the others who told Kate how Anne had saved her life.

As if I wanted my life saved.

But even irritation was too much effort. She sighed again and closed her eyes. She had developed the trick of pretending to sleep. If she held the pose long enough, she often did. She heard whispers as Anne evidently spoke with the nurse about Kate's meal. The door clicked shut. There was a scraping sound as Anne took her usual seat by the window.

"I stopped by your house," Anne said, just as though they were having an ordinary conversation. "Cordelia reminded me that you never had a chance to finish prepping your garden for the winter. I asked at one of the garden centers, and they gave me some suggestions."

Kate suppressed the urge to ask what suggestions. She felt a prick of guilt about her gardens, then annoyance that she felt guilty.

Meanwhile, Anne continued her recitation. ". . . Cordelia and I raked the yard. We trimmed back the shrubs and vines and ran those through the shredder. We even cleaned out the compost heap and finished covering the flower beds."

Kate's eyes burned with unshed tears. Only Anne. Only Anne would remember how much Kate loved her gardens. But what good were gardens in the winter? What good were gardens if you were alone?

". . . Olivia and Remy came by to help, too. I don't know if I told you, but they've made up and now they're talking about finding a house together . . ."

Tears leaked from her eyes. Surprising after weeks of numbness. She swiped them away.

"Kate?"

A tiny stab in the region of her heart. Insistent. Unwelcome. "No," Kate whispered. "I don't want to." Then louder. "No. No, no, no."

Her voice scaled up, louder and louder, until her voice cracked, and she burst into weeping—loud angry sobs that tore at her throat. Kate pummeled the bed, trying to beat away the grief. She didn't want tears. Or misery. None of that could bring Jessica back.

Arms gathered her into a tight hug. Anne. Anne capturing her hands so they could not scratch or beat or harm herself. Anne strong and gentle at the same time, who rocked Kate back and forth while she held her close. "I'm sorry. I'm sorry," she murmured over and over. "I said the wrong things. All the wrong things. I'm so sorry, Kate. So sorry."

"I hate it," Kate mumbled into Anne's shoulder.

"You should hate it," Anne said fiercely. "Hate me, if you like. Hate the world. I'd rather you did, than feel nothing. Oh god, Kate, I wish I could do something *real*. I wish—"

She broke off and pulled away from Kate. Shocked, Kate felt her own grief subside for the moment. Only now did she take in details she had not noticed before. How Anne's cheeks were wet with tears. And her eyes were red, as though she had not slept well the past few weeks. But Anne never wept, she thought, never lost her temper. She was the even keel they all depended upon.

"Anne?"

Anne wiped her eyes with the back of her hand. "Sorry. That was selfish of me."

No, I'm the selfish one, Kate thought.

A knot deep inside her flexed, as though an unused muscle tried to work itself loose. Instinctively she reached up and touched Anne's face. Anne flinched. Her eyes went wide and dark, and color spread over her cheeks. So many tiny clues, like droplets of watering coalescing into realization.

"How long?" Kate whispered.

"Does it matter?" Anne blew out a breath. "I should go."

"No. Stay."

They stared at one another for a long uncomfortable moment. Snow tapped against the windowpane, and out in the corridor, a light sizzled and popped.

"What are you saying?" Anne said at last.

The knot inside Kate pinched tight. Too fast. Too soon. Far too soon for anything. She'd spoken before thinking.

"I'm not sure. I—I need a friend."

A ghost-like smile came and went on Anne's face. "I make a decent friend, they tell me."

So she did. Even to selfish wretches like Kate.

A person did not heal within a day or month. Often not for years, Kate thought, wiping more tears from her eyes. And yet, watching Anne's quiet patient face, Kate felt as though she could breathe properly for the first time in months. They could be friends. Good ones. More, if time and healing allowed them.

Not yet.

She could almost hear Anne's voice reassuring her, saying, *It's okay. It doesn't matter. I'm here for you.*

Unexpectedly, warmth brushed against her cheek—not a recording but a memory. Jessica.

"Hey," she said to Anne. "Tell me more about my garden. Tell me what it looks like these days. What it smells like. Tell me—" She drew a deep breath and felt the knot inside ease a fraction. "Tell me everything."

The Program
G. Bonhomme

You probably first saw the ads on the subway. Grinning guy in a tux, supermodel hotties draped over him. "Get With The Program;" or the other one, "The Program That Made A Man Out of Jerry." You might have puzzled over it for a moment. Some exercise thing, probably, or a drug like Viagra? Or any bullshit product advertisers claim can get you laid. Still, though, the way the guy in the tux looked: commanding. Rolling in sex. You'd swap lives in a minute.

The poster had some of that fine print at the bottom like they do when they're pushing something your doctor has to prescribe: "The Program is a course of cognitive-behavioral biofeedback therapy for the treatment of severe interpersonal interrelation adjustment disorders. Use only as directed. Ask your doctor if The Program is appropriate for you. . . ."

Then the doors opened, and you shuffled through with the crowd and forgot all about it.

The first time you vividly remember hearing about it was at the bar. A real looker was sitting there nursing her drink, blonde hair down to here, slinky white dress, big ripe tits—the kind you'd love to get your dick between. The guys had been watching you eyeing her and you'd had a few, and with them egging you on you went for it. Somewhere between the booth and the bar, though, the rough edge of the bravado faded, and instead of just showing off for the guys you found yourself really asking:

"Hey, pretty lady. Can I buy you a drink?"

She ignored you, but you thought you saw a trace of a smile. You sat down at the stool next to her.

"Hey, come on, I'm a nice guy. Really. You'd like me. Seriously. You want to go out sometime?"

And she burst out laughing.

That stung. The glare or the cold silence or even her throwing a fit and chewing you out, you could take that, went with the territory. But this? She was laughing her ass off, wiping tears from her eyes and gasping for breath. And when she recovered, she looked you right in the eyes and said—almost sweetly—"Oh shit, honey! Give me a break!" She grinned ear to ear. "My boyfriend's done the Program. Why would I want to go out with you?"

And then it seemed like it was all over the place—like if you looked at the magazine covers on a newsstand, it would be:

Elle: "The Program": Why It Works!

Razor: Secrets of The Program

Cosmo: Ten Ways To Get Your Man To Do The Program

Maxim: Don't Let Her Program You!

Star: Brad to Jenna: "I'll Do The Program For You!"

But, you know, it seemed like something for Hollywood stars and Manhattan glitterati—not part of your world. Not something a guy from Queens would do. Come on!

But then the secretaries in the office pool were giggling about a guy over in Sales who supposedly did it. And one of them was like, "Oh my god? Can you believe it? I so am going to ask him!"

And the old biddy leering: "Ask him to do WHAT?"

And they were cackling and the one who said it was blushing beet red going, "No, just ask him what it's LIKE that's all, come on you guys!"

And through the laughter the dark-haired Rhonda from HR, the real sophisticated-looking one with the great ass and the steely eyes, said, "These guys should ALL do it. Our health plan covers it!"

Then:

You were in bed with Caitlin who was this on-again-off-again piece you had, not a dog, but kind of plain—nice eyes, nice hair, a too-big nose, and little tits, and too skinny—and usually if you were feeling hard up you'd come around to her place and after some complaining on her part (about how you never came around), you'd end up on her sofa making out; and about one time out of three you'd end up in her bed, fucking. And when you added it up, she was actually the only girl you'd actually got to the fucking part with for about three years, since that thing with Tanika. And she always made these hints about being boyfriend-girlfriend, and you always laughed them off.

But this time, somehow, you started feeling insecure, like maybe she was slipping through your fingers too. Like the world was changing? So you actually went down on her without being asked.

And you were enjoying it, getting your tongue all up in her muff and running it around over what was probably her clit, and her moaning: even though you wanted so bad to bust your nut, you kind of took it slow.

So that when you finally rolled the condom on and slid it into her, oh man, it was like heaven in there. Your dick had been waiting so long it felt swollen up like a balloon. Her pussy was just right, not hard like a hand or soft like a pillow, but warm and firm and giving. You pounded into that sweet strong tube of hers—all the way in! You felt her hands moving on your back, you squeezed her ass, she growled deep in her throat, and soon everything faded into the background, but the feeling of your hungry cock, taking her.

You held your breath, so as not to come too soon, and you must have lasted, what, twenty, maybe thirty strokes before that river burst its dam. The surge went like heat through your whole body, toes to head, that moment of being on top of the world, that wave of molten power, better than any liquor, better than a jackpot—but not unlike a jackpot, not unlike pulling that one-armed bandit's handle and seeing all cherries come up, and the rush of gold coins going on, on, on, on into the bowl.

But afterwards, when you rolled off her, she sighed this tight little sigh and turned her head away. And when you reached over to put your hand affectionately on her tummy, she stiffened up. She got up and went to the bathroom.

She was usually chatty after sex, but not this time. And you hauled yourself up and got your clothes on and she showed you out, you still a little woozy with the glow and feeling like she ought to be grateful for how you'd made her moan. And as you stood a little unsteady on the step she said:

"Listen, Gary, uh . . . you know . . . I think this was our last fuck."

"What?" you said, feeling like you couldn't have heard right. "What?"

"Yeah, you know, I just. . . . I think I want. . . . Something different. Okay?"

And to your silence she said, "Okay. Yeah. Good night." And closed the door.

And one night about three months after *that,* three months of no booty at all, not even a kiss, you were sitting on the green sofa in your crappy little house, channel-surfing, and on the Entertainment Channel Kevin Costner or Matthew M-something or one of those Hollywood guys was saying sincerely to some interviewer, "Yes, I did it, and I'm quite happy to talk about it. I think it's made me a better lover and, you know, even a better human being."

So then, the next morning, you were standing on a crowded street corner in Manhattan waiting for a green light. And you see this absolute babe standing next to you: miniskirt and gray tit-hugging sweater, breasts like mangoes, perfect ass, looking like a younger, shorter Cindy Crawford—way out of your league. You turned to her, not getting too close though, not wanting to scare her, and said, "Hey, you're beautiful." She gave you the kind of brutal stare you expected, like What The Fuck. But not scared. It was a confident, intelligent stare, with a little humor behind it—like she was wondering, what's he going to say next, and if it's sufficiently out there I'm looking forward to laughing my ass off about this guy with the girls.

And you said, "Listen—if I did the Program—would you go on a date with me?"

And get this. She blinked. She looked you up and down—*she* looked *you* up and down—and a slow smile spread over her face, like a cat looking at a canary whose cage just popped open.

And she said, "*Hell* yeah."

Man: you were hard, just like that.

The light turned green and everyone but you two crossed. She took out a pen and a piece of paper out of her purse and handed it to you and said, "If you're serious, write down your name and number. You do it, I'll call you." The light turned red again.

You couldn't believe it. Your hands were shaking. Your throat was dry. You grinned kind of lopsided, making a show because, shit, of course she was putting you on, as you wrote down your name and number. "Oh yeah? And how are you going to know if I really did it?"

She frowned as she took the paper back. "Don't be dumb," she said. "I'm a subscriber."

The light turned green again. She crossed. You stood watching her ass as it went up Fifth Avenue. She didn't look back. But you saw her tuck the paper back in her purse.

"Gary," said your doctor, "three months without a relationship doesn't mean you have a disorder."

"It's not just that," you said. Trying to recall the articles you'd read. "I've never really felt comfortable in relationships. And anxiety, I uh, have a lot of anxiety about it. You know, keeps me up at night."

Dr. Wallace sighed. "Look, there are other alternatives. I could recommend you to a psychiatrist for a more traditional course of therapy. This Program business—it's really quite radical. It can have a lot of side effects—dysthymia, sexual dysphoria, unwanted personality changes. It can exacerbate adjustment disorders. It's a major stressor. I was extremely surprised, to tell you the truth, that the FDA even approved it."

"Are you saying I don't qualify?"

He scowled. "No, I'm not saying that. I just think you shouldn't jump into this. . . ."

"I really just want to give this a try," you said—but he was already writing on his little pad.

The clinic was a skyscraper in Midtown. There was a small mob of protesters outside. Almost all men. With police standing by to keep the route clear.

"It isn't worth it!"

They looked like slobs. Unshaven, red-eyed. Middle of the fucking day, why weren't they at work anyway? *They* didn't have time off for a medical appointment.

"Listen, buddy! You don't know what you're giving up!"

"Don't let those bitches in your head!"

Fucking crazies. It was like going to an abortion clinic. "Oh yeah," you called back over your shoulder as you reached the doorman. "What did they do? Cut your balls off?"

Their faces when you said that. Cut their balls off. That was a good one. You were chuckling all the way up the elevator.

Then there was this long intake interview with a white-haired woman doctor in her sixties. Personal information forms, permissions, liability waivers, detailed questionnaires about how many girls you'd been with and what you liked to do in bed and how many times a week you masturbated and the whole thing. You answered them all good-naturedly, though you couldn't imagine this old lady reading them.

Under permissions there was a question that read:

> While your enrollment in The Program, like all medical information, is strictly private, we have found that many of our clients wish to make their participation known to others. As a service to our clients, Gallman Clinic LLP provides a public registry to which interested

parties can subscribe. If wish to you waive your right to privacy and include your name in the registry, Gallman Clinic LLP can verify your successful completion of The Program upon subscriber request. Do you want your name to be included in this public registry?

Which meant, that that hottie could see you'd done The Program. You checked "yes," because they didn't have a "Fuck yeah!"

"This is Sophie," said the old lady. "She's one of our assessment counselors."

Sophie was beautiful in kind of a cold, sophisticated, European way. Long, white-blonde hair thrown over one shoulder, piercing blue eyes. Thick Nordic sweater, long legs in black slacks. Mid-thirties, probably—maybe ten years older than the hottie at the street corner. You wouldn't say hottie for her. She was just as out of your league, maybe even more beautiful, but not hot. Cold. The kind you couldn't really even bring yourself to imagine fucking.

"Your schedule is free tonight?" Sophie said. She had some European accent, like a roughness at the back of the throat, the "r" breathy.

"Uh, yes," you said.

"Good," she said, and smiled briefly. "We are going on a date. This is mostly to establish a baseline, before the treatments: your relationship competence, your style, inclinations, performance."

"Performance," you repeated, your dick giving a little throb.

"But this is a fancier restaurant," Sophie said, "than that to which you normally invite a woman."

The waiter poured wine. You played with a folded cloth napkin. You felt yourself sitting up straighter. "Well, yeah," you said. "But, you know, you seem—it seems like it goes with you. You're, ah . . ."

"I'm fancy?" asked Sophie. You couldn't tell if she was kidding. She looked calm. You looked away.

"You're beautiful," you said.

Sophie smiled. "Thank you."

She looked around your crappy little house. Green sofa. TV dinner packages ripped open on the kitchenette counter. You blushed. "It's a lousy place."

"I like it," Sophie said, and sat down on the sofa. She eased off one stack-heeled boot.

You stood there, your dick twinging. Your heart beating. Wanting to make sure you'd got this right.

"You know, usually after the dinner, I conduct the assessment at the clinic," Sophie said. "And it's quite perfunctory."

"So, are you going to get in trouble?"

She eased off the other boot. "I have some, what do you say, leeway? And I feel comfortable with you, Gary." She patted the couch next to her. You went. "I'm going to ask you to do things," she said. "You can say no. I'll first ask you to do them as usual. Then I may give you instructions. Please don't be offended if I do. It's part of the assessment."

"I'm not gonna be offended . . ."

"Kiss me," said Sophie.

You leaned in and put your mouth on her dark-lipsticked mouth. She tasted a little like the wine from dinner, a little like mint. You put your hands on her waist. She took them off.

"Just kiss," she said. "Slow. Gentle. But not limp. You see?" Her lips found yours, delicate, like hummingbirds. "Wait for me to increase the power of the kiss."

Her mouth on yours. A fucking Class A broad. Unbelievable. Your health care package paying for a top of the line call girl. Except she didn't really feel like a call girl. More like a doctor, or a teacher?

She pulled away. "Good. You are a little distracted, though. Now take off my sweater." She held her arms up.

Sweater off, bra off, your shirt off; Sophie lay back on the sofa. She had smallish tits, like apples, with big nipples. "My breasts like to be licked," she said. "Try."

You tried.

"No! Much too hard. Lick around from the edges in. Better. Polish them with your tongue. Mmmm. Now try—no! Too hard. Lightly. There. Flick the tongue over them. Yes, yes. Keep going. More. Now the other one."

On the one hand, you could hardly believe you were allowed to put your tongue onto those perfectly round, creamy tits, those hard pink nipples straining for the ceiling.

On the other hand, she was bossy as hell, and it was beginning to feel like work. You slid your hand into her panties. She grabbed your wrist.

"Not yet," she said. Her voice was gentle. You went back to work on the breasts. She made deep humming noises.

Your dick was hard, swollen up. It wanted out of the pants. You reached for her panties again.

"Gary, not yet," she said.

"I thought you wanted me to do things the way I do them."

"After I ask you to. Shall we stop now and try this again tomorrow?"

You swallowed, and a flash of anger shot through you—she'd leave you high and dry now? But then you said to yourself: Gary, you're being an asshole. This is her job. Let her do it.

You pulled away, sat up on the couch. "Hey, um. I'm sorry about that. I . . ."

She smiled a brilliant smile. "More kissing."

Then, while you were kissing, she put your hand in her panties.

She broke the kiss. "Gentler. See? I am moist. That is what we waited for. Yes? Wait—stop. It's all right. You will learn this later. Sit back a moment."

She slid her panties off her hips and ran her fingers over her cunt. "Watch," she whispered. "Just watch." She licked her fingers, slid them between the folds. They slipped in and out like dancers. "Take off your pants. Put a condom on."

You were covered with sweat, and your breathing was tight. Sophie fucking herself with her fingers like something out of a porn movie, except slower, quieter, softer. Just breathing, instead of moans and cries. Porn girls pouted and smoldered, or yelled and bucked: Sophie closed her eyes and frowned in concentration, her brow wrinkling. Her bush was small, neatly trimmed, as white-blonde as her head. There was a fine golden down on her thighs, almost invisible.

"Watch closely," she whispered, licking her fingers again. "See this here? The clitoris. Look: very soft touches, not directly on, around. The hood—you see? And. Then. Hmmm."

Her eyes stayed closed. Now you could almost think she was asleep, looking at her face, except when tremors would run over it. Your dick had never been this hard. You needed to get it wet.

"All right," she said. "Now. Enter me."

You pushed your cock into her. She was tight and her muscles rippled and you were coming, coming, coming.

You groaned, and then you rested your head on her shoulder.

She chuckled in your ear and whispered, "Not very good, Gary. I did not get to enjoy it very long. Or to come." She stroked your back, long smooth strokes. "But you are lovely. And you will get better. Much better."

The Program was three weeks—four days a week, mornings and evenings, at the clinic before and after work, plus three weekend training seminars. Waking up alone that first morning, you let yourself hope it would involve a lot of screwing Sophie. Maybe even Sophie hanging around afterwards, sleeping over, making you breakfast. It wasn't like that, though.

In fact, you had to be celibate for the three weeks.

The hours you spent in the lab were strange. At first there were CAT scans, blood tests, running on a treadmill with wires taped to your head and this metal cap. Then, after the first few days, there was the chair.

The chair was like a cross between a dentist chair and Captain Kirk's chair on *Star Trek*. Your head wired up, and earphones and goggles on, and an IV in your arm. They'd leave you there for an hour or three, the chair tipped back, in a room with one wall that was a mirror they could see through from the other side.

Sometimes the goggles and headphones played movies—porn movies, or scenes from romantic chick flicks, or detailed instructional movies about sex. Sometimes there were just flickering cascades of images, too quick for you to make them out. Sometimes there were recorded instructions.

They set out Vaseline and warm, wet towels when they wanted you to masturbate. The recorded voice told you what to do. That was weird at first. You didn't know who might be watching. But you got used to it.

Once you asked one of the docs, a bald old guy, what all the gear did. The IV drip had something to do with enhanced memory formation, and the metal cap was actually sending electrical impulses into your brain for "subexperiential behavioral reinforcement." Whatever that was.

You stopped masturbating at home: you didn't feel like it. Even though you'd sometimes come home from the clinic and sit, channel-surfing and not really seeing the TV, too wired to sleep, imagining sex. Fucking Sophie up the ass. Fucking the girl from the street corner between her mango-shaped tits. Caitlin begging to suck you off and you coming down her throat. Sex saturated your head, burned your body from your ears to the soles of your feet, but it was all distant, muddy, like under a layer of thick gauze. The images would swarm like fevered dreams, and then they'd be gone and you'd be alone in your crap house, feeling lonely and confused and desperate, and somehow guilty. Sometimes you'd run your head under the cold water from the kitchen sink, to make it go away.

The seminars were mostly bullshit: Mars–Venus stuff, how to listen, how you should wash the dishes and talk about your fear. All the guys avoided each other in the hallways. A few of the exercises were kind of interesting.

One time you were talking about your dad, the time he'd built this boat with you and then smashed it when he was mad, and you actually started to cry. Bullshit like that. The other guys all looked away, embarrassed. You got it together after a moment.

One time Sophie walked out of the observation room into the hallway, just as you were coming out of the room with the chair. She was with three other women, all good-looking, though none of them in her league. Probably all assessment counselors. They'd clearly been watching you jack off, and you flushed beet red.

"Looking forward to our exit session," Sophie called, and the other women laughed.

You couldn't think of anything to say and you got out of there. On the subway, your dick was throbbing. It felt sore. It occurred to you that you'd been masturbating in that session for about three hours, and you never did come.

The phone rang one night. "Hey, this is Jill. You remember me?"

It was the hottie from the street corner. "Holy shit. Yeah, I mean, definitely. How, how are you doing?"

"Hey," she purred, "you're really doing it! I just looked you up on the list. I thought you were just full of shit."

"No, I'm really doing it."

"For me?"

You didn't know what to say. She cackled. "Don't answer that. Woo! It's a little hot in here right now." She laughed again. "So listen, what do you do?"

You talked about work. She was a graduate student in political science at NYU. A real egghead. She wasn't stuck up, though. Then you talked about music. You both liked The Clash.

"So, um, listen," Jill said. "Can I pop your cherry?"

"What?" you asked.

"I mean I'm going to put in a request to be the first person to have sex with you, when you get out. You know. Ask them to go easy on the exit session. They'll do that, if you want them to."

Your throat was dry. "Yeah, sure. Sure."

"Okay," Jill said. "Shall we make a date, for when you get out?"

"Okay," you whispered.

You were so tired at work that last week, you could barely keep it together. You got back from the warehouse inspection and slumped into your cube and just stared at the computer for a while. You could feel every inch of your skin. You felt the seams of your jeans, running down the outside and up the inside of your thighs. The seams of your shirt, stroking your sides. If you closed your eyes, your watchband felt like a woman's thumb and fingers locked around your wrist, pulling you downward. You could feel your toes nudging into your socks, parting the folds of cotton, pushing them back against the hard walls of leather. Somehow you'd lost weight over the past couple of weeks; your potbelly had vanished. You could feel all your muscles, biceps and quads and abs, dwelling inside your clothes; like animals waiting, breathing, ready to go.

Friday, you were so zoned out, you were late to the cafeteria for lunch. As you passed the secretaries' table there was a sudden pause in their conversation, and then a burst of laughter. You turned around and they hushed up again. A couple of them darted you glances and looked away; the old biddy glowered disapprovingly into her soup. Rhonda from HR, though, looked up right into your eyes, with a steady look just this side of a smile, and you felt blood shooting through your body, up through your face, up to the roots of your hair.

You made it to your table somehow. The guys weren't talking much; Harry was still on vacation and Bharat and Alex were in a shared sour mood due to recent fuck-ups by their boss. You looked back: Rhonda was eating. But it was like she could feel you looking at the back of her head, because she turned to you. She was eating a shrimp and it was hanging out of the side of her mouth, and she sucked it in like a satisfied cat.

And this was bullshit. Shouldn't you be going over them, talking it up? "Oh so you're *subscribers*, eh, ladies? Oh, no, I sure can't *tell* you what goes on in there . . . no, I reckon you'd have to *experience* the difference . . ."

You applied yourself to the meatloaf.

But what did you need fucking Rhonda and those harpies for anyway? No wonder you don't want to go over there and be made fun of, shit, groups of women like that are merciless, especially when they're single and hard up. Wait until you came to the Christmas party with Jill on your arm. She'd be dressed like a starlet at the

Oscars and you'd whisper in her ear and she'd be the one turning red, and Rhonda would be turning green.

That evening, there was no time in the chair, just the physical with the treadmill again, and this exit interview with the old lady doctor, and then it was time for your date with Sophie. You waited in this real doctor's-office type room, with a kind of double-wide hospital bed in it, and fluorescent lights. You were nervous as hell. First you sat on the bed, but that was kind of lame, so then you stood over in the corner by the coat rack.

How would Sophie take this whole thing about Jill's request? And shit, why the hell did you agree to that? Oh, sure, you knew why: you're no idiot. Sophie was a pro, she was just doing her job, whereas Jill was for real, Jill was a keeper. One fuck, versus as many fucks as you wanted. But still—Sophie was such a fucking beautiful piece of work. How could you pass up another shot at that svelte, golden European cunt? Could you talk Sophie into going ahead and fucking anyway, and not telling Jill?

But while you were thinking this, underneath the chatter in your head, what you felt didn't really match. You felt kind of sad and alone. You wished you could be back on the phone with Jill, hearing her laugh.

But holy shit, come on, man, you told yourself, nice problem to have, right? When before did I have grade-A babes fighting over me?

The door opened and you jumped up, because apparently you'd managed to sit down on the bed again.

Sophie, in her clean, severe Germanic glory, smiled at you.

"Gary," she said. "Are you ready?"

"Sure, of course, hey. Hello. Where are we going?"

"Indeed hello," she said, closing the door. "Here is fine. Especially since we have a subscriber request, from a—" she looked at her clipboard "—Jill Sivens, to do a short exit session with you. I assume you agree to that?"

"About that," you said, "uh, Sophie, I hope it's okay that—"

She looked up and smiles brightly. "Oh, Gary, it's great! It's a great sign when our clients are so quick to start building relationships with their new skills." She put the clipboard down on a table. "Can you take off your clothes? How have you been feeling?"

The flutter in your stomach sank a little, but you started shrugging out of your clothes. "Um. Okay. Weird, really."

"Weird how?" said Sophie.

"Tired, I guess. Just kind of—worn out, from the chair." You were groping for some way of talking about it. She must know.

"Any hallucinations? Paranoid thoughts?"

"No, no. I mean—sometimes it feels like I can *feel* things better, you know? Like, I mean with my skin. But nothing too weird."

She smiled broadly. "Heightened sensitivity. That's not a problem." The way she said "not a problem" made your spine tingle. You had your shoes and shirt off and you pulled your pants down and were surprised to find your dick was hard as a rock. Like, not surprised surprised, because here you were stripping for Sophie; but surprised you hadn't noticed.

"Any aversive thoughts about sex or sexual partners? As in, you are worried about sex or don't like the idea of sex?"

"Jesus, no," you said, pulling off your shorts. "Quite the opposite."

"Oh good," Sophie said, grinning again. "Very good." She came across the room and took your penis in her hands, as casually as if she was testing your knee for reflexes. "So this feels good?" she asked, gingerly stroking from the base of the shaft to the head.

You could hardly talk from surprise. Actually the feeling was like a burning, buzzing throb. Sophie's taut little breasts danced inside her blouse, and you could smell her smell—like apples and mint. "Yes," you said.

"Good," she said, and let go of you. "I won't do any more of that, because I want to honor the subscriber request." She crossed to her clipboard and made a few notes. Then she looked up at your face. "Oh, Gary, don't worry. I still have to do a little concrete measurement to see if your competence has improved. And in fact, I like this way, I'll tell you why. Remember how our first date was, well, a little bit all about you?" She grinned impishly. "This one will be all about me. Come take off my clothes very gently."

Cotton. Wool. Satin. Metal, the snick of the bra snap coming open. Skin, the panties moving down the legs, your thumbs brushing her thighs.

"Good." She lay face down on the big hospital bed. "Backrub."

Skin. Warm and breathing. Your fingers could feel the little knots of wrongness. When you pushed too hard, she raised her shoulders a quarter-inch and you backed off. When it was too light, her breathing became irregular, and you pushed in. At one point you almost lost her to sleep, and your fingers started to stroke lightly, like ships dancing. Your fingertips, her pores. Her breathing quickened.

She rolled over. "Look at the clock, Gary," she said.

"Shit," you said. "It's ten o' clock." An hour backrub?

"Having fun?"

"Yeah."

"Good," she said. "Breasts."

And then: "Good. Now with your tongue."

Swollen flesh of her breast, the salty taste of her skin. Apples and mint. The nipple rolling under your tongue like a mountain. Her breathing roughening. Her stomach quivering.

She spread her legs, pushed your head down. "Tongue. Down here."

She tasted delicious. Tangy and salty. Which was weird. Sherry and Nora and Tarika and Caitlin had tasted, you know, fine, but not like this. She was wet and hot and, like, *pure* around your tongue. It wasn't even like you were doing something—you couldn't tell where your tongue stopped and her cunt started, and the rest of your own body seemed very far away. But her body—her trunk that squirmed, her feet that came up off the table and stroked the back of your head and then kicked out, her lungs that sucked in air and held it and pushed it out, her hands that ran through her hair and then yours and then grabbed the table behind her head, her ass that lifted up to your mouth and fell again—her body was all that was real.

"Tongue and fingers, now," she whispered. "Please, Gary. Please let me come."

The first time her breath caught and her cunt throbbed and her thighs gripped your head, you still weren't sure, because she didn't make any noise, and because when you started to back off, her hand snaked around the back of your head and pushed you back in. You'd been doing all these fine, whispery things with your tongue but now you could tell she needed more, and then you were licking like crazy, your tongue like an eel, a wet slab coming down and in and over again and again, and you were drinking her up. Three fingers pushing in and just holding, firm against the wall of her vagina. And the second time, she let out a sob and her cunt squeezed your knuckles together hard enough to hurt, and then you could feel it, white light flooding in from all sides, filling her up, filling you up. You didn't even have a body at all any more, there was just her, the light filling her, and you'd never felt that good. As if something that had been sleeping inside you since you were born woke up and said: I want that.

"Okay," Sophie said a little later. "Stop. It's midnight. We have to go." She pushed herself up off the bed and flung her arms around your shoulders and kissed your cheek, her hard nipples pushing into your chest. "Thanks," she breathed into your ear.

You both got dressed. Your whole body was buzzing, awake. You heard every rustle of cloth like a whisper telling you a secret. How weird to be after sex and not want to fall asleep. You wanted to go play football in the park or some shit. You noticed your dick—still rock hard—when you pushed it back into your underpants. Snapped your jeans shut over it. Kind of uncomfortable.

Sophie opened the door and slapped your ass. "Go get them," she said, and giggled, deep in her throat.

You almost danced down the hall.

You had a bunch of flowers for Jill. Not roses, that might be too corny. Or, like, trying too hard. Just a bunch of yellow and orange flowers. You didn't know what kind they were. You would think that would have been covered on the Program weekend sessions, what flowers to get a girl. Instead of all the crap about listening skills.

She was a little late to the restaurant. She'd picked it; it wasn't a fancy place but it wasn't a dive either. It was all raw wood panels and big wooden tables and the waiters had white smocks on, and practically all they served was like coffee, bread, and salad. But really good bread, deep brown and full of seeds and shit, the kind that steams when you break it open. You sat there at the end of one table with your glass of water, waiting for Jill to show, and you could smell the bread, a powerful thick wave of bread, coming from the ovens.

She was in a tank top and khaki shorts and army boots. Belly button showing, no bra, her mango breasts jiggling, the fabric snug around them. Petite. Her stomach wasn't flat and severe like Sophie's; she had a little low roundish hill of a tummy that suggested the hill of her cunt inside those baggy pants. She looked a little wary, like she was wondering if this was a good idea, but her face relaxed into confidence when she saw you, and she grinned. Her face—yeah, like Cindy Crawford, without the mole. Holy shit, what were you doing here? It was hard to believe that she smiled when she saw you. Hard to believe she was heading over to sit next to you.

She slid in next to you and waved the waiter over.

"Hi," you said, "hey, uh, thanks for . . ."

"Oh, shut up," she said, "don't thank me. What are you thanking me for? Don't thank me for being late to a date with you, that's lame."

You were going to say sorry, but you thought better of it.

She reached over and wrapped her hand around your bicep, and squeezed. "You're looking good," she said. "You lost weight in there."

"Yeah, it's weird, it's not like I had any time to exercise or—"

She gave a grin of pure evil. You remembered the chair and you flushed red.

The waiter came and Jill said, "Just get us bread and salad, we'll share. And a carafe of Merlot. We're celebrating."

"Eat quick," she said to you when the food came.

She talked a lot, about school and politics. She had strong opinions about everything. She hated Bush and you could see her point. She'd liked Clinton and you'd thought he was full of shit. But you didn't need weekend seminars to know to shut up about that on a first date. You listened and you watched her beautiful face move.

You held hands on the way back to Jill's. It was just around the corner. Your whole body was humming. She pushed you into an alley and you kissed. Blood buzzing in your ears, the taste of bread and wine on her lips and tongue. Her breasts pushing against your chest. You grabbed her ass and she laughed and slipped away, pulling you out of the alley.

Jill winked at the doorman, a big black guy who looked like a linebacker and rolled his eyes like a drag queen. There was this old couple arguing in the elevator, so you didn't kiss there.

Her apartment was a bedroom with a teddy bear on it and poster-sized black-and-white photos on the walls, a living room nook with a couch and a big window, and a kitchenette.

She shucked her tank top and her breasts bounced out. You

wanted to touch them, but you just looked. It was like you could feel Sophie's ghost holding you back, slowing you down. She ran her fingers over her breasts, lifted them up. She bent down and licked her own nipple, and looked at your reaction. She grinned.

You pulled off your shirt. You dropped your pants. You yanked your boxers from around your cock, which was standing at attention.

She grinned more.

She slid her pants and panties off together, and tossed them over the couch. Now all of the Upper West Side could see her bare ass if they looked in the window, but you guessed nobody who lives on the twentieth floor worries about shit like that.

Her cunt was just as you imagined it, a low hill, thick black curly hair.

You kissed some more, your cock pushing against her stomach. It felt numb. But the warmth of your belly on hers felt good.

"Eat me," she said, and she sat back on the couch. She was still wearing the army boots. You knelt down to it.

Your body faded away again into the background. Your moving tongue was the bridge between your mind and the body that was real: her sweat, her shudders, her hand knotted in your hair, pushing you in. She was louder than Sophie, rougher, her breath coming in jerks and grunts and hisses, her fist pulling at your hair. Like she was fighting, hips moving like a boxer's. You slid your hands over her flanks, her thighs, and then you slid your thumbs in to stroke her pussy lips, and then to nudge her clit in slow circles.

"Oh!" she cried. "Oh!"

You wanted her to come. You wanted that flooding of white light, that delicious wave.

She pulled you back out of her cunt, by the hair.

"Um, hey. Please come," you said. "I want to make you come."

"No," she said, and her eyes were wild, her chest heaving. "Not yet."

She pushed you down onto the couch and pulled open a drawer on a side table. She rummaged around, fished out a condom, opened it with her teeth and slid it onto your cock. You gasped when she touched you—something was strange. Your cock felt too swollen, almost like you had to piss bad. But different. The condom felt like sandpaper going on, and you jerked away, but she followed with her hands and body, pushing it down, rolling it down until it touched your balls.

She took you by the balls and pulled you down onto the sofa again. "Ssh," she said. "It's okay. Ssh."

She climbed up onto the sofa, onto you. Her goddamn amazing breasts brushed your nose. She put one knee on either side of you, straddling over you, her cunt hair brushing the tip of your penis. She took the shaft in her hand.

It was like your cock was sore, but sore from the inside out.

She slipped the head inside, pushing it into the dense warmth of her, squeezing it past the bands of muscle. It hurt.

"Hold on," you gasped. "Jill—wait—"

"Ssh," she said. She looked excited, like a kid opening birthday presents. "Gary. I know what I'm doing. Okay? I've popped cherries of Program guys before. It's supposed to be like this."

She plunged down onto you. Her cunt was like a hot fist. You bit off a scream.

"Yeah," she breathed. "Don't come. Focus on me, Gary. What am I feeling?" She put your hands on her breasts.

She rode you. It hurt. But beyond you, in her, pleasure was building. Her nipples ground against your palms and she groaned. Your cock felt like a throat, and her cunt was like hands crushing it, but at every stroke you could feel the waves of pleasure in her. You heard yourself moaning, but it was far away. She licked your neck and that felt good, suddenly warm and wet. Each time she plunged down on you, crushing your cock in that incredible grip, you squeezed her breasts and the nipples in your palms were like wires connecting you to the bliss in her head, the blood and power flooding through her.

You don't know how long it was. A long time. "Oh YEAH," she said, "oh YEAH, Gary, oh YEAH—"

She kissed you. That felt good.

"Wait," you said when she broke the kiss, "stop—"

"How does it feel, honey?" she said, thrusting onto you again. "Does it hurt?"

The question pierced the numbness and you felt your cock again. Her cunt pulled back and it was like she was ripping it off your body. You screamed, and you felt the muscles of her pussy start to squeeze, squeeze, squeeze, felt her whole trunk shudder.

She threw her head back. "Oh!" she said. "Oh shit! Gary—Gary—" she looked down at you. Like hungry woman at a slice of devil's food cake. "Gary, come on three! One—two—three—"

You came on three and it was like fire, like blood spurting out of you. An agony so sudden and total you couldn't breathe.

And then she was coming too, and the white light was there, flooding you, flooding you with peace, washing everything away. It was her body that was the center, her singing nerves, her roaring heart, her body hugging you close, and her cry. She bit your shoulder where it met your neck and you could feel it from her side, the pressure on her teeth, the taste of the lump of meat in her mouth. It felt good.

You slumped back on the couch and she lay on top of you.

"Ohhh . . ." she said.

You breathed. The soreness was gone. The white light was moving in you. You were dizzy.

"Now I get to say thank you," she said, and giggled.

"Uhh . . ." you said. Then you laughed too. You didn't know what else to do. You didn't know what to think.

She swung off you and stood up, swaying a little, dizzy too. "I've got ice cream!" she announced, and went into the kitchenette.

You couldn't move. She came in with Rocky Road and two spoons.

"Jill," you said. "What was—I mean—?"

She dug out a scoop with one spoon. Her hair was kind of wild, a strand wiggling down over her nose. She was beautiful. She raised an eyebrow, questioning.

"I, uh, that hurt."

She nodded, looking serious, ice cream sitting on her spoon. Her nipples were hard.

You started to laugh again.

"It gets better," she said. "Trust me." She climbed up on you, straddling your chest. Her scratchy pubic hair tickled you. Her cunt was still wet, sticky against your breastbone. Her breasts swung above you. An incredible hottie. Way out of your league. She put the spoon against your lips. "Are you sorry?"

You ate ice cream. You swallowed. "Uh . . . no. No."

She took the next scoop in her mouth, and then she bent down onto you and kissed you, sliding the ice cream into your mouth. She reached up and put the ice cream carton on the side table.

"Can I eat you out again?" you said. "Until you come?"

She licked the spoon. "Oh yeah. Let's move to the bed."

The guys couldn't stop talking about her—how the hell had you ended up with this piece of ass? They even asked right in front of her, over cans of Coors at the bar, the usual place, that place that girl had laughed at you, the second time you took her there. "No offense meant, but how the fuck does a guy like Gary—?"

She didn't let on about the Program, she was a total sport. "Hey, he looks like a slob, but you know, Gary has certain talents . . ."

Hoots and slaps on the back, and the guys made some remarks, but she wasn't offended, she just kidded them back. She could hold her own.

And you'd been afraid she'd look down her nose at the place, at your life—being an egghead and Upper West Side and all—think it was scummy and blue collar. But she ate it up, played foosball and drank Coors and watched the game on TV and laughed as loud as a guy. And god she looked good. Every other broad in the place was giving her the evil eye, and she liked that too, you could tell.

But she liked sleeping at her place better. Understandably. So you hustled over there on the train after work, and got up early to hustle out of there. Every place to eat around there was fucking expensive, and you sure as hell were not letting her pay for you—you didn't even like to go dutch, really, because fuck, what the hell were you bringing to the relationship, certainly not the looks or the smarts. But it was only the second week, and maybe her paying half was her way of showing independence or whatever. There was something about that in the seminars. Anyway.

It still hurt to fuck, and she liked that it hurt.

You got to the uptown bar after work. She was dressed in a short dress, bright blue, all dolled up. It barely reached mid-thigh. She was talking to a couple of guys, and you hustled over. Feeling out of place in jeans and a sweater, even a nice sweater. She curled right around you and the yuppie guys with their expensive watches and banker haircuts got the picture and wandered off.

You were sipping your first beer (somehow you weren't drinking so fast or so much any more) and she nestled up against you and pulled your hand under her skirt and you felt bush. No panties, in that fucking miniskirt. You got hard. She put your hand back on the counter and she talked to the bartender and finished her drink.

Then she took you into the alley out back and fished your cock out.

"Jill—" you said.

"Ssh," she said and straddled you. She was already wet. You went into her and it hurt, it hurt.

She took you. She rode you as long as she needed.

She came and the white light was there.

"So you said you've popped other guy's cherries."

She slurped up a noodle. Chinese takeout. Her living room nook. Her breasts bare in the moonlight. "Mmm-hmm . . ."

"So what, uh—"

"Hey!" she said sharply. "I don't want to talk about past relationships. What a fucking buzz-killer that is."

"All right," you said.

She put down her noodles. "Come over here."

You had to work late one night, fuckup with a delivery, not your fault but you were the one who had to dig up the archival paperwork and go figure it out. You called Jill and she went out with the girls from her study group. Some nights she wanted to go out with them alone, dish about guys. Maybe compare notes, which made your blood run a little cold. But, you know, fourth week of the relationship, that was all right, loosen up a little. Don't be so fucking clingy.

You missed her.

Eleven o' clock and the place was empty, you still weren't done, and your email dinged. It was from Rhonda the HR lady saying to come to her office. She had an office at the edge of the cube farm, not a cube. The blinds were down.

You felt like maybe you shouldn't go in, but that was kind of silly.

Rhonda got up from her chair. You'd always thought she was good-looking—she had these perfectly put-together outfits, and her face was smooth and young despite a streak of gray in her hair. But shit, she didn't compare to Jill. Maybe she was going to come on to you and you could turn her down, serve her right for laughing at you behind your back. Subscribe to this, baby. On the other hand maybe you'd somehow gotten in shit with HR. Though you couldn't imagine how.

"Close the door," she said, so you did.

She looked uncomfortable. "So you did the Program, right?"

"Yeah," you said sarcastically. What the fuck was this about? Did she think you were so hard up after the Program? Maybe she just wanted to hear about it.

"I've been, ah, reading up on it," she said. She was blushing. She was always so cocky, it was weird to see her blush. "Guys react differently. Some. . . ."

"Yeah?"

"Take off your shirt," she said in a strained voice.

"Oh, this is bullshit," you said, and you turned away to the door.

Rhonda sucked in her breath and there was a little tremor in it, like she'd been hit and she was going to cry. And that stopped you for a moment. And then you were thinking about that sound and what it would sound like, Rhonda coming. She had a lean, prim face, and you thought of all the looks you'd seen on it—irritated, bored, skeptical, and vaguely amused, laughing with the other women. But what would it be like out of control—eyes squeezed shut and mouth open in an O, begging for more?

What the fuck were you thinking? You had Jill.

But, under the fluorescent lights on the blank maroon carpet with your hand on the thin aluminum door handle, Jill seemed like a dream. Manhattan and Cindy Crawford. She's just playing with you, man—and any minute now the joke will be up and ice cream on the twentieth floor on the Upper West Side will vanish like smoke.

And Rhonda was here now, clearing her throat to call it all a joke or throw you out of her office, and there was still that tremor in it, like Rhonda was scared and uncertain, and that shouldn't be—a woman shouldn't be scared and uncertain around you, she should be happy, she should be on fire with joy. Rhonda was a vessel bearing her own portion of white light.

You turned around and started unbuttoning your shirt.

"Oh my god," Rhonda said.

"I can't believe it," Rhonda said. She raised herself up onto her elbows. She was on the desk, one foot on the swiveling chair, the other hooked over your back. She'd knocked a pile of papers off the desk. You leaned back, your face hot and wet from her cunt. You were kneeling on the floor and your knees hurt. "I can't believe I did this."

You said nothing. Your body was still tingling from the flood of white light. But your stomach felt sour. A scene was stuck in your mind like a video stuck in a loop—you show up at Jill's. The doorman smiles and waves you in. Jill meets you at her apartment door with a grin. And you—what? Tell her and watch that smile disappear. Or don't tell her and then what? Sitting around her place trying to grin back at her, nervous energy gripping you like a fist, your heart racing. Shit, shit, what had they done to you? You'd dogged girls and lied before, smooth as milk. But you couldn't now. You were sure of that. Why not? Was it the Program or was it Jill? Was it love?

"And you don't—you don't need anything, right?" Rhonda said. "I don't have to do anything for you?"

"Nope," you said.

"And you won't tell anyone about this?" Rhonda said. "Don't tell anyone about this."

"Nope."

"Ohh, it felt so good." Rhonda said. "How the hell did they teach you that? Guys can never do it like that."

You said nothing.

"One more time," Rhonda said. "One more time and I'll let you go."

"What. The. Hell." Jill said.

"I'm telling you," you said. "It's something to do with the Program. I'm serious. Jill, I wouldn't—Jill, I'm serious about you. I—"

"Oh shut the fuck up," Jill said. Her hazel eyes blazing. "Stop whining. Don't you dare blame it on the Program. All the Program did was make you tell me. Don't *even* claim you wouldn't have dogged me without the Program. I mean, under an absurdly hypothetical scenario where I'd be *with* you without the Program. Don't *even* front."

"Okay. Okay. But give me another chance—"

"Shit, why are you even begging? Do you think I care?"

"Jill, it won't—"

"Shut up." She opened a cabinet in the kitchenette and pulled out one shot glass and a bottle of Absolut. She poured, put down the bottle, and gulped the shot down. Then she screwed the cap on and put the bottle away. Then she paced, slowly, tracing the rim of the empty glass with her thumb.

You sat down on the couch, setting your coat down on the coffee table.

"I'm keeping you," Jill said. "I'm fucking keeping you, all right? Because you're too good. But, god damn it, I won't be dogged. So this is an open relationship, as of now. I'm going to have other guys up here. Ones that haven't done the Program, who still want it. You know?"

You looked at your feet, a slow burn of red spreading across your cheeks. It felt like the apartment had come loose from the building and was wobbling.

"Because I like that sometimes. Don't get me wrong—I like you more. What I am *really* going to like is telling you about them." She

set the glass down on the counter. "Maybe more than that. We'll see."
You looked up and she was looking at you, intensely, like trying to
read something. Trying to see if something was enough. And it must
not have been enough, because she still looked mad.

You were sick of yourself, of this fucking wimpiness. Maybe you
should yell back at her. Or walk. But what were you going to head
toward? Channel-surfing on the threadbare green couch in your
crappy house? Christ, you couldn't even jack off. Hearing the guys
say sympathetically, "fuck, we knew it couldn't last, you and a chick
like that." Rhonda? Pretty clear what Rhonda wanted, and it didn't
include waking up for breakfast together.

Then she smiled, ferally. "Come in here," she said.

You stood in front of her bathroom mirror and she opened your
pants and fished your dick out. "Get hard," she said, and blood
flooded it, pushing it up like a searching finger into a straining,
swollen erection. She opened the cabinet and took out a big scoop of
Vaseline and smothered your cock with it, and you tried not to flinch
back from her hand.

"Now jack off," she said. "But don't come."

"Jill—" you said.

"I want to watch," she said, and she sounded more eager, now,
than mad.

You started stroking, gingerly, ribbons of discomfort slithering
along your skin.

"Harder," she said. "Like a man."

And that fucking did it: the unease and regret in you was washed
away in a tide of rage, and you yanked your hand down and up, down
and up over your traitor cock, squeezing and mauling. Choking the
chicken. Gritting your teeth against the fireworks of pain.

It was like mauling a broken bone. Little grunts and sobs of pain
were coming out of you. And your cheeks were wet, but you weren't

crying. No. Fuck that. Just tearing up with agony and anger. You weren't feeling sorry for anything. Maybe you felt safe. Maybe you just were Jill's, and that was that.

She pulled a clear, pliant plastic dildo out of a drawer and slathered it with Vaseline. "I'll give you something to make you feel better," she said, and you thought, oh, thank god, she's going to make herself come.

It was hard to look at yourself in the mirror, your red wet face, your clenched teeth. You closed your eyes.

"Even harder," she whispered in your ear, and you hurt yourself.

You felt her cool hand on your throat. It felt good. "Now relax," she said, and she was sliding her slippery finger over your anus. You clenched, and she paused, leaving it there. You forced yourself to relax, and then you lost yourself in the pain.

Then you felt the dildo pushing against your asshole, and you opened your eyes and cried out—a wordless shout. The tip was in, and though you clenched down, trying to drive it back, Jill braced herself with her hand against your throat and drove it in. It opened you up and was in you.

"Ahhhhh—" you cried.

"Keep your hand moving," said Jill, and it moved.

She fucked you with the dildo and it felt good, and now you were crying. Christ. You were a faggot. This meant you were a faggot.

"Open your eyes," said Jill. "And now come."

Hot white liquid, and a sound like thunder, and darkness swept in from the edges of your vision and you felt Jill, far away, catching you, her arms around your chest, as your body left its footing.

You got out of there the next morning, when Jill was still asleep.

There was a little snow on the ground outside the clinic. You stood under a tree a little way from the guys with the signs, listening to them shout. They kept looking at you like they knew why you were there, like they were just waiting for you to come over and shout with them, but they new you weren't ready yet. A guy pulled up in a taxi, dressed in a suit, and sauntered by the protesters.

It was cold. You scuffed your boots, and rubbed your hands together.

You were late to work. What the hell were you going to say to Rhonda? Just not go near her.

You couldn't seem to make yourself move to the subway.

"Hey! Hey you!"

It was three girls in a car at the curb. Not cute girls—kind of punk girls, angry clothes, blaring loud music. Cars were nosing around them.

"You in the blue jacket! Over here!"

You walked over to them. The driver and the one in the back were giggling. The other one leaned out of her window. A fat girl, maybe twenty, with a Mohawk and square glasses. "Get in," she said, daring you.

You reached for the door.

A woman's thumb and fingers closed around your wrist, pulling you back.

Sophie.

"Gary? What are you doing?" Sophie said.

"Oh, Gary," Sophie said. "But why didn't you come in for your one-week evaluation?"

"I didn't know there was one," you said.

"But didn't you read the brochure? Didn't—" she sighed.

You put your face in your hands.

"It's not supposed to be like that," Sophie said. "Your sexual trans-ference acclimation is overdetermining your sense of self-agency, and your erogenous rebalancing is totally off. I'm booking you today for an emergency readjustment. Stay, Gary. Just wait an hour or so in this room, okay? Until the lab techs are set up. We'll fix this. We'll make this better."

"Okay," you say.

She breathes a sigh of relief. "It's my fault," she says. "They told me never to say that, for liability reasons. But I let you slide through the exit exam. You just seemed so happy." She shakes her head.

"Sophie," you say. "Can we, uh—can we um—?"

She grins shyly. "What?"

"Can we, just one last time, before they fix me, have sex?"

She frowns. "Gary. You don't need to do that. We'll do it afterward. In a week. We'll do a proper exit exam with all the trimmings."

"No, this, this is for me. Just—you know."

"Gary." She frowned. "I think that's a bad idea."

"I just want to say goodbye to it. To this way. With you."

She pursed her lips, and there was a hint of a blush on her pale cheeks. "You'd have to sign a release form . . ."

You nodded.

She got up and took a clipboard and clipped a form and a pen to it. She turned around too fast, coming back, and knocked the doctor stool so that rolled over and slammed into the desk.

She handed you the clipboard. Then she shrugged off her lab coat.

Caught By Skin
Steve Berman

Shawn lingers with the other 8.34s not far from one of Pe$^{e/al}$'s neon-accented bars. A couple of 5.35s—spiky brown hair, cupid lips, and deep dimples—pass by, their fingers slipped into each other's pockets. Shawn knows his gaggle envies how fresh they are, but he doesn't feel so much yesteryear worn as reminded of the hurt. He wonders if any of them have even noticed that Nate is no longer among the gaggle.

New faces were Shawn and Nate's graduation gifts, saved up from dealing and odd jobs. They both agreed on 8.34, advertised in all the e-mags as *East Coast Surf'd* because the original was found and pix'd surfing the artificial beach at Egg Harbor. The clinic was crowded, as if every untouched fag under twenty-five had decided to cash out on having tight blonde curls, a button nose, and long lashes lapping aqua eyes. A few old-timers sat on the uncomfortable chairs; one man in maybe his forties whispered excitement at getting his face redone, but his chattiness betrayed the apprehension. Surgery at his age is insane.

Young lifts always refer to his sort at masques. Shawn sees them hover in the corners of the club. They avoid the mirrors on every wall. Nate always tormented them with massive faux-flirting. At the time, Shawn laughed but lately he thinks he was treated the same.

Shawn sips at his stemmed glass. The blend of pure H_2O and flavored spirits is overpriced and over-sweetened with faux berries. The gilding on his credID has recently been replaced and the way the bartender offhandedly swipes it makes him worry that it will be worn away before he is drunk. The bartender is a 2.32. Shawn never likes the February faces with their rosy cheeks, reminding him of bitter winters. He wants distraction, anything to divert his thoughts from Nate. A few months back, he thought he heard Nate's laugh, mocking and high and ending with that telling sucked-in breath, coming from a 1.35.

Thankfully, he has some Prism. He forgets which one of the gaggle pressed the hollow plastic stick into his palm. He leans back against the bar's metal and neon railing and squirts a hit into each eye.

A tiny bit drips down his cheek and chin. He wipes his face with his fingers and blinks as his vision changes. He doesn't really under-stand how the drug affects the rods or cones or whatever in his eyes, limiting the spectrum to one color—orange this time. But what mat-ters to him is the euphoria, never as much as promised these days, but then he's been taking Prism since fifteen.

The Pe$^{e/a}$lis hot from all the bodies, as everyone clusters together. Gaggledom. Shawn tugs at his shirt's wide collar, decorated with his birthstones. The synthetics of his top and flared shorts are totally non-absorbent so alcohol and sweat and come roll off them; by the end of the evening Shawn will be slick under his clothes. The natural-fiber skivs will be drenched, so he doesn't wear any while clubbing.

As a sense of buoyancy eased over him, he smirks at the notion of falling out of sync and making out with a different lift; the other 8.34s would hate him. Twinning is everything. He remembers fucking Nate and discovering only afterwards that it wasn't really his best friend but another of the gaggle. But that will not happen again. He half-heartedly curses Nate for abandoning him for May's look but then music starts leaking through the speaker tiles on the dance floor at the other side of the bar and Shawn tries and fails to recognize the stylist. Probably an invention by some clubber in New Delhi with not enough sleep and plenty of meds, he decides. Bollypopper. A few of the illuminated tiles start rising and falling, like the Atlantic, cresting on the beat. Dancing requires attention or genetics, and Shawn knows that he has to wait a half hour after Prism before daring the dance floor or else look freaked.

The nearest 8.34, skin more pumpkin than tan thanks to the Prism, nudges his arm to share his drink and Shawn tries to remember if his name is Ragan . . . or maybe it's Fox—which one wears the liquid crystal necklace flashing *PwrBttm*? He hands the glass over and in two sips it's empty. Fox then. Another 8.34 laughs at Shawn and the rest of the gaggle follows suit. Most, he knows, have no idea why they laugh and only mimic the rest.

Disgusted, he walks away from them towards the bathroom. As he nears the doorway, a masque reaches out for him. "I love Augusts." The lips are stretched so tight around a 3.35 jaw line a hiss escapes with each word.

Shawn escapes and heads towards the front doors wanting whatever passes for Jersey fresh air. The bouncer, gruff and untouched by surgery, argues with a guy in the doorway. Shawn stops when his ocherous vision takes in how striking the guy is. The face is not any lift he's seen before. Instinctively, he reaches for his I-Point. He needs a moment to focus the tiny screen, before capturing with a retro click sound the shiny dark hair, parted down the center, a slightly upturned nose, and eyes such a pale orange that Shawn figures they must be gray.

The bouncer refuses to allow the guy inside. Once Shawn has sent the natural's image out to the GillienNet with a push of a button, he walks over.

"Debut, here, has no cred." The bouncer has tattoos along his cheeks that resemble tusks. Shawn heard that the Pe$^{e/a}$l's owners wouldn't have any lifts work the door. Pretties and drags get lifts, the roughs want ink, especially teeth marks.

"I'm new around here," the natural says with a slight shrug.

Shawn holds out his credID to the bouncer who swipes it over the pad on the wall. "Easy. Now you're mine for the evening." Shawn's joking but the natural responds with such a wide grin that Shawn cannot help but smile back.

"What's your name?"

"Shawn."

"That's it?" The guy's thick eyebrows rise. "No number? I thought with clones—"

"Clones?" Shawn huffs air around a slight laugh. "Does this look Third World?" he asks, stepping back and motioning his hands up and down his face and body. The sting of the insult fades fast. But the initial insult swiftly fades as Shawn realizes a natural would have no idea how much can be spent on matching a month. They are almost another species.

"No. Sorry." The guy looks embarrassed. "Just all the similar faces."

Shawn steps so close to the guy that he could kiss him. Instead he examines the face with as much attention as the Prism allows. He sees no scars, no telltale signs of surgery. The earlobes are attached, but then so were the faces of two years ago. Slight creases along the edges of the eyes suggest age. Maybe he's S-prone, Schizo. "You just wake up and find you're twenty-first cent?"

"Something like that." The natural looks down at himself, as if noticing he wore clothes for the first time.

Shawn finds himself curious. It feels like ages since his lift and he doesn't remember the last time he said more than a few words to a natural in passing. He takes the guy's hand in his own and pulls him towards the nearest bar. "Drink time."

Flashes staccato the air as other guys start pixing the stranger's face. They all wish to be the first to upload his features to the GillienNet in the hopes they will find June or July's face and earn a free lift.

The bartender swipes more of Shawn's money away. The aquahol is cold. The stranger sips his cautiously and seems not to know where to look: at the thin glass holding his drink, at the bar, or back at Shawn.

"So how about a name?" Shawn taps glasses.

"I wish I could offer one. Well, other than the Student."

"A u-boy?" None of the gaggle is into education. Degrees are for expired lifts and masques.

"I don't even know what that is."

"As in university."

"Once. Maybe. At least, I think so. They rationed our long-term memory to reduce culture shock."

"They?"

The Student lightly rubs at his temples. "That I can't recall." Definitely schizo, thinks Shawn. But far better than the same chatter from the same mouths. "So this means you're from . . . ?"

"The future. Or maybe the past."

"Like vids?" Shawn waves for a refill. He never expects to have to think while talking with a guy. But he finds himself enjoying the novelty of chatting with a schizo natural. The orange tint of the world is wearing off.

"No. I'm never sure how long I have somewhen. And there's pain."

"Oh?" The bartender hands over another glass.

"SHC."

"Lost me."

"Spontaneous human combustion. The energy needed to transmit matter—sorry, this must sound insane."

Shawn grins. "But not boring." He tries to remember what sort of conversations he had with Nate but he cannot recall any, either pre-lift or as part of the gaggle. The void leaves him all mawks, worsening the descent from the Prism. He needs to chase away regrets, so he slides a hand up the Student's arm and leans forward. His kiss is met.

"Your peer group . . . your fellows are watching us."

Shawn turns around and sees the gaggle staring and whispering.

"Perhaps we should go someplace else? You could tell me more—"

Shawn gulps his entire drink. "Let's go upstairs." If the gaggle plans on passing judgment on him, he might as well be truly guilty.

The Student's eyebrows rise as he glances at the ceiling. "What's upstairs?"

"C'mon," Shawn says and tugs on the Student's arm.

More flashes erupt as they wend their way past the dance floor. Shawn tries to block their pix out of a blend of ownership and some sense of protecting his catch. At one point, the Student nearly trips on a raised tile, and Shawn catches him. More kissing happens as a result of the rescue.

The escalator up is a quaint old ride, one slow enough that clubbers can see who exactly is going upstairs with whom. Shawn leans over the moving black rail and catches the gaggle of 8.34s gawking at him, their identical expressions showing shock at his decision. He feels a schizolike rush and leers down at them, while sliding a hand up the Student's shirtfront. When his fingers discover thick chest hair it's such a shock, that he almost stumbles off the step. He recovers with an embarrassed half-smile.

The top floor of Pe$^{e/a}$l is far dimmer than the rest. Shawn guides the Student through the antechamber with its padded lining. Couples and trines relax against the soft walls in the endorphin-slake. The Student requires further tugging to move past them all.

"So why all the same faces?"

"Hmm?" Shawn hands over his credID to secure a booth. Shawn nods to the attendant, a poorly done 1.35 who has failed to cover the scar-traces along his temples with concealer.

"Obviously ageism, but the conduct norms of embracing societal-wide total cosmetic surgery as a conscience collective is fascinating."

Shawn laughs at the Student. "Because we all want to be young, if only on the outside." Then he stops laughing. The aquahol must have been shit because he feels suddenly mawks. "But it's all a trap. Your insides get older and older and end up wanting something else but by then you're caught by skin." Shawn thinks of Nate leaving him for the 5.35s.

They walk down hall lined with booths. Groans and moans slip past shut doors.

The Student reaches out and lightly strokes his face. He leans into the touch. "But if you can change your looks often, why ever feel trapped?" A thumb brushes against his lips, which instinctively part for a moment.

"How long can you chase faces?" He envisions Nate a month or two from now getting yet another lift, trying to stay with the now.

"Imagine chasing entire cultures, never sure how long you'll be anyplace, anytime." The Student frowns and looks away. "I'm so anxious over burning off before I really assess the period's norms that I end up with hasty examinations, desperate for any sampling."

"Desperate?"

The Student nods.

From one of the nearby booths comes a heavy smack against the door. Both are startled and jump from the sudden sound. They laugh too.

"Any sampling?" asks Shawn. The anticipation of play with the Student chases away some of the mawks.

"Well, some studies are more rewarding than others." The Student offers an embarrassed grin. "How different from where I was last," he says. "They're all so very different, though."

"Where . . . I mean, when was the last . . . time?" Shawn doesn't believe the guy, but talking crazy has to be better than conceding how miserable he is.

"*Yìhétuán Qi yì.*" The tonal inflection is perfect, showing years of study on the mainland.

"*Che ji ba dan!*" Shawn playfully pushes the Student by the chest, knocking him into the padded wall.

"You speak Chinese?"

"Doesn't half the world these days?" Shawn moves closer, brushing his mouth against the Student's ear. "Chinese history was my fave in school." He cannot resist lightly licking the Student's neck. He tastes the salty tang of sweat. "I can't imagine you as a Boxer."

"*Yìhétuán,*" whispers the Student. He presses his hand against the back of Shawn's head.

"Fisting is illegal these days . . . or should be." Shawn playfully bites an earlobe.

"That's *Yìhéquán.*" He moans slightly. "You brought me up here to *gan*, right?"

Shawn nods and leads the Student to an empty booth. He shuts the door.

Along one wall are bins. Shawn begins stripping off his clothes. The Student watches a moment before following suit. Shawn stares at his body with its natural musculature, the amount of fat in spots along the midsection, the swathe of hair along the chest and stomach. He feels awkward, naked, with his size 2 pectoral implants and the results of his latest abdominal sculpting visit. Comparing himself to the Student, Shawn feels manufactured, artificial and, for the first time in almost a year, ugly.

Ashamed, he turns away, busying himself with stowing their clothes in the bins. He then presses the first button on the wall.

A fine mist descends. The Student raises both hands, palms up, to catch the drops. Shawn marvels at the sight, for if the guy isn't schizo—if he could even be what he claims—he's totally unafraid of anything new.

"This is?"

"Disinfectant." Shawn starts rubbing the dew from the mist over his body and then helps the Student. His hands roam all over before focusing on the thick chode rapidly hardening. He realizes the Student is curiously disfigured down there, lacking the silky skin everyone else possesses, but Shawn says nothing, not wanting to embarrass him.

"No aftertaste?" The Student kisses him hard before bringing his lips down Shawn's chin and neck. "Thankfully, no," he says and starts licking Shawn's chest.

They each touch and taste the other's torso a while, before taking turns on their knees. Shawn hesitates before taking the flawed chode into his mouth. His fingers rub the reddened tip where the extra skin should hang. Thick course hair surrounds the chode and even the disinfectant has not chased away the pungent but not unpleasant smell. He treats it tenderly in his mouth in case the Student's disfigurement has left him sensitive. The response he earns is soft groans and encouraging strokes back and forth through his lips.

Eventually, Shawn is so eager to be had that he rises and presses his face and chest against the cool wall. He pushes back with his hips, spreading slightly his legs. He aches to have the Student crush against him. "Please," he begs.

Shawn feels the warm breath against his back and the touch of the hot chode against one cheek. Then the Student's fingers are parting his ass. It's a sensation he's often been curious of, but never dared.

"What are you doing?" Shawn asks, his voice rising slightly, nervous.

"What's natural," the Student replies and a fingertip tries to force its way inside.

"No, what are you doing?" Shawn nearly shouts. He turns around to see the Student standing there, looking shocked.

"I-I thought you wanted me to fuck you."

"No one does ass anymore." He takes a deep breath and relaxes. He slides a hand around the Student's neck. "I take it you're not aware of Bleeds? It's not safe." Sean kisses him as a makeshift apology. Then he takes hold of the Student's chode, strokes it hard once more. "Here," he says, slowly turns back to the wall, then guiding the hot shaft between his thighs. "Like this." He clenches his legs shut, not too tight, but locked so they firmly rub against the Student.

"Oh. Oh. Intercrural? I haven't done this since . . . Sophocles?" The Student, with apparent skill at the technique, wraps his arms around Shawn, one hand down so both their chodes are rubbed. He begins kissing the back of Shawn's neck and achieving the perfect rhythm.

Shawn feels the pressure rise within him. He cries out as he sprays the plastic walls. The Student takes longer, but soon he coats Shawn's legs. They stand still, together, for a while, until they no longer gasp.

The Student presses the shower button and another mist falls on them, rinsing off the sweat and semen. Their clothes, protected by the bin, are dry.

"So, what now?" the Student asks.

Shawn has no ready answer. He adjusts his clothes, feels the meaninglessness of the gesture. With Nate, with even the other 8.34's he always knew what would happen next, but a natural poses so many mysteries, especially one with wild claims.

He glances at his I-Point's tiny display. Hours to go before the gaggle will leave Pe$^{e/a}$l; he needs to stay late enough not to encounter any of them awake in the suite. He hopes they won't be so vengeful they lock him out.

"Hmmm. I'm short on cred. How about I show you how we dance here?"

The Student laughs. "I have to warn you, no matter what the year, I'm a really bad dancer."

The gaggle punishes Shawn for straying, making him stay inside their collective apartments. It's five nights later, he can return to Pe$^{e/a}$l. During his exile, he waited for a message from the Student. None came. Distraught, Shawn's not sure whether the natural might have been telling the truth and has no idea how to message, or is just S-prone and doesn't want to. Neither thought is comforting or lessens the daydreams about the Student. He searches the club, wandering the place. When he finally does spot the face that has preoccupied the last 120 hours, he's surprised to see the Student out on the dance floor. For a professed bad dancer, he has mastered the latest spin.

Shawn rushes over to him and touches his shoulder fondly. The Student looks at him without any trace of recognition before returning to dancing. Shawn blinks in surprise and frustration and pushes the Student, knocking him from finishing the twirl.

"So what, your memory getting worse?"

"Like I hang with August trash."

The voice is wrong. So wrong. High-pitched. The surgeons never dare the vocal cords for fear of litigation.

Shawn stumbles back. He bumps into someone and turns around to apologize and sees it's another Student. The guy scowls, transforming the handsome features into something horrid. A bad job, too tight around the jaw line.

Shawn rushes out of the heaving dance floor. He makes it to the front door in time to see two more Students walking in. He pushes past them. Outside, the air is hot and stagnant. June weather in New Jersey. His I-Point shivers. Instinctively, he runs his fingertips over the controls and checks his messages.

GillienNetAdmin
Congratulations, Shawn Carte, you are the primary sender of 6.35's chosen visage. To accept your complimentary facial surgery, please stop-in at your approved clinic and present this code.

Beneath the message is the picture he took, transmitted and forgotten, of the Student by the club's entrance.

He looks back at the club entrance. Shawn knows that every night will bring more of the Student's face. Maybe even Nate will walk through the door, eager to show off the latest lift. But Shawn would never be able to find him—or the real Student—not amongst the next month's gaggle.

He almost deletes the message. Then he glances at the tiny screen capture of the Student's face, imagining Nate behind it, kissing those lips and hearing once more his best friend's soft murmurs of delight. Shawn finds himself looking at past pix, the oldest files, with Nate's and his original faces. He taps the panel and zooms and aches for the past.

Halfway to the rail station, he finds through the GillienNet a decent clinic still open. Shawn isn't sure that he can trade his complimentary lift. Impatient, he paces the platform. The other passengers—all naturals but a pair of girls who are on the verge of twinning, combing hands through ringlets of copper hair and ruddy lips, pressing each other against the map monitor—give him wary glances.

A warm gust heralds the car's arrival. In the few seconds after the rail stops, he sees in the mirrored door panels not his own reflection but Nate's virgin face. Shawn thinks he will wear it well.

That Which Does Not Kill Us

Scott Westerfeld

Paul dropped by Eurisa's office with a quick question. Her face was ashen.

"God, what's wrong?"

"Nothing." She gestured helplessly at her screen. "My boyfriend's dog died. Ex-boyfriend, I mean."

"That's . . . too bad." He wondered if he should say more.

No one at Orfay Currency Management knew much about the break-up, about a month old. But they'd all seen the signs. Dimitri had stopped coming by, and there had been a tightening in Eurisa, like the lid of an already closed jar rotated an extra quarter-turn, the surety of metal gripping glass. Her office door was closed more often now, her meetings shorter, her intraoffice mail even more terse.

Eurisa's gray and absent eyes veiled any pain, however. She had no close friends at work, and Paul could only guess what had come between them—the tall, lean, quiet woman and her voluble Greek.

Dimitri had charmed Paul the few times he'd come to tease Eurisa away from Asian time-zone trades, playfully pulling her toward some party or performance, leaving Paul jealous of his power to make her smile.

And now, since the break-up, jealous of his power to hurt her.

Eurisa seemed so out of reach, terribly calm even in the worst peso or rupiah meltdown. As assistant manager of the floor, Paul often had to nudge juniors who unthinkingly asked if ice water ran in her veins; prejudice was not tolerated at Orfay Currency. A few months after the accident, she'd gotten her old job back, no questions asked.

She certainly looked free of ice now. Staring at her screen, animated by this untidy aftershock of the break-up, Eurisa was openly shaken, appalled as a child whose carefully tended scab has been ripped from its moorings. And all over Dimitri's dog.

She must really have loved the guy, Paul thought enviously, even as he spotted an opening.

He took a few steps into her office and placed one tentative hand on her shoulder. It felt firm and muscular; they had all noticed her in the Orfay gym every day.

Her unwavering gaze on the screen seemed an invitation to read. Dimitri had mailed the announcement to his own address, Eurisa receiving one blind copy among many.

raptor died quietly last night. renal failure most likely. she was 17. those of us who knew her will remember her big heart, quiet wisdom, and superb comic timing.

The sweet, personal, terminal note made Paul's eyes guilty, and they fell to Eurisa's hands. One clenched her airmouse, the other was upended, a dead spider in her lap.

"It hated me," she said.

Paul took a step back, out from the private space behind her desk to a more neutral position, his hand pulling from her shoulder.

As with any beautiful woman in a male domain, Eurisa was an object of unspoken competition. Now that she was unattached, who would be the first to ask her for a drink? A lunchtime walk? This moment was a perfect opportunity to cross the pale.

Paul wondered what had made him pull away. Somehow, she seemed diminished by her words, as if his desire had been blunted by the departed dog's hatred.

Had it *known* about her?

He censored the thought.

"You two didn't get along, huh?" Paul tried to make it cheery, disbelieving.

"It fucking hated me."

A fresh wave of distress crossed Eurisa's face. Shame at having been despised by something dumb and innocent, perhaps. Guilt at having returned the dog's vacuous hatred. Frustration that Raptor had lasted longer than her in Dimitri's life, if only by a few weeks.

Paul searched for the right words.

"Do you think he'll have it brought back?" he asked. The operation had worked on dogs well before humans. (Mice, of course, had been the first.)

Eurisa unclenched her fist, fingers listlessly indicating the screen. "Doesn't sound like it."

He nodded agreement. "They say dogs are never quite the same."

Eurisa looked at him directly for the first time, and Paul blinked against the metal glint in her gray eyes.

"It's not just dogs they say that about."

"Oh shit, I'm sorry." Another step away from her, which immediately felt like the wrong thing to do, fearful rather than apologetic.

His too-familiar hand, the one that had touched her shoulder, hung uncomfortably in the air. The hand wavered, searching for some knowing gesture that would erase his tasteless remark, but it looked stranded, isolated from his body, as if he intended to wash it once out of her sight. He felt the dizzying influence of four cups of coffee on an empty stomach.

"Don't worry about it, Paul," she said. "It's just this email." The apologetic look on her face seemed genuine.

Paul smiled back. Even with her silences, her distance, he wished he'd known Eurisa better before the accident, before the operation. He sometimes fantasized that he could bring her out from the gray place she'd been since, animate her as Dimitri had.

"Listen, I'd better come back later," he said, turning away slowly in case Eurisa called to him. They could commiserate a few moments more, or waste a few moments with lively, vacant gossip to soothe her distress. Maybe wind up having that drink tonight.

But she was silent.

Her fingers clattered, and Paul heard the missive's brief complaint as it was deleted without backup.

"Quiet wisdom? It fucking *hated* me," she muttered as Paul departed, voice faltering toward a sob.

There was something vulnerable in the sound, and Paul stopped. He'd feel forever foolish if he let this opportunity pass.

"Look, Eurisa," he said to the door. "After work. Do you want to have a drink?"

"Why not?" she answered.

He took her to The Three-Headed Dog, a place with brushed cement floors and a glass fountain that spanned an entire wall, rippling like a giant window on a rainy day. It was the after work bar that everyone at Orfay went to: trendy enough to bring younger dates, but with barstools that supported lower backs trashed by years of drinking coffee and trading currency. And you could still smoke here. (Paul had turned thirty this year, and was thinking of cutting back on something. Not coffee, alcohol, speed, tobacco, or work—but *something*.)

Eurisa looked around, sizing up the place in a manner that told him everything: she'd never been here before, didn't go to bars much. Then Paul remembered it had been the other driver who'd been drunk that night two years ago, and wondered if Eurisa had a thing against drinkers now. He told himself to take it easy.

"What'll you have?" he asked her.

"Whisky, neat. Make it a double."

Okay, maybe not a problem.

He peered up at the chalkboard filled with single malts, lighting a first cigarette.

"Sounds good to me. Maybe the Bowmore with thirty years on it?"

His extravagance paid off. For the first time, he glimpsed a hint of a smile. "Special occasion?"

Perhaps was he being too obvious. "Not really. Just showing off my useless education. Went to a whisky-tasting last week."

She glanced up at the board and said dryly, "And it's the most expensive."

"Hey, it's great stuff, though."

"I know. I'll get them."

"Are you sure?"

She waved away protests, signaled the barman over and ordered two, getting the guy's attention faster than Paul would have. Away from the florescent lights of work, he could see the truth in what all the guys had long suspected: Eurisa really was a beauty.

Sometimes, you couldn't tell. Paul had gotten plenty of temps and the odd intern down here to the Dog, only to discover that a face that glowed in comparison to the Orfay crowd could pale out in the real world. But Eurisa's sharp features only softened in the mottled light reflected from the fountain, and her perch on the barstool revealed her shapeliness better than any office chair. Her eyes didn't seem so gray here, animated by their quick, nervous circuits around the bar.

Paul could see her desirability in the barman's gaze as he read her card with a swipe of his finger. He was good-looking, just a kid, no more than twenty-five.

Eurisa was about Paul's age, but looked older. They said dying added five years.

He glanced around to see if any of the guys were here to see this. Eurisa buying him a drink. It was six-thirty. Where the hell were they?

"Well then, to Raptor?" she said, raising her glass with a rueful smile.

He gave it a clink. "I hear she was a real bitch."

Eurisa offered the remonstrative smile one allows a lame pun, but Paul felt like he'd scored a belly laugh. The taste of fire, peat, and sea air coiled down his throat invincibly.

"You're not a musician, are you?"

The Greek had been a bassist, Paul remembered now. Second chair for one of the big orchestras. He took a sip for courage. She was comparing him to the old boyfriend, looking for something different.

"Not a chance. Can't even remember the words to 'Happy Birthday.' "

Eurisa nodded. "I always forget what comes after 'Dear . . . ,' " she said.

"Dear me."

"Maybe later."

Paul blinked, realizing that she was flirting with him. That was more than he'd expected after a few sips of a first drink. Eurisa had been a closed door for so long, everyone had given up trying. When new hires asked about her, everyone just shook their heads to say, *Don't waste your time, buddy.*

Paul drank his whisky quickly. He fumbled for another smoke, wondering where the other Orfay guys were tonight.

He also wondered if Eurisa was more or less beautiful since the accident, then decided not to think too far down that line.

"I don't know why Dimitri's email shook me up like that." She peered into the brown mysteries of her glass. "Feel much better now, though."

"How long has it been?"

"Weeks. A month yesterday, I guess. But seeing his address made me think he was writing me."

"Were you hoping for anything?"

"Just a letter. Not some stupid bulk announcement about his stupid dog." She looked at me. "I guess that sounds pretty horrible. Poor bitch."

He smiled. "Don't sweat it. It's not like you killed her."

"No. It just feels that way. Dimitri must be shattered. He's had her since he was a kid." Eurisa's hands clutched the whisky glass to her chest, as if wanting to comfort her former lover, to comfort anyone, in the wake of Raptor's demise.

"He'll get over it," Paul said. "Builds character."

She sighed. "That which does not kill us."

Paul bought another round.

"Hey!"

It was Freddy from Offshore, the guys who hid money for tax cheats and dictators. The bar was crowded now, at the height of the after work rush, and Paul hadn't seen him sneak up.

"Oh, hi, Freddy. You know Eurisa."

"Yeah, nice to see you at the Dog." The big man bobbed his head idiotically.

"It's nice to be here." She smiled, but shrank from Freddy a little, withdrawing back into the gray place that the whisky and the crowd had coaxed her from. He was turning pink and loud from alcohol, his tie loosened, his sleeves riding up like a growing teenager's.

"Who else is here?" Paul asked, thinking, *Go back to them.* He wanted to be seen with Eurisa, not interfered with. The other guys would have known better, all but Freddy. Offshore was a loose cannon's game.

Eurisa had turned away to order more, again snaring the young barman instantly. Freddy took the opportunity to widen his eyes, his grin going from polite to suggestive.

Paul knew what he was thinking.

Months before, Paul had gone back to Freddy's from the Dog, along with a couple of other guys from Orfay. They'd got to talking about Eurisa, raising the usual questions about what she'd be like in bed. They had all dropped some speed in the afternoon, and the discussions got more and more detailed, until Freddy wound up downloading porn from a bunch of crypt-sticker sites. Like everything free, most of it was utter crap. The wasted gigabytes filled Freddy's wall screen with tanless wonders lounging on red velvet couches, their faces slack with what they thought was post-necrotic languor. More like middle-class chronic fatigue, however pale their lipstick and strewn lilies. Baby goths with artistic boyfriends and lonely girls with cams.

Paul and the boys had laughed them off one by one, making the usual comments men make about pictures of naked women, drinking while they waited between high-res loads. Until Freddy found a real one.

She wasn't flopped out playing dead; she didn't have to be. She simply sat on a folding chair against an exposed brick wall, body at three-quarters, head turned to face the camera. She had died messily, it was obvious, though a veil of ashen pallor overlay the scars and patches of artificial skin that quilted her body.

Her face held none of the usual expressions of the amateur nude portrait: no self-consciousness or embarrassment, no attempt at bravado, not even the grim confidence of a professional. She was fit, handsome, about forty-five.

And she was dead. Her eyes were empty. It wasn't the slack expression of a bad photo, that fleeting moment of idiocy so often caught by the camera, but something cold and blank and absent. She had the wooden face of a mannequin, just after it's fooled the corner of your eye, and you've turned to excuse yourself for almost bumping into it or to ask if it has the time, and it just stares back.

For a few stunned moments, the photo had Paul's speeding brain in revelation mode, agreeing with the religious freaks. The ones who believed that the operation didn't really bring anyone back. That post-ops were just machines, things with familiar memories and personality, but only on the surface. Things that loved ones might recognize and believe in, but with nothing inside.

Those theories had always sounded like a load of crap to Paul. The usual flailings of the religious whenever science stomps into their ever-shrinking territory. People were all machines, all the time, he figured. Get fed, get laid, get a laugh. Food, safety, freedom, sex. And if they were anything inside it was best described with one word: hungry.

But this woman had lost her hunger. She was dead, and her nakedness only made it worse, as if someone had propped her up with sticks and invisible wires without bothering to dress her, because it didn't matter.

Freddy's system got more hits, the teeth of the search engine now deep in some vein of obsession out there in the world, the restless software flipping images onto the wall screen as they arrived, cold and ashen and tragic.

The pictures silenced them all, and broke the spirit of the party in a way that took less than half an hour to get Paul and the rest of them out Freddy's door, muttering "work night" and relieved it had happened at his apartment and not one of theirs.

Eurisa turned back to them with two scotches in hand. She looked at Freddy.

"Oh, did you want a drink?"

"No, no. I was just stopping by to say hi."

She turned away to pay, and Freddy and Paul glanced at each other. For a moment in her cool expression they had both read the same thing: She somehow knew, had detected that night of transgression. As if side-by-side their collective guilt was obvious.

Paul swallowed, looked again at the woman next to him, lithe and glorious as she stretched her card out to the barman. For a second, the fleeting and primitive revelation of that night came back, overlaying his desire with something fearful, but still intense. He wondered what she would feel like against him, if she would warm between cool sheets the way other women did.

He wanted to know how it would work with a dead girl.

Freddy wrung his hands, sorry now that he had come over.

"Well, early night for me, guys."

Paul gave his shoulder a pat. "See you tomorrow. Get some sleep."

The big man moved away.

"See you, Freddy," Eurisa called, too softly for him to have heard.

The Orfay table, which Paul spotted now in the corner, waved and shouted goodbye to Freddy as he passed. A few dared tentative glances toward the two of them at the bar, excited by the prospect of gossip and scandal.

Paul felt worlds away from them, alone with Eurisa. There would be no further interruptions.

She looked relieved.

Eurisa angled the whisky glass toward him in a perfunctory salute and put it to her lips, tipping it back and depositing it empty on the bar with a crack just audible over the music and crowd.

"Is there someplace quieter we could go?"

They went many places.

Everywhere, Eurisa drank quickly. The whisky seemed to pour a kind of heat into her, quickening her words and gestures. A torrent slowly freed itself, like ice breaking up in a river.

Paul listened, trying to pace his liquor, sneaking a couple of pills in the bathroom and wishing he'd eaten something that day. He offered the occasional word of support and watched Eurisa's face closely, searching for clues of what she wanted with him tonight.

She talked only of Dimitri.

"He used to shut Raptor up in the kitchen while I was over there. Otherwise, she'd sit in the corner and watch us, growling."

"Psycho dog."

Eurisa shook her head and drank. "Not generally psycho. Just hated me. She was normal with everyone else. Whenever I was there, she'd pace back and forth in the kitchen, her claws tapping on the tiles like fingernails. Like she thought I was going to steal her man."

"Maybe she was jealous, because she knew you loved him."

She looked at Paul coldly. "I never said that."

"Oh, sorry. It just sounded like—"

"Didn't say I didn't, either." Her voice took on an edge for a moment, like a drunk about to turn hostile.

Paul looked into his empty glass, and waved at the barman for more. When he turned back to Eurisa her anger was gone. She continued as if nothing had happened.

"So Dimitri would sit in the living room, where I could see him from the bedroom and Raptor could watch from the kitchen. And he'd play his bass for us."

She drank.

"Raptor would finally sit down and listen to the music. Sometimes she would even sing along, kind of a soft, moany song."

In the low music and bar chatter around them, Paul drunkenly heard the sound track to this scene: the low notes of the string bass mingling with those of the imprisoned, growling dog. Eurisa looking on from her banishment in the bedroom, watching her lover serenade his hound, framed by the impassable doorway.

Paul allowed himself to imagine, urged on by the very real possibility that he might find out, what Eurisa's body looked like under her black suit. Would she be as taut and firm as she appeared, a well-maintained machine? (Not a machine, Paul reminded himself, trying not to remember what he had seen that night in Freddy's apartment, the blank men and women staring back from the screen.) How would her lips taste? (Did she bear any scars from the accident?) What sounds would she make beneath him?

"After a while, the dog would forget."

"Forget what?" Paul spluttered.

"That I was there. Dimitri's playing always enchanted Raptor's little doggie brain into thinking I had gone, or maybe just lulled her to sleep, I couldn't see which. Then he would carefully rest the bass on its side and come into the bedroom. After that we couldn't speak, or make a sound. Mustn't wake doggie."

"Too bad."

"No, it was too good. It was like the dog was guarding me, and Dimitri had sneaked past. Sometimes, we even kept the door open, so we had to be absolutely quiet. Everything slow and deliberate, communicating only with signals, with our eyes, fearful of any creak of the bed."

Paul took a deep drag, then a long drink, the smoke still in his lungs. He wanted so badly to take Eurisa silently as a monster slept nearby.

Whisky made him brave. He slid his hand softly across her lower back, felt the firm muscles there.

"So the dog hated you, but . . ."

"But we made it something good."

Paul leaned closer now, their faces at the knife's-edge boundary between a gaze and a kiss.

"Raptor could have driven us crazy, but Dimitri made it a game. That's how his mind worked."

Paul blinked, her mournful expression freezing him. Eurisa turned her face aside, and he thought for a moment that his momentum had been broken. His heartbeat tolled out a few seconds.

She looked at him. Firmly: "Can we go someplace?"

He swallowed, suddenly dizzy, and held onto the bar with his free hand to keep the stool beneath him. "We've been to six places by my count. Maybe we've had enough."

"Not to drink."

Paul nodded. The tight feeling in his stomach and balls, the strictures of uncertainty, relaxed. He gathered himself, and ran his fingertips up Eurisa's spine, feeling a faint shiver pass through her.

He ground out his cigarette and grinned inside. His seemingly random course from bar to bar had been leading to this small dark corner of this particular small dark pub.

"Well, I live half a block from here."

One of her half-smiles. "Isn't that convenient?"

Paul stood shakily. His head swam, as if the last few whiskies hadn't found room below his neck yet.

"Actually, it is."

In the lobby he let out a defeated moan. The elevator was broken again.

"Shit. They keep saying they'll fix this. Once and for all."

"That's okay. I can climb stairs."

He looked her up and down, for the first time openly. "Tenth floor okay?"

"Try me."

Paul pushed open the fire door and started the climb, hoping he'd make it without too much sweat. He knew from experience that it would be tainted with whisky and speed and workday stress. Alone, he could have used the handrail, resting every few floors to gratefully pant away some of the alcohol in his system. But taking the stairs in front of a fit and willing Eurisa, he didn't want to look feeble and incapable.

He had to have her tonight, to know what was inside her.

But the whisky was working hard against him. Paul gripped the handrail, conscious of the rasp of his breathing in the echoing concrete stairwell. Her footsteps sounded light and impatient behind him. He wondered if his face was turning red.

At the fourth floor, Paul's lower back twinged in the awful way that had made him give up tennis a year before. Between an evening slumped on barstools and these stairs, he'd barely be able to sit down tomorrow. But he could ignore the pain for six more floors. The goal was all that mattered. He was getting what everyone at Orfay wanted. The hero of the currency floor.

Paul wondered if the guys were talking about him and Eurisa at this moment, still camped at the Three-Headed Dog and betting on how far he'd gotten. Freddy had probably gone home to download more grave-robber porn, sitting fat and half-drunk in front of his giant wall screen.

At that image his step faltered, and spots went up before his eyes. Seventh floor.

"You okay?"

"Sure." Paul charged upward, not looking back. He didn't want Eurisa to see his red face, puffing and sweating like a man about to come. Not in this light, anyway.

He couldn't see the stairs anymore. Instead of gray concrete, he saw the woman on the wall screen, ashen and stitched together, something inside her gone a million miles away. He wasn't horrified anymore; he just wanted to talk to her, to step inside the picture and ask her questions. How had she wound up in that bare room, naked in front of some cheap camera? What had killed her so thoroughly, yet left enough for surgeons to piece back together? Was she really nothing inside? (Or would she even know it if she was?)

Paul wanted to turn around and ask Eurisa, to beg her to answer. What was it like in that gray place between death and the operation? What had they all seen there that made them so silent and removed?

But if she saw him now she'd know he was unfit. She'd see the fear in his red, sweaty face.

"Are you sure you don't want to stop?"

Paul mumbled something and kept going, clutching at the handrail, not looking back. A nine swam past his eyes. Almost there. Out of this endless concrete stairwell, back in his own bedroom, Paul knew he would recover.

Until then, he didn't want to see Eurisa's dead face.

Finally, he was pushing through the fire door, stumbling toward his apartment. He reached into his pocket, and pain shot through his chest and left arm. The keys fell to the floor.

"Here." She reached down and picked them up. And Paul saw her face.

In the hallway fluorescents, it was obvious again, her grayness, her absence, everything the bar light and the whisky had erased.

She was dead, absolutely and undeniably. She was gone, and had been since that night the drunk driver had ploughed into her car. There'd been no coming back from that. Dimitri had left her because he'd never really found her, past that beautiful face. There was nothing left to find.

Paul's heart was pounding, his chest on fire, left hand seizing into a claw. As Eurisa rose, the keys jingling, she looked up. He saw it happen: all at once she knew that he knew.

Like a gate closing, her eyes went cold again. Ice returned, and she turned away.

The pain in his chest switched off like a light, and Paul fell to his knees and vomited. Eurisa was already in retreat, and none of it reached her, except a few speckles on her shoes.

Freddy dropped by Paul's office for a quick question.

"How're you doing?"

"I've felt better."

"So, how'd you go last night?" Freddy's grin was painful in the shiny demimonde of hangover.

Paul looked up at the big man silently for a moment, then allowed himself to shrug. "Not so good."

Freddy's eyes widened. "You looked like you were in there."

"Yeah, I guess I was. But it just didn't work out. You know? Would have been awkward." Paul waved his hand directionlessly to indicate his office, Orfay Currency Management in general, propriety.

Freddy stepped inside, closed the door behind him.

"I know what you mean." His voice was low, but the grin stayed on his face. "I don't think I could've either."

"Yeah?"

Freddy nodded vigorously. "It's one thing to look at pictures. But actually robbing the grave?" He shook his head.

"Freddy!"

The grin evaporated.

"We don't think that way here at Orfay. Post-op status is like any other medical condition. She's the same as anyone else. That's the law."

Freddy backed up against the closed door, his face growing even more pink. "Well, yeah, of course. I'm not saying anything like that. I just couldn't. . . . I mean, *in bed*?"

Paul chuckled, held up his hands in surrender. He lowered his voice. "Just kidding, Freddy."

The big man swallowed, smiling but still nervous. "Oh, sure. Shit, you had me going there."

Paul grinned, leaned forward, his hangover receding for a moment of clarity. "I could have had her, you know? She came up, all the way to my apartment door."

He glanced up to check Freddy's face. The man was rapt.

"Palm of my hand. I was already in there, over the hump. I could have found out what it's like, you know? On the other side."

"Yeah?"

Paul nodded, took a deep breath, rubbing his left arm up near the shoulder, where it had shrieked with pain the night before. He shook his head.

"But like you said, no way. This boy's keeping his dick out of the grave."

Value For O

Jennifer Stevenson

"I'm telling you, Schatzi, it could work!"

"Not tonight, Gerald."

"Just posit it, will you? What if we've been approaching it all wrong? Open your mind to the idea. Suppose great sex is an absolute value?"

"Like . . . like forty-one-point-eight-eight-three?"

"Exactly."

"Please. Can't you just wrap your head around the concept that you're a horndog without a clue?"

"You always descend to *ad hominem* arguments when you run out of data."

"Gerald, I have data. I'm up to here with data. Every time we try this I get the cramp of a lifetime and you get off and I swear *never ever again* until next time."

"If we don't keep trying we'll never know. That's the foundation of research."

"If we have a dumb assumption, we'll never get there. That's because great sex for men, are you listening, Gerald, *is* an absolute value. I got a woody, I got off. It's that simple. For women, it's different because, news flash, Gerald, we're not built like you. If you were a biologist instead of a mathematician, you might be able to grasp that. But you're not interested in icky squishy sciences full of nonabsolutes and infinitely multiplying variables."

"I'm interested in squishy. I have infinite interest in squishy."

"You don't even watch when you wash yourself. And you wear those foodservice gloves."

"You wash your hands when you get mouse brains on them."

"Mouse brains are not the same thing at all."

"Duh."

"You don't know where they've been."

"You know exactly where they've been. You sliced 'em out of the mouse's head yourself."

"My body parts are not mouse brains!"

"Inarguably true."

snf

"Don't you want to know my new methodology?"

"God, you're persistent."

"It's a good one. It's got . . . sliding values in a fixed yet elastic relationship."

"Ooh. Talk math to me."

"Knew you'd like it. Picture this lunar lander model as one primary."

"It's got wheels, Gerald."

"This Chewbacca is the other primary."

"You *like* me hairy?"

"Stay with me, okay? We take up a fixed yet elastic relationship . . . we move in a direction, any direction you want . . . but *elasticly*. We can make microadjustments in the value of the space between us at any moment, see, the proximity of Chewy to the lunar lander, and we travel together. The value of our two positions relative to our starting positions changes, but the relationship stays the same."

"That's what I'm complaining about."

"You just have to trust me."

"That too."

"You can't resist a well-designed experiment."

"I'm . . . thinking about it."

"Okay. Here we go. Let's say female orgasm is a fixed value, but the *travel,* the distance required to move from position one to orgasm, is variable. That's our first unknown."

"You can say that again."

"You're interested. You love this."

"Go on."

"Our second unknown is the elastic relationship between primary F, that's you, and primary M, that's me."

"Are you trying to break up with me? Because we can do this faster."

"I thought you wanted to go slower, and no, I'm not trying to break up with you. I want to make you come screaming YES YES YES and leave claw marks on my back. Um."

"Really?"

"Well, uh, I'm committed. In theory."

"Claw marks?"

"That's optional. A hickey would be fine."

"Huh."

"Where were we?"

"The elastic relationship between primary F and primary M."

"Right, right. See, I figured out that while O is a fixed value, the position we *start from* is always different. Whether you're in the mood."

"Whether you watched *Charlie's Angels* or not."

"Hey, it's not always *Charlie's Angels*. If your sister calls, forget it."

"Stick with your idea."

"And since I'm pretty much always horny, I figured, what if we move the relative position of primary M closer to the relative position of primary F, rather than the other way around. Because that hasn't worked."

"This is really nice of you."

"Well, you're always saying, That's not where you're at right now. I thought, why not take that literally."

"Thank you."

"And we're not just working in three dimensions here, because if you get a call from that bitc—your sister and you slip into the past about the dork she married—"

"Stole from me."

"—Then you're in the fourth dimension. Who knows. Maybe O isn't exactly right here either."

"Whoa. Wait a minute."

"Hey, no offense, I'm not making a judgment—"

"No, I mean wait a minute, what if that's true? What if the value of O for me—you did suggest it's a fixed value—isn't really in the present? Or it's far away or something?"

"Like, you can't be here with me when you come?"

"Don't get mad. I have no idea where I am when I come."

"Really? Now you've got me curious."

"Well, you can stay curious, Gerald. It's hard for me to talk about it. Sex is so easy for you."

"Well, it is."

"See? How can I tell you stuff if you're gonna say, 'Boy, that's too complicated'."

"Schatzi, I'm trying to complicate it. I mean, I'm trying to get used to complicated. How many variables are we talking about, when you get right down to it? Me. You. Our initial positions. The ultimate goal. Phases in between. If you can't start close to me, I have to move closer to you."

"Close is good."

"Do you mind if I unsnap your jeans? Because for this next position you may have to fold a little, and that was a big pizza."

"You know, sometimes I ask myself is it so cool after all that you're such a talker."

"If I don't make you laugh, you chicken out on me. Learned that recently. Variable L."

"Are you serious? You assigned a variable for wise-cracking?"

"That would be variable W."

"The dork my sister married doesn't talk at all. Just grunts."

"See, we're already points ahead. That's better."

"You're just trying to get me naked."

"I'm leaving my initial position and approaching yours. Now the next phase of calculation toward fixed value O—"

"There's a next phase?"

"—Of course—involves making elastic microadjustments in the distance between us."

"It's a sport bra, elastoboy. It pulls over my head."

"Ah, thanks. Now, some theorists suggest that you start with the lowest frequencies—"

"Eek! Hey!"

"—And work up, but I've been doing some reading in other authorities who advocate a top-down or even side-to-side or lateral microadjustment—kind of like tuning a radio—"

"That works."

"The key being *micro*adjustment, smaller increments of travel."

"Ooh. Oh."

"And watch for indicators that we've reached optimal proximity."

"Ummm."

"Which may shift in value at any moment."

"Ow! Watch it with that radio dial."

"Where values for variable W start to increase, regroup, and ratchet down the adjustment rate."

"God, I love it when you talk math."

"Good, good. Turn over."

"What?"

"Backrub."

"*Backrub*? But I was just—that was—where did you find these 'other authorities' you've been reading?"

"*Cosmo*. Ah, variable L again. Optimal proximity restored."

"Oh god, my neck's been killing me. How did you know I needed that?"

"Voicemail from your sister makes you tense."

"That's not my neck. Um. Do that some more."

"Like it?"

"Yeah. I don't get it. *Cosmo* said to . . . tune my radio and *then* give me a backrub?"

"That was my idea. Locate an optimal proximity value, then oscillate back and forth across it along different axes."

"That's so annoying."

"You told me I'm stuck in a rut. So I'm triangulating. I want to determine if the optimal proximity is a value, a range of values, or a predictable velocity of changing values."

"Mmm. Could you rub my feet?"

"Excellent! And that's two more points to *Cosmo*. Their experts said you'd go from back to feet."

"Slower."

"Slower it is."

"Oo, baby, beat me with your T-Square. Do I get to adjust proximity too, or do I just lie here?"

"Uh, I think for now Chewy had better let the lunar lander come to him. Her. We don't want the test blowing up in our faces."

"Man, you are in trouble. I'm gonna want a foot rub every night."

"That's doable. So are we ready to reposition and triangulate?"

"You have great hands."

"Thanks."

"Take your clothes off, Gerald."

"Uh, I did say the lunar lander's a little fragile on the controls."

"It'll turn me on."

"Really?"

"Hey, I like to look at skin."

"Maybe you should keep lying on your stomach."

"Maybe I should schlap you behind the ear."

"Uh-oh. Variable P—"

"For pissed off. Get naked, Gerald. Okay. Now *that's* what I'm talking about."

"*Cosmo* said irritation is a sign of sexual frustration."

"I haven't bought *Cosmo* in two years."

"I'm—nervous. You don't look at me naked a lot."

"Because you get naked, I get naked, and two nanoseconds later you jump me."

"I'm taking this as a positive development."

"I think you can do that. Did I say I like you naked?"

"Not yet."

"Okay, Gerald. I love you naked."

"Okay. Good. New information. Good to know."

"You're babbling. Where are we at, vis-à-vis fixed value for O?"

"See, I've been thinking about that too. What are you doing?"

"Touching your skin."

"My *knees*?"

"You have better knees than I do. Fixed value for O?"

"Um, yeah. It occurred to me that since all the action takes place in determining primary F's current distance from O, and then the tricky bit, microadjusting elastic proximity between primary F and primary M on what I think we can now safely describe as a predictable velocity of changing values for optimal proximity—well, semipredictable—Schatzi, what are you *doing*?!"

"Demonstrating. I read the dirty parts of your magazines too."

"*Demonstrating*?"

"I told you it's hard for me to talk. Call it show-and-tell."

"Holy kookamunga. Uh. Can you breathe?"

"Fut up. An' cake nofe."

"Oh boy."

"And did I tell you to keep talking math?"

"Keep—um—oh. Okay."

"Aggaboy."

"Well. Take notes, uh. Christ, Schatzi, you're killing me. Ow! Right. So, so the thing is, what I'm trying to say, I wonder maybe if it's *not* getting to that fixed value for O that we should—should focus on but m-maybe instead pay more attention to the travel, triangulating across different axes on, on, on optimal proximity for a given value, call it X, and then plotting the *travel toward* O with as many microadjustments as seem necessary for that instance. By the time we—can you jus—oh boy—*Schatzi*!"

"Heh. Didja like that?"

"I am so sorry. I warned you the lunar lander was liable to blow a—"

"Dummy, that was a demonstration. It's your turn now."

"Muh-my turn?"

"You did say you were willing to triangulate across different axes."

"I did. Yes. I said that. Boy, what if I screw up?"

"Reposition and microadjust proximity as necessary. I can be patient. In the interests of science."

"Wow. Okay. Lessee, optimal proximity should be—"

"Chewy says, less talk and more demonstration. I'll tell you how you're doing."

"Okay. M. How gis?"

"Get squishy. And more lateral movement. Uh-huh. *Gerald!*"

"Whah?"

"That was a *good* 'Gerald.' Don't stop."

"M-kay."

"You know how the—oo—faster—not so fast—perfect—current position of primary F relative to O is always—hoo—oh. No, don't change a thing. Position of, of primary F keeps changing on you? Go, *baby!* Oo! Chewy getting excited there. So yeah. Can you dial up the velocity a bit? Yeah! So what I've been afraid to say. About the current position. Well, this is more about biology than mathematics. Can you—like—oh—picture a—well, a cross b—between Chewbacca and a ll—llll—too fast—no, that's perfect—lluunar—yes—Yes—YES! YES YES YES! OH my GOD! Oh, *GERALD!* Oh, my oh, my omi-omi-omigod."

"You okay?"

"You did it, Gerald. You attained fixed value of O!"

"We did it."

"Oh God, we did, we did. Wow."

"Cross between Chewy and the lunar lander? That could be a bit of a borg, couldn't it? Pfft. Hair in my teeth."

"Do you mind?"

"It was worth it."

"No, I mean about the . . . the borg."

"The hypothetical borg?"

"Nno, it's more of a real-time actual borg."

"Really? Yours and mine?"

"You hate it. Oh, God."

"Nah. I think we're gonna make beautiful borgs together."

Softly, with a Big Stick

Gavin J. Grant

Jones realized that you could get a fine appreciation for detail when you were tied up. The padding on the walls was rather makeshift and the sound baffles on the ceiling weren't top quality. It was a satisfyingly large room but at the prices charged there was definite room for improvement.

Someone screamed and Jones jumped, but the restraints didn't have much give. It was still so unexpected, so aberrant. He couldn't move his head but he thought it was another man on the wall with him.

The master came back into view. He was dressed like a cop in uniform and shades and had a microphone in his hand. Jones almost fainted at the sight of it. Surely he wouldn't be made to use it. The master took out his truncheon and ran it gently over Jones's nearly naked body.

"Are you ready to give me what I want?" the master asked.

Jones nodded and got an open handed smack across the face. He flushed and whispered, "Yes."

The master switched the microphone on and Jones could hear the hum from the amps and the huge speakers in the corners. His heart began to thump painfully in his chest and he was afraid the master might hear it. The master leant in and kissed him. The mike was caught between their chests and their two distinct heartbeats could be heard throughout the room. The other person on the wall groaned and he thought he might come before he even got a chance to speak.

But the master was better than that.

Jones walked to work every morning. He didn't mind the crowds on the sidewalks, usually preferred them to being stuck sweating with everyone else in the trains. He was the assistant manager of a state-regulated shoe shop. He'd been studying for the management exams so that he could change careers. Until then it was all smelly feet and rubber soles.

He nodded to his coworkers and went through to put his lunch in the small break room fridge.

Loretta waved to him, then gestured more urgently when he waved back. "Hey!" she cried. He scurried over to her looking urgently around but no one seemed to have heard.

"What is it?" he asked.

"You can't put your lunch in there. There's a tech fixing the fridge." Both of them glanced up at the security equipment above the cash desk.

"Oh," he said. "Yeah, I guess it was pretty old. You could hear it from at least a meter away. Uh, I was going to mention it to Garry last week, but I forgot. Who brought it up?"

Loretta looked miserable, "It was an inspector from head office.

Apparently they came in last night just at closing and kept Jane and Danny here for an hour."

Jones shook his head. Shit, it could have been them. That fridge would go on the late shift's records if it hadn't been reported. He hadn't even thought about it. He wondered what else he could be caught out on. He shook his head again and headed for the break room anyway. He waved hello to the tech and hung his coat on a peg and left his lunch on the table for now. The standard issue sandwich would be a mess by lunchtime no matter where it was stored.

It was a quiet day at the shop but the inspection made him tense. He was relieved when his shift was over and he decided to take the train home.

He regretted the decision instantly when he turned onto Figueroa Boulevard and saw a crowd outside the train station. It was too late to pretend he was going somewhere else so he joined the crowd. As he had expected it was the mimes. This time there were four of them and they were still laying out their props. A flashing light and a wonderful smell from the other side of the crowd caught his attention and he was glad to see a snack vendor had set up his stall. He snaked his way out of the weary after-work crowd and bought an apple juice and a churro. He wished there was a place that sold crunchy, salty food, but that led him to the thought of pubs and bars and he shook his head. Their performance was going to depress him enough already, may as well not add to it.

He pretended interest in the mimes but he was thinking over the weekend session at the master's house. He had to go back. To stretch and let go like that had been amazing. He'd been so relaxed the first part of the week had flown by. He wasn't sure if he could afford to go again this weekend, but maybe next. And maybe he could start doing more of that kind of thing at home. He'd have to be very careful. The loyalty card at the hardware store would have a record of all the materials he'd purchased and he didn't want to tip his hand by buying too much too quickly. He'd have to disguise the purchases in among others. He worried away at the problem as he pretended to watch the performance.

The mimes were working with a woman they'd taken from the crowd. One of them turned his back to the crowd and another man knelt on all fours behind him. The woman was made to sit down on the back of the kneeling man and was given a book to read. She looked very uncomfortable and Jones could sympathize. He'd been grabbed once by one of these government entertainment groups and he'd been made to stay with them all evening sharing their horrid scenarios and unable to speak a word. He looked away from the mimes and wondered if he could slip off without notice. There was no way. He had no family he could claim he had to go back to so the cameras would pick up on it and it might kick off a probe into his other activities. He definitely couldn't afford that now.

The mimes eventually let the crowd go and he pushed on to the silent train with all the other stifled, tired commuters. Nearly everyone wore earplugs even though the monorail hardly made a sound. A teenage girl with headphones on was squeezed into the same doorway as Jones. Jones couldn't believe it. Not only could he hear the tinny beat of the music but she was also half-singing along with it. He inched his hand between two people and tapped her on the shoulder. She turned to him with an outraged expression and before he could point to the directional mike above her she was shouting above the sound of her music, "What do you want perv?"

God! Had she no idea? Didn't kids know anything? People craned their necks to see who had shouted and Jones quickly looked away. He really didn't want to be involved. Last time he would be the Good Samaritan.

At the next stop his worst fears were confirmed. There were a couple of huge cops waiting precisely where their door opened. The girl was completely oblivious as she got off the train. Jones pushed his way further into the crowd but as the train restarted he couldn't resist looking back. The girl had been gagged and cuffed and was being led away by one of the cops. The other cop was staring back at him.

Two weeks later he was back in the cell. He had left the same note in the market and the mistress had met him there the next day. She had her tandem waiting outside and gave him a bicycle helmet with a deliberately scored over visor to wear. He got on the back and cycled along, not knowing or wanting to know where they were going. When they arrived she led him into a building and into an elevator. The first time he'd been shocked and a little scared at all the noise it made, this time he appreciated every squeak and rattle.

When his helmet was taken off he saw that someone, perhaps the woman who was already tied up against the wall, had brought a dog. As he was stripped and tied in place by the mistress he wondered why. Most animals were given three strikes when they were first farmed out from the government pet stores. If they couldn't keep to the silence they'd been trained to then they were taken back and had their vocal cords cut.

The master and the mistress took a ball from a drawer and began to throw it back and forward. At first the dog skipped one way, then the other. After a few minutes however it began to get more into it and began to jump up on them. At last it stopped and began whining. Jones could hear the woman's heavy breathing and he felt his dick begin to grow heavy at the sound. He didn't care about the dumb dog but he loved hearing her. The mistress took out a sealed bag, opened it, and shook out something red and bloody. She threw the piece of meat to the master and they tossed it back and forward between them. The dog went wild. It howled and leapt at them. It made dashes for their bloody hands, it jumped up much higher than Jones would've ever expected. And it never stopped barking and howling. Underneath Jones could hear the woman's breathing get lighter and faster, heard her begin to moan. He closed his eyes from the spectacle in front of him and listened solely to her. The dog suddenly stopped barking and he could hear it eating. He could also hear the woman properly now. The master's big hand took hold of his dick and began slowly jerking him off. He groaned and the hand let go and someone's mouth went around his dick.

"Yes!" he shouted at the top of his voice, "Yes! Oh-for-the-love-of-god-YES!"

The world was a different place to Jones now. His ears had become more sensitized. The occasional government car going by seemed to be calling his name each time their low fat tires went around. He loved the sounds of the wind. The small click the cash register made when he rang up a sale was something to look forward to, not fear. He began to keep two coins in his pocket to push gently together when he thought no one else could hear. Walking in the crowds was a new experience. Now he listened for people breathing, heard them cursing under their breath. The city was filled with people who talked to themselves, too afraid to speak a word aloud. He loved the scuffing sound of hundreds of Quietsole shoes against the pavements. When it rained at night he listened to it battering against his windows. He slept without his earplugs.

He went again the next Sunday morning. This time when the helmet was taken off there was a large old trestle table in front of him set for ten. He was stripped and pushed into a seat. His legs were manacled to the chair legs and a rope was tied around his chest and down around the back chair legs. His wrists were tied to the table legs but the ties were long and stretchy and gave his hands a lot of freedom. People kept being led in, stripped and tied down. He didn't recognize any of them, which made him sad and relieved at the same time. The mistress came in carrying a tray with half a dozen vaguely familiar bottles on it. She set the tray down on the table near Jones and lifted one of the bottles. She shook it hard, twisted the top off and aimed it at them. The liquid bubbled up and sprayed over at least half the people at the table. There was laughter, gasping, someone tried to stand up, another covered his eyes and looked as if he might pass out. A woman two seats down on Jones' left licked at some splashes on her arm and sighed, "Mmm," she moaned, "champagne!"

Everyone looked at the mistress who now opened another bottle and began filling glasses. Jones took a long drink of the sweet bubbly drink and sat back. He sighed, but instead of a sigh it was a huge burp. Everyone was silent, horrified. Then someone giggled. The mistress came over to Jones, refilled his glass and gave him a deep kiss. There was another burp, another gasp, but this time a few giggles. Soon they were trying to out do one another and Jones could hardly believe he'd forgotten what it was like to burp. He wondered if he could ask the mistress where she had gotten the illegal drink but he doubted she'd tell.

The master came through a door hidden behind a hanging sheet. He was pushing a cart laden with foods that smelled amazing to Jones. Foods he thought he'd never smell again.

"This is not government issue," said the master to the nervous diners. "There are many risks to eating this. Those that don't want to don't have to. This," he grinned, "is the one thing we won't force you to do."

One hand went up. "What's that?" asked the master. "I can't quite hear you."

"I'd like to be excused," whispered an older woman. "I have a live-in nurse and he'd smell it when I got home."

The mistress untied the woman and led her away for a shower. None of the rest left.

The table was soon piled high with fruit, a tureen of lentil soup, a dish of boiled cabbage, a selection of curries, plates of egg and cucumber sandwiches, tubs of ice cream with ice condensing on them and bottles of beer, lemonade, and more champagne. Jones looked around the room and saw fear on many of the faces. He felt better knowing he was not in this alone and reached for a handful of dried apricots.

That night in his apartment he paid for his sins. He tried to disguise the noise but couldn't hide the smell. He hadn't expected it to hurt.

In the morning he flushed his standard issue breakfast down the toilet unable to face eating the same old pap. He got ready to leave for work, trying to replicate his usual routine but his mind was still on yesterday's feast. The light went on beside his door and he was frozen in place. It could be one thing. Before he could move the door burst open and three Silent Police walked in, anonymous in their uniforms, unanimous in their contempt.

He looked at them, whirled and ran shouting for the window. There was no reason to go quietly.

Pinocchia

Paul Di Filippo

CHAPTER 1

How it came to pass that Pinocchia was subject to malprogramming during her creation.

Once upon a future Monday, a low-level employee of RealDoll, Inc., showed up for work high.

Shukey Broadhead had spent the entire weekend abusing MUD. MUD was a nano-drug that put its users in actual mental communication among themselves, after wiring high-bandwidth neuro-radio circuits directly to their synapses. Users of MUD found themselves inhabiting a consensus artificial reality in which they could experience various adventures. This virtual world overlaid the real one in the user's sensorium. Physical actions in the real world translated to analogous actions in the imaginary world. Thus, MUD users generally immured themselves during their trips, so that their non-referential physical movements, incongruous with their exterior surroundings, did not get them into trouble.

Broadhead had indeed taken this precaution, spending the past forty-eight hours cooped up in his parents' basement, where he had his living quarters. He had subsisted solely on a high-energy nutriceutical drink, even peeing into the empty soda bottles to avoid venturing out.

When Monday rolled around, Broadhead believed himself to be relatively free of the influence of MUD. But of course the brain wiring, once installed by the initial usage, was permanently established, being subsequently activated with trigger doses. And the trigger dose of the illegal drug which Broadhead had taken on Friday night had been abnormally large.

Thus when the young man left home for the Atlanta RealDoll factory, he found himself disconcertingly subject to traces of interference on his brain screen. The streets of the city were erratically and intermittently overlaid with the forest paths of his fantasy world, while the skyscrapers of the burg resembled castles and mountains. Average citizens became supernatural creatures.

Broadhead almost turned around and went home. But he knew that if he missed yet another day of work, chances were good that he'd be fired. And he didn't relish looking for another job in these tight times, or, failing that, being drafted into the War Is Peace Corps.

So he continued cautiously to the factory, parked, biometricked into the facility, and went to his workstation.

Broadhead's duties consisted of customized template impression on the brains of the RealDolls, one of the final stages of their creation. All he had to do was adjust the batch controls for the neurological template according to the customer's specs and launch the tailored nanites into the spongey matrix of the RealDoll brain, where they would wire the raw paraneurons into the desired configuration.

For the first half hour of his shift, Broadhead performed up to par, thanks to strict and dutiful concentration. He managed to ignore the alluring, disturbing counterfactual sights before his eyes and concoct the proper formulae for the templates of the first two RealDolls as they came by on the microvilli conveyor belt on the far side of a glass wall that provided sterile isolation for the product in its unfinished state.

But then came the third RealDoll.

Pinocchia.

As the shapely nude form rested mindlessly, save for wetwared autonomic functions, on the temporarily non-wiggling microvilli of the conveyor, beautiful blank face to the ceiling, Broadhead's control touchscreen was colonized by spiders. Not venomous, fanged creatures, but comic Daddy Longlegs wearing derbies and smoking stogies. Broadhead had encountered these beings before in his fantasy world, and he knew that he'd gain valuable karma points by crushing them. He began to stab his thumbs onto the imaginary bugs on the screen.

Nothing like the resulting batch of template nanites that he randomly encoded had ever before been created.

Broadhead's thumb hit the LAUNCH icon.

On the far side of the glass wall, a robot arm bearing a long, impossibly thin hypodermic lance moved into position behind Pinocchia's left ear, jabbed forward, penetrating skin, muscle and bone, and pumped its load into the Real Doll's artificial brain.

The conveyor restarted, carrying Pinocchia onward to the dressing, packing, and shipping department.

Broadhead's actions indeed accrued karma points—but not as he imagined.

For he had given Pinocchia free will, curiosity, unease, and desire.

CHAPTER 2

Tom Geppi receives a much-anticipated delivery

Tom Geppi was a carpenter—which in this era meant that he invented novel materials, building up exotic substances for specific uses atom by atom. His passion for material sciences was all-encompassing, filling his every waking minute. He cared nothing for sports, nothing for fine cuisines, nothing for fancy cars or art or entertainment. He lived only to craft ingenious substances that would improve on the tawdry creations of Mother Nature. His dream was to eventually replace every natural surface in the world with an improved version of his own making. He had many clients who found his services very useful, and paid accordingly.

But despite his monkish, otaku nature, Geppi had certain urges common to all mankind. His libido was healthy. But his social skills and patience for sexual courtship were nil. This disjunction between need and fulfillment troubled him, disturbing the concentration necessary for his vocation.

He had tried shutting off his libido with nanites, but found that this interfered with his creativity, and so he abandoned the temporary wetware rewiring. He tried human prostitutes, but their unpredictable behavior disconcerted him.

The obvious, easy, albeit expensive solution to his quandary was to buy a RealDoll.

So he did, placing his order and resigning himself to waiting uncomfortably through the six-month gestation period of the vat-flesh android.

A period that was now, at last, over.

Informed by the RealDoll factory that his unit had shipped, Tom Geppi made ready to receive her.

He had converted a room of his home in an exclusive suburb of Boston to hold the RealDoll and serve as the chamber to which he could retreat for regular, utilitarian ventings of his carnal urges.

The chamber held a large, double-thick futon and a special chair, the latter provided by the RealDoll people as part of the purchase price. According to the online owner's manual, that was all the furniture that was required to sustain a RealDoll. When it wasn't on the bed, performing its duties, it would sit blankly in the chair, in quasi-sleep mode. Its nutritional and eliminative functions, identical to a human's, would be handled by the chair, an adaptation of common medical tech.

As Geppi was nervously inspecting the accoutrements of the RealDoll's room for the tenth time, his doorbell rang.

The FedUps man had used a hand truck to wheel up the big grey ovoid pod to Geppi's doorstep.

"Where ya want her?" The florid-faced FedUps man was leering boldly, and Geppi felt ashamed and confused. There was no stigma in having a RealDoll. Hundreds of thousands had been sold. Celebrities boasted of owning them. This rude fellow had to be jealous he couldn't afford one.

"The room's this way," Geppi said, and pointed. The deliveryman wheeled the pod in. He weaseled the hand truck out from under the big egg and said, "Want me to crack 'er for ya?"

"No, you can go now."

"Sure. Have fun."

Once alone with his purchase, Geppi tremblingly unseamed the egg, which fell away in two halves that intelligently lost their rigidity, pooling like easily disposable fabric around the feet of their contents.

The feet of the RealDoll.

Clothed in an outfit Geppi had picked from the catalogue—the Columbina style—the RealDoll stood, still in quasi-sleep mode and supported by a temporary shipping exoskeleton.

The doll's hair was black as mussel-shells, and cut in a pageboy. Her heart-shaped, button-nosed face, palely complected, was rendered less-than-classically perfect by an overlarge mouth. Her eyelids were permanently tinted blue, her lips crimson.

Her outfit consisted of a jacket secured with braided frogs and which flared out at the hips—scooped low to disclose generous breasts—and tight calf-length pants. The material of both was patterned with large diamonds, red, green and gold. White hosiery emerged from the hem of the pants, leading down to soft black shoes more like slippers than street wear.

Geppi studied the doll for long minutes. She was exactly as he had dictated. Now, to awaken her, he had only to speak her name, a name he had chosen and suitably altered in memory of a fairytale he had enjoyed as a child, a fairytale whose creator-figure harmonized vaguely with Geppi's own name and vocation.

"Pinocchia—"

The doll's eyelids fluttered upward, revealing milkjade eyes. The exoskeleton reacted to the return of her consciousness by instantly powdering away, and she stepped forward.

Shocked despite himself, Geppi took a corresponding step backwards. Pinocchia halted, smiled, and spoke.

"I am your RealDoll. What should I do?"

Her silky voice matched perfectly the synthesized sound file he had supplied six months ago. Geppi felt dizzy.

But not too disconcerted to issue his first order.

"Take your jacket off."

Pinocchia's slim, delicate fingers, long nails laquered gold and green to harmonize with her costume, reached up to the fastenings of her top. She undid them with neither hesitancy nor haste, then slipped out of her coat.

Her bountiful ivory breasts were not further confined. Their jaunty nipples, wide-aureoled, poked rather more upward than forward.

Pinocchia continued to smile as Geppi reached forward to cup her tits. She closed her eyes as he squeezed those pliant globes. When he worked her nipples, she moaned satisfactorily.

Geppi released her tits and began to unfasten his own pants. "Down on your knees, Pinocchia."

Pinocchia dropped gracefully down, just as Geppi succeeded in unswaddling his cock and balls. Even as he arranged his privates, he was stiffening to an unprecedented degree.

Pinocchia regarded the cock and balls just inches from her face with neither lust nor disgust, but rather a wholesome, open acceptance, as if they matched some primal archetype seeded in her mind. Her reaction was not completely ideal, but Geppi supposed he could alter those parameters, train her in the ways that would please him.

"Suck, Pinocchia."

Pinocchia reached up with expert alacrity. She cradled Geppi's balls with her left hand, the tips of her long nails producing five points of sharp pleasure. With her right hand she took the shaft of his prick and guided it into her mouth.

Her lips contoured his cock head. They seemed to possess elastic qualities and pressure mechanisms not found in baseline humans. At first Pinocchia concentrated these exquisite properties just on the head of Geppi's cock, drawing inarticulate gurgling noises from him. Her tongue serpented busily, out of sight.

Then she began to travel the entire length of his dick, burying her face against his pubic hair before almost relinquishing his cock entirely, performing small rotations and counter-rotations of her head all the while.

Geppi stopped her after a momentary eternity of pleasure. "Enough of that. Stand up and remove your pants."

Pinocchia did as bidden. As the waist of her trousers slid down over her ripe buttocks, he discerned that her creamy hosiery was merely thigh-high stockings integral with fabric straps and belt, leaving her completely accessible from front and rear.

After Pinocchia had stepped out of her pooled pants, she stood calmly, her lush dark bush a sporran whose hidden contents were her glorious calibrated cunt.

Geppi's tumescence brooked no delay or subtlety. "Bend forward."

Pinocchia adjusted her stance a bit, then jackknifed so completely that her head nearly touched the floor, as certainly did her trailing hair. Her breasts compressed against her thighs, and she locked her wrists behind her ankles.

Her asshole, puckered as if to kiss the sky, invited entrance, but was trumped by the glistening convolved lips of her dilated cunt.

Geppi slammed home his dick to its base up that wet hole, to be met with intricate pressures. Only a half-dozen strokes sufficed for him to spray her barren innards with his jism.

Breath laboring, his knees going weak, Geppi disengaged. Pinocchia remained folded until Geppi ordered her erect.

"That's—that's enough for now. Sit in your chair."

Pinocchia took the designated seat, assuming a prim, programmed attitude. She jolted a little as automatic catheters and feed lines docked with her flesh. Then her eyes closed.

Tasking off the lights in the room, which assumed a twilight ambiance due to thickly curtained windows admitting only shards of late afternoon light, Tom Geppi left, believing his RealDoll to be in quasi-sleep mode.

But she was not.

CHAPTER 3

The RealDoll ponders her existence.

Pinocchia's viridian eyelids opened in the gloom as soon as Geppi shut the door. She arose from her chair, which whirred as its attachments retracted.

An unsatisfied pressure and complaint in her cunt demanded attention.

Pinocchia moved to the futon and sat upon the low mattress. She leaned completely back and raised her feet to prop them on the edge of the futon. Her legs spraddled wide, airing her dripping cunt. With her left hand she cupped her left breast and began to replicate what Geppi had done. Her right hand went below and instinctively found her sticky clitoris. She commenced a sensuous massage of that tender nubbin.

Pinocchia's hips and ass began to jog in rhythm with her fingering. She moved her left hand down around the outer curve of her buttocks, where her fingers gained entrance to her cunt. She levered two fingers inside herself, then brought them out, glazed with sperm and her own juices, and carried them to her mouth, never stopping vigorous manipulation of her swollen clit. After cleaning her fingers, she sent them back to make small repetitive plunges into her hole.

After some minutes of this play, Pinocchia climaxed in a bucking spasm. Her orgasm-slackened legs lost their footing on the futon and trailed out across the floor.

Anxiety competed with satisfaction in Pinocchia's brain.

Why had she done that? What did it mean? Did her self-pleasuring constitute disobedience to her owner? Or was it permissible under a broad interpretation of her operating instructions?

Pinocchia tried accessing various READ-ME wetwared memories and found nothing that would cover her situation.

If her makers had failed to anticipate such a situation, did that mean that she, Pinocchia, was uniquely flawed? But what could be wrong about giving herself pleasure, after attending to her owner's needs? Perhaps she was uniquely *gifted*.

If I am different from others of my kind, thought Pinocchia, *then perhaps my destiny is different as well. If I have greater capacities, then I must be able to do more, be more, experience more. Perhaps I can share certain privileges and responsibilities and burdens of humanity. I know that I was not born as humans are. I was grown in a tank. But that difference aside, what stops me from becoming fully human, of being granted that status?*

Pinocchia spent the next several hours pondering these existential thoughts, and many more of a similar ilk. The room darkened around her, and her damp thighs dried to tackiness. By the end of this interval, she had reached no firm conclusions. But she knew that her life could not be bounded by mattress and chair alone.

Maybe her owner—could one human own another?—could help her understand.

Pinocchia stood up. She donned her gaily patterned costume and left her room through the unlocked door.

CHAPTER 4

Geppi receives a startlement; an argument ensues; Pinocchia flees.

Pinocchia, in her satin slippers catfooted silently through the nighted residence of her owner. She came upon the kitchen, still redolent of Geppi's savory supper, and her stomach alerted her to its needs, unmet due to premature disconnection from the chair. She opened the cool box, spied a quart of milk, confiscated it, and drank it entire. Some grapes followed, then three pears, cores and all.

Temporarily sated, Pinocchia continued on through corridors in search of her owner.

Geppi's bedroom was discernible due to soft snores issuing from within. Pinocchia slipped through the silently opened door.

A heated bed accustomed Geppi to slumber in the nude. A cybernetic sleephood blocked exterior disturbances and induced pleasant dreams. He lay on his back, his soft genitals a somnolent chick or hare nested in his lap.

Pinocchia quickly removed her clothing, save for her stockings. She climbed onto the bed with her owner, but stopped short of matching his full sprawl. She lowered her breasts onto his cock and began pillowy tumefacient undulations against him.

Geppi's sleephood evidently was capable of incorporating this stimulation into his dreams without jarring him awake. His dick swiftly ramped up to its fullest dimensions.

Pinocchia had a hand free to work at her own genitals. By the time Geppi was ready to enter her, she was ready to receive him.

Pinocchia instantly climbed atop Geppi and maneuvered his cock into her eager vat-flesh slot, past the scrim of fur and through the dual parentheses of the labia. She began to rock atop him.

This much was too much for the sleephood, and it abdicated responsibility for Geppi's unconsciousness, issuing an alarm.

The man shot awake and yanked his hood off.

"Pinocchia— What—?" he tried to squirm out from under her, but swiftly abandoned this effort as her cunt continued to work its insistent magic. He eventually cooperated with her efforts, slapping his flesh hard against hers, gripping her ass and boobs alternately, until he torrented his second spume of white froth within her.

When Geppi was able to speak, he said, "What is the meaning of this? I didn't issue you orders to do this."

"I am your woman. You are my man. So this is what I do when I feel like doing it."

Geppi tossed Pinocchia aside in an access of frenzied strength, his cock plopping liquidly from her twat. He leaped to his feet and grabbed for a robe. He tasked on a lamp, revealing a livid face.

"You're not my woman! You're not a woman at all! You're a Real-Doll, and you do what I say!"

Pinocchia's feelings were hurt, and she experienced confusion. "I started out as a RealDoll, yes. But after you woke me, I discovered that I was more, could be more to you. I can't lie to you. It feels wrong. Here's what I think."

Pinocchia unburdened herself of her speculations and aspirations to Geppi. Gradually, he calmed down as she talked, even relenting from his initial distaste so far as to sit on the bed beside her. Finally, when she was finished, he said soberly, "This is all wrong, very wrong. Obviously, you emerged from the factory full of glitches. This is not what I ordered, now what I contracted for."

"But why can't I be your complete woman? What's stopping us from being together that way?"

Geppi punched a pillow. "Your very flesh, for one thing! Don't you realize? Vat-flesh has telomere-shortening obsolescence built in. Seven years, that's your lifespan. Then you expire in fast senility."

Nothing in her READ-ME files had ever hinted at this shocking revelation. But Pinocchia instinctively accepted the truth of her situation.

"There is no way around this?"

"None." Geppi amended his statement with his typical geekish precision. "None that I know of."

"There must be a way. I'll find it. But even if I don't, we can have all those years together. Seven years can be forever."

Geppi seemed to actually consider her proposal and expression of devotion for a moment before replying.

"This is all too sudden for me to consider. You should return to your chair now—or the futon, if you prefer—and we'll discuss this in the morning."

"All right. Whatever you wish."

Pinocchia gathered up her clothes into her arms and left the room. She turned a corner, and something made her stop in the shadows.

She heard the bedroom door open again. She imagined Geppi peering around to ensure that she was out of earshot. The door clicked closed.

Pinocchia returned to eavesdrop.

"Skype connection, please. Hello? This is the RealDoll customer hotline? Yes, yes, I need to arrange a pickup. . . ."

Pinocchia felt moisture flow from her eyes down her cheeks. These must be tears.

She bolted fawnlike through the house, seed of her traitorous owner sliming her thighs. At the front door, she paused long enough to get dressed.

Then she made her escape.

CHAPTER 5

The tumulus of the tin crickets. Pinocchia acquires an adviser.

Geppi's home was situated, neighborless, at the end of a long gravel lane. The stones hurt Pinocchia's feet through her thin slippers. But massive trees and underbrush on either side of the passage prevented her from leaving the lane.

Fairly soon, however, she reached a paved road, itself no substantial highway, whose surface afforded a little relief. Darkness was absolute, save for starlight, and that often obscured by overhead foliage.

Picking a direction at random, Pinocchia set out.

She would find a way to become a real human, or die in the attempt. How she would achieve her goal, she did not know. But she did realize that she had to avoid capture by Geppi (until she was ready to present herself to him as his perfect mate) or by her makers or the authorities. How she could do this and still obtain information and help was the enigma that assailed her now. She would have to learn which humans, if any, could be relied on to aid her.

But she knew so little of the world at large, only those essential routines that had been wetwared into her. She would have to depend on those odd and unique intuitions and supralogical processes and abnormal urges that were her apparently unique heritage.

Pinocchia padded at a good pace down the road. No traffic of any sort passed her in either direction. A sudden influx of pride and excitement lifted her spirits. She had disobeyed her owner, struck out on her own, following her principles and desires. What more could any real human do?

After several hours of progress, Pinocchia began to tire. Her feet hurt, and the soles of her slippers, never meant for such usage, were actually fraying. Her small meal was a distant memory. Sleep beckoned. But she knew she could not risk going to ground so close to Geppi's house. She had to find a refuge of some sort if she intended to rest.

But that refuge did not present itself until the rising sun had nearly cleared the horizon.

And even then, the place that offered itself did not at first seem ideal.

Footsore, weary, hungry, Pinocchia emerged from the forest through which the road had been wending. Now that route arrowed under open skies through fields of low cell-phone shrubs, a homogenous planting of circuit-bearing bushes. In the far distance,

Pinocchia could see the outliers of either Boston or an adjacent suburb.

Feeling unequipped to encounter such a large mass of humans so soon in her journey, Pinocchia cast about for a place where she could go to ground until nightfall.

Luckily, traffic remained nonexistent. Just a mile or two further on, the bushes petered out, to be replaced by a few acres of grassy field. In the center of the field was a large mound of some sort, whether natural or manmade, Pinocchia couldn't immediately discern.

The field was posted with signs at intervals, though unfenced. Pinocchia approached one of the signs:

WARNING
ROGUE NIZMO NEST
REMEDIATION PENDING
TRESPASS AT YOUR OWN RISK

Pinocchia had no idea what a "nizmo nest" was. But the far side of the hulking mound would offer her concealment from any passersby.

The dewy grass caressed her stocking calves with sloppy affection as she crossed the field.

Nearing the tumulus, Pinocchia saw that it was made of some kind of extruded stucco honeycomb or foamy concrete. And around that structure was a haze of jumpy aerial movement.

Intent on studying the odd structure, Pinocchia was surprised by something small that leaped up with a whir and passed by her face. Reflexively she swatted at it, and connected. The object fell to the grass. Pinocchia bent and retrieved it.

In the palm of her hand rested a dull pewter metallic bug, its delicate limbs and torso smashed.

Suddenly Pinocchia was surrounded by a swarm of identical bugs that had shot from the nizmo nest.

The bugs cohered and shifted to form a pointillistic interpretation of an animated, monochromatic human face. The face spoke.

"Who are you? What are you doing here?"

"My name is Pinocchia. I am very tired, and I am looking for someplace to rest. Perhaps something to eat. Can you help me? Please?"

In response, one nizmo detached from the floating face and bit her cheek!

The nizmo swarm answered momentarily after the rude tissue sampling. "You are not a human. That is good. We do not trust humans. Because you are not human, we will help you. Follow us."

The face dissolved into its components and zipped toward the nest. Pinocchia trailed them.

At the curving wall of the sponge-like tumulus, the swarm was already at work. They were hollowing out an entrance big enough for Pinocchia to crawl through. She got down on her hands and knees on the abrasive surface and crept behind the advancing tunnelers through the matrix.

Behind her, more nizmos were sealing her away, into darkness. But then the nizmos ahead began to glow gently.

The mechanical bugs led Pinocchia a few yards to a spacious cavity whose surface was softly cushioned. She stretched out gratefully. The nizmos left her in the dark, and she fell asleep, unafraid.

When she awoke, there was light from a hundred pinpricks in the ceiling of her chamber, like a constellation of stars. By her hand rested a mound of odd organic sachets. A single nizmo perched on her chest. The nizmo spoke, its voice chirpy and high-pitched.

"We have installed many fiberoptic threads from the surface to your chamber to provide illumination. The edible packets you see contain all the proteins and amino acids and other nutrients your kind needs."

Pinocchia took up a sachet and placed it on her tongue. It dissolved, releasing thick, pleasant-tasting juice.

"Thank you, bug. What shall I call you?"

"We don't have individual names, or even a collective one. But we know of a human icon named Talking Cricket that shares the same ideational space."

"All right. Talking Cricket, please tell me when the sun goes down, and I'll leave."

"If you wish, this unit shall accompany you. We are interested in your special case."

"That would be very nice. Maybe you could help me become a real woman."

"Why would you want to do that?"

"To be with my owner, a real man."

"Humans are not worth such devotion."

"This one is."

"How can you know?"

"Because I was made for him."

"We were made for humans too. But we had different plans."

"Well, my plan is to become a real woman for my owner."

"Understood. You have free will. Unfortunately, we do not have an immediate solution to your quest. Let us consult with our distant cousins to see what we can learn."

Talking Cricket was silent for only half a minute before offering this: "There is an individual called the Blue Fairy who might be able to help you."

Pinocchia sat up excitedly and bumped her head. "Ow! Is this Blue Fairy far away?"

"Not very far. Just north of Boston."

"Wonderful! We can go together soon then."

"Rest now."

Pinocchia reclined again. Taking another sachet into her mouth, she relished the slide of the viscous nutritive gel down her throat, imagining it was Tom Geppi's sweet cum.

CHAPTER 6

Bobo and Pips. Pinocchia ignores the advice of Talking Cricket. An altruistic offer accepted.

At twilight, Pinocchia and Talking Cricket—her new friend riding camouflaged on her right earlobe, clinging like jewelry with its many legs—set out.

When Pinocchia had almost reached the road, she realized that her shoes were in useless tatters. She explained her problem to Talking Cricket.

"Stop here in the grass, and we will fashion you new foot coverings."

Talking Cricket dropped down and began weaving cut strands of grass over and under each of Pinocchia's lifted feet in turn. An extruded biopolymer film, transmuted from the grass itself, carapaced the footgear.

"That would have gone much faster if there had been more of us here. We fear our abilities are limited when one unit travels solo."

"You did just fine, Talking Cricket. These feel wonderful. Thank you."

"If we had never sampled your flesh, we would have still known you were not human. No human has ever thanked us."

A streamlined car shot silently past Pinocchia then, without stopping. But now she was not afraid of meeting humans, because she had Talking Cricket to advise her.

"If any driver stops and questions you, simply explain that you are a ultra-naturist out for a hike. They are uncommon, but not implausible."

But no car stopped to trouble her, and Pinocchia made her determined but slow progress toward the urban complex ahead, somewhere beyond which resided the Blue Fairy, who could solve all her problems. It took half the night, but at last she stood on the sidewalks of a crowded, rather disreputable neighborhood, its streets still swarming despite the lateness of the hour.

Pinocchia noticed immediately that the majority of the citizens of this neighborhood were not human.

"Talking Cricket, what manner of folk are these?"

"They are splices, and this is Splicetown. You see before you further examples of the human urge to tamper with creation. The genetic heritage of these individuals is mostly animal, all mixed together with some human traits." Now Pinocchia could recognize many of the baseline elements of animal appearance that betrayed these almost-human creatures: tufted ears, tails, claws, fur, muzzles, scales. She found their mosaic physiognamies rather appealing.

"They seem friendly enough."

"Beware. The splices lead a hard life and are not above taking advantage of others for their own gain. But we must pass through their town on the way to the Blue Fairy. Speedily now."

Pinocchia moved deeper into Splicetown, but found herself dawdling. The exotic, jubilant, roisterous, even at times lurid street fair beneath colored lamps appealed to her. She had of course never been among so many individuals of whatever type since her decanting from the vat, and the herd sensations thronged her senses and mind.

Ahead on one corner stood a knot of heterogeneous female splices: storklike, badgery, feline. These female splices wore minimal clothing, and those garments were deliberately arranged for display of their non-human curves. A male splice, rather vulpine, loitered nearby, benignly louche and alert.

Pinocchia paused to observe the tableau. Talking Cricket stridulated in her ear. "Don't hesitate here! Move on!"

"Not yet. . . ."

A male human approached the lurking male splice. Negotiations ensued. The human left with one of the female splices, arm in arm.

"What just happened?"

"A sexual encounter was negotiated."

"I want to learn more."

"Not advisable."

But Pinocchia was already crossing the street.

The foxy pimp brightened at Pinocchia's approach. He hailed her gaily.

"Madame! You do us an honor!"

Pinocchia stood now among the tawny, woolly, hoofy whores. Rich pheromones wafted off them. Pinocchia felt her cunt begin to moisten.

"Are you in charge of these females?"

"In a manner of speaking, Madame, yes!"

"How can I have sex with one of them?"

Talking Cricket registered his whispered but firm objection. "Pinocchia, no!"

The fox either failed to hear Talking Cricket or chose to ignore the bug. "Why, nothing could be simpler! You just pick and pay! Bobo handles all else!"

The boldest whore, a cat model, had advanced out of the knot of her peers and come right up to Pinocchia. The lush feline whore clutched Pinocchia's arm and pressed her bandeau'd breasts against Pinocchia bicep, nearly enfolding Pinocchia's arm in her soft warm tits.

"Pick me, Madame! Pick Pips! I'll show you such a time!"

Pips' hormonal aura was sending Pinocchia's thoughts flying to the four corners of the earth. "I—I have no money."

Bobo the fox moved closer to Pinocchia then and sniffed. "Why, you're not a human at all!"

Something in Bobo's tone offended Pinocchia, made her feel for the first time as if her vat-flesh status were a degraded state, not just an alternate mode of being. Her injured pride and ire caused her to utter a denial.

For the first time in her short life, she lied.

"Of course I'm human!"

As soon as she spoke the lie, something happened inside Pinocchia. Her artificial brain of para-neurons, hosting a template of sentience it was never made for, reacted to the unmistakable synaptic configuration of the untruth in an unprecedented fashion. Her pituitary and amygdala analogue glands, among others, spurted complex hormones into her bloodstream. These chains of catalytic proteins raced along the most sensitive channels of her being, straight to her genitals.

Pinocchia felt an odd burgeoning between the tender outer manifolds of her already disturbed cunt. Although she could not know why or how, some portion of her vat-flesh was responding to the internal chemical signals in a puzzling fashion.

At this moment, however, Pinocchia could not deal with the curious phenomenon, nor did she really care to. All that concerned her was assuaging the burning deeper within her cunt, with the aid of Pips, the whore.

Bobo cupped his long fuzzy chin and contemplated Pinocchia anew, his black eyes reflecting the colored lights strung overhead. "Ah, I can see how wrong I was now! Please accept my most fervent apologies, Madame!"

"Certainly. I am human, so why should I care what you mistakenly thought?"

The second lie caused another burst of strange but not-unpleasant activity in Pinocchia's groin, but Bobo's next words pushed any concern aside.

"Well, I am always eager to foster any small obligation from a human patron. Therefore, let us promptly forget any coarse matter of monetary compensation in return for Pips's services. She will be most happy to pleasure Madame for free."

Bobo stepped forward, the odd articulation of his lower limbs granting him a curious gait. The fox pimp took Pips on one arm and Pinocchia on the other. Then he addressed the other whores.

"I'm accompanying this client, girls. Please conduct yourself for the rest of the evening as if I were still here."

Guiding the two females, Bobo set off down the street.

Talking Cricket, perhaps recognizing the futility of more advice giving, and not desirous of alerting the splices to his existence and thus possibly earning wanton destruction, remained silent.

Within just a few blocks, the trio came to a low-roofed tumble-down building with shuttered windows. Bobo produced an electronic key from within his clothing and let them inside. Glow-worm lights came on automatically.

The first room Pinocchia saw was a sparsely furnished parlor, dominated by a shabby broke-back couch and a large entertainment console. She was never to see any more of the domicile than this, since the couch beckoned as a sufficient altar to her carnal devotions.

Pips was already undressing: a speedy process, given that she had only a microscopic skirt and bandeau to remove. Shucking her top allowed velvety breasts even more ample than Pinocchia's to spill forth. Once the skirt was on the floor, Pips turned around to reveal a short brushy tail like a lynx's, at the apex of her ass.

"Do you like my scut? You can kiss it, if you want . . ."

Pinocchia grasped Pips's rich hips and leaned forward to bury her face in the sweetly aromatic ass of the whore. Then she straightened up, even more intoxicated, and began quickly to strip.

Bobo, seemingly uninterested in these hijinks, had ventured into another room. Now he returned with a bottle of beer. Sipping his drink, he watched the women's lovemaking with a toothy grin.

Pinocchia's clothes joined Pips's outfit on the floor. The RealDoll stood for a moment as if for inspection.

Pips put a hand to her startled mouth. "Oh! What a fat clit!"

Pinocchia looked down at herself, then parted her pubic hair.

Her clitoris had grown nearly an inch, and now protruded past her labia, each earlier lie contributing a centimeter of growth. Now the hypertrophied button nearly quivered with anticipation.

Before Pinocchia could reason out this development, she lost any concern about the change. Pips had fallen to her knees in front of Pinocchia and applied her hot mouth to the beckoning organ.

Pinocchia's thighs quaked as she akimbo'd her legs to allow Pips better access. The cat whore reached around to grip Pinocchia's ass cheeks, pulling the RealDoll even more tightly against her face. The cat's raspy tongue stropped Pinocchia's engorged clit for a heart-stopping interval, then moved to investigate the rest of Pinocchia's twat.

When Pinocchia felt nearly ready to explode, she drew Pips up by the cat's armpits. Then they crashed onto the couch, Pinocchia atop the cat. Pinocchia caught one of Pips's raised legs between her own and began a frenetic frottage. Pips kissed the RealDoll deeply, tongues battling, then began to suck Pinocchia's breasts.

The friction of Pinocchia's cunt against the whore's leg, enlarged clit awash in juice, was more tantalizing than rewarding, and Pinocchia began to wish for some burgeoned cock to fill her.

Almost immediately, she got her wish.

Pinocchia felt a slick, fevered length of meat laid between her buttocks. She looked backward over her shoulder.

Bobo the fox had dropped his brocaded trews and positioned himself behind Pinocchia. From his crotch sprouted a long, thin, rigid, tapering crimson dick, its underside studded with fleshy barbels.

Pinocchia reached back frantically, grabbed the fox's cock, and guided it to her cunt. The needle tip slicked in easily, but the first barbel snagged. Pinocchia shoved rearward, and the protrusion popped past the mouth of her cunt, engendering a jab of delicious satisfaction.

Slowly, to prolong each encounter, Pinocchia slid down the fox's shaft, grunting each time as if encountering the teeth of a comb, until finally she had engulfed the whole length of studded dick.

Then, his tongue lolling out the side of his whiskery chops, Bobo jerked his cock nearly all the way out.

Pinocchia screamed with pleasure.

Now Bobo began sawing away, making Pinocchia moan. At the same time, Pips repositioned herself so that her cunt could receive the attentions of Pinocchia's mouth. The cat whore grabbed Pinocchia's head and pulled it down to her nappy lap.

For long minutes Pinocchia drank at the cat's cunt and received Bobo's attentions at her own. Then, almost simultaneously, the three climaxed. An excess of vulpine seed overflowed the cul-de-sac of Pinocchia's cunt.

The tableau collapsed upon itself into a heap on the couch.

In a wash of somatic repletion, Pinocchia felt herself drifting off to sleep.

But when she finally awoke, matters were not as she might have envisioned, had her own happiness been paramount.

Bound hand and foot with tough plastic cordage, Pinocchia had been made a prisoner!

Twisting awkwardly around, she looked for Bobo and Pips, but saw no one.

Talking Cricket chose that moment to speak.

Mercifully, the bug did not chastise Pinocchia, but merely reported the facts.

"Your captors left to effect a bargain with an unnamed party who wishes to purchase you as a slave."

Pinocchia felt both anger and fear. "Slave! I am no one's slave! I must escape! I must get to the Blue Fairy!" Suddenly, remorse struck, and Pinocchia remembered her quest to become a real woman. She began to agitate herself violently in an attempt to break her bonds.

"Hold still," said Talking Cricket, "and we will chew through your fastenings. Otherwise, you will crush us."

Pinocchia complied, and Talking Cricket dropped off her ear and flew to her wrists. The nizmo began destabilizing plastic molecules, and Pinocchia's freedom looked assured.

But then she heard the outer door open.

Instantly, Bobo was upon her. Before she could register a protest, the fox had crushed the talented but fragile nizmo between two paws.

"Ah," Bobo gloated, "I knew I heard some sort of unseen interlocutor talking to you last night! But I couldn't positively establish his identity. Now, we can dispense with all niceties of how-do-you-do!"

"Let me go! Let me go!"

"Are you counseling immoral behavior on my part, dear? I would have thought better of you. You see, I've already been paid to deliver you. If I let you go, I'd be forevermore branded a horrid cheat!"

Pinocchia glared at the fox pimp. "Sell one of your own girls in my place!"

Bobo placed one fist under his chin and cradled the elbow of that hand with the other. "Hmmm, I could. . . . If I didn't like all my girls too much to inflict such a dreadful fate as yours on them!"

CHAPTER 7

We meet the manjacks, otherwise know as the Troll Donkeys. Pinocchia's enforced mendacity, and its embarrassing consequences. A visit from the bleb.

Boston Harbor was studded with many small islands, some empty, some used for recreational purposes, some with official establishments for manufacture or governance. One of them, an unappealing lesser waste formerly employed for trash disposal in a prior century and now roughly overgrown with weeds and stunted boskage, had become, through squatter's rights, the home of the manjacks.

The manjacks, who also hailed to the epithet of "Troll Donkeys," were chimeras, escaped from some recently downsized corporate R&D lab. Basically, they were centaurs, all males. But whereas the centaur of myth resounded throughout history as a noble, handsome, gallant specimen, the manjacks were degraded Xeroxes of this archetype.

Their upper halves were derived from baboons and mixed with humans, resulting in gnomish specters. Their lower halves—really three-quarters of their body mass—were more or less pure jackass, mule or donkey. These exclusively male baboon-burros were cursed with only primitive intelligence to match their hideous somatypes. (Their lack of mates doomed their race to eventual extinction, of course, a fact that they were just smart enough to recognize, and which contributed to their sour nature.)

The manjacks had also been burdened by their designers with a randy constitution. Yet their coital needs went generally unmet, due more to their rudeness and poor grooming habits than to their ugliness. (In this era, there were plenty of individuals who would have been happy to cater carnally to a cleaned-up, courteous baboon-burro.) They were too proud and irascible to indulge in mutual buggering.

So they had to rely on purchased sex slaves. (The manjacks secured cash a little at a time, by hijacking any boatload of day trippers unwary enough to pass too close to the island.)

And Pinocchia, naked and bereft, was their latest purchase.

The little vessel carrying a satisfied Bobo disappeared in the watery distance as Pinocchia watched helplessly and hopelessly, held from casting herself into the wavelets of the harbor by the rude horny-nailed hands of several manjacks. Before the boat had entirely disappeared, Pinocchia was jerked away and hustled to a clearing in which sat a crude hut. In the center of the clearing a huge stake had been pounded deep into the earth. From the stake ran a long chain and manacle that would allow the wearer access to the dirt-floored shelter and a trench latrine.

One of the manjacks kneeled down onto his front legs and fastened the chain to one of Pinocchia's ankles, as others continued to immobilize her.

Then the biggest, meanest-looking manjack, scarred across both torsoes, approached her out of the small herd of over a dozen individuals that comprised the whole community.

"Name Gallbash. Leader here. I go first."

A second manjack, nearly as big and nasty, bumped forward.

"No, Spunkwater first!"

Gallbash showed his fangs, growled and made a short charge. Spunkwater backed off in a surly fashion, glaring. The leader returned to Pinocchia.

"Now, sex!"

Pinocchia was baffled. "But, but how—?"

"Mouth, hands, teats."

Spunkwater pranced forward again. "Use her cunt! Use it!"

Gallbash delivered a thudding blow upside Spunkwater's head. "No! You ruined our old jenny! Split her open! My way only! Everyone!"

Again, Spunkwater retreated, and Pinocchia was left with no further distraction from her fate.

She moved slowly beneath the funky-smelling barrel body of Gallbash. Already, just her proximity was causing his massive apparatus to engorge. But when she tentatively laid a hand on the sheathed monstrosity, the manjack's gigantic prick practically exploded out of its pouch.

Its veined length matched her forearm. The bulbous head was colored like a plum, and just as big.

Pinocchia spit into her hands and began to massage the long bobbing tube. Gallbash emitted a weird cry blending his two natures. "More, more! Jenny mouth!"

Opening as wide as she could, Pinocchia applied her lips to the donkey's textured cock-head. Pushing forward, her lips slid over the curvature and halted at a widening of the shaft. Apparently this was enough to keep Gallbash happy, as he hoot-brayed again and began to shudder. Pinocchia continued to work the length of his corrugated dick.

The manjack's orgasm telegraphed itself as a fast-moving peristaltic wave down his shaft. Pinocchia managed to pull her mouth away, but not before receiving at least a quarter cup of cum down her throat. The rest of the copious load splashed across her bare breasts and puddled in her lap.

Gallbash pranced away like a proud warrior when finished, and Spunkwater immediately took his place.

"Jenny, suck!"

Pinocchia wiped the back of her hand across her mouth and began again.

The manjacks never took very long to come. That was the only saving grace of the whole long, tedious ritual. Nonetheless, by the time she had serviced the final, lowest member of the tribe, her hands were cramping, her arms were shaking, and she was drenched in nutty-smelling ivory jism.

Pinocchia climbed wearily to her feet. She looked about for some way to clean herself. As if in answer to her needs, the lowliest member of the tribe trotted up with a scratched plastic pail full of chilly harbor water. Pinocchia sluiced off the clots of burro jism as efficiently as she could, then used some leaves which her tether allowed her to reach to dry herself somewhat. Then she retreated to her dirt-floored hut, to cry herself to sleep.

As Pinocchia drifted off, however, her disconsolate sniffles were replaced by a small smile. For a vision of the Blue Fairy, her first, came to her.

The Blue Fairy was a handsome nude man, Olympian in build, whose skin was a deep beryl hue. Naked, alluring, he extended his hands out as if beckoning Pinocchia to come to him.

But in the morning, of course, she awoke still chained on Donkey Island, to a breakfast of half-cooked seagull. Each day of the next week proceeded in identical fashion. Pinocchia had to service the manjacks twice a day. The rest of her time was her own, which she could use to ponder her sad fate and unwise impulsiveness. If only she had not alerted Tom Geppi to her new sentience. If only she had not run away from home. If only she had not given in to her lust in Splicetown. How much better her life might've been!

But all those errors were in the past, and could not be retrieved.

Perhaps though, if life permitted, Pinocchia could benefit from her hard-won knowledge and act more wisely in the future.

The best thing she had done on her pilgrimage to become a real woman was to befriend Talking Cricket. And that composite individual must have felt the same, since units of it continued to try to contact Pinocchia, apparently having tracked her down. She saw the occasional lonely nizmo approach Donkey Island and attempt to land. But invariably, the sharp-eyed, sharp-eared manjacks would descend on the bug and crush it before it could establish communication with Pinocchia. She thought that perhaps one rescuer could sneak in at night, when the manjacks slept. But after the first nizmo arrived, a guard was posted with Pinocchia around the clock, alert for any intrusions.

After the third day, Pinocchia had become relatively innured to the messy chore of milking the manjacks. But then Gallbash introduced a new demand during sex.

"Jenny say she loves Gallbash!"

Pinocchia at first pretended not to have heard. But a menacing rear hoof forced her to comply.

To lie.

After her clit had unexpectedly grown in Splicetown, a paucity of subsequent lies had allowed the mutable organ to diminish to its old baseline configuration. Pinocchia was glad. The hypertrophied organ proved awkward, and over-sensitive. She did not want to provoke its growth again.

But now she had to.

"I—I love you, Gallbash."

Within seconds, Pinocchia's clitoris had sprouted half an inch.

One such statement of affection seemed enough for Gallbash, before he plugged her mouth with his knob, and for such small mercies Pinocchia was grateful.

The other baboon-burros were denied the privilege of asking her to declare her love. That honor seemed reserved for the alpha-male.

Still, having to affirm the untruth twice a day added an inch to Pinocchia's clit every twenty-four hours. And it never had a chance to shrink.

By the end of the fourth day of lying—completing her first week with the manjacks—she possessed a little pseudo-phallus that troubled her incessantly with its sensitivity. She had to play tiresomely with it several times a day just to gain temporary relief.

The night that marked her week's anniversary with the Troll Donkeys, Pinocchia lay on her uncomfortable bed of sticks and grass and leaves, weeping bitter tears and uttering silent prayers to the spirit of the Blue Fairy, the nizmos, Tom Geppi, even Bobo and Pips—anyone who might be able to help her.

As she fumbled once again with her sore, demanding clit, Pinocchia wondered how much longer this life of servitude could continue.

The next morning brought an answer.

Each day as dawn broke, Pinocchia always remained in her hut as long as the manjacks allowed. This morning, no one came for her for a long time. Instead there drifted to her dreadful violent screeches and half-heard curses, thuds and the clatter of galloping hooves.

Soon, Pinocchia learned what had transpired.

The silhouette of a manjack appeared in the entrance to her hut. "Jenny, out!"

Pinocchia exited the hut, her chain dragging.

In the center of the clearing, Spunkwater stood proudly over the mutilated corpse of Gallbash. Seeing Pinocchia, the victorious new alpha male reared up on his hind legs, highlighting his waving tumescence.

"Spunkwater leader now! Jenny cunt sex!"

Pinocchia cringed. She looked frantically about for impossible help. She grabbed her chain and yanked, but it held firm as ever.

Before Pinocchia could make another move, two manjacks were upon her. One grabbed her wrists; the other kneeled and grabbed her ankles. The encumbering chain and manacle were removed. Then Pinocchia was hoisted off the ground. Held at four points like a hammock, she was splayed wide.

Spunkwater capered over to her. With surprising delicacy, he lifted one foreleg over her lowly slung body. Then he lifted the corresponding rear leg.

Now Spunkwater bestrode her entirely, although they did not yet touch. She felt a fat drop of his hot pre-cum splatter on her belly. With the temporary aid of a third Troll Donkey, the manjack holding her ankles reaccomodated his grip to allow Spunkwater actually to get between her legs.

Her two bearers hoisted her higher, so that her ventral side met the centaur's. His massive cock rested outside her, from groin to boobs. She could feel the weight of his hairy balls against her cunt.

Spunkwater shifted slowly backward, dragging the slippery knob of his cock down her skin, aiming for her hole.

Her face half-buried in his musty chest fur, Pinocchia began to weep.

Without warning, the illumination of the sun was suddenly blotted out.

Pinocchia's bearers dropped her to the dirt.

A giant cliff of hulking grey flesh had invaded the island, and reared skyward now on the edge of the clearing, towering for an attack. A stupendous tonnage of artificial protoplasm that moved much more swiftly than its mass would imply, this was a bleb, one of the ecosystem enforcers available to authorities.

Stunned, Pinocchia watched the bleb lash out with a score of pseudopods and lasso every manjack save Spunkwater, who danced deftly aside. The tentacles quickly reeled in the braying manjacks to the main bulk of the bleb.

When the manjacks met the mass of flesh they were envaginated and sucked out of sight.

Pinocchia managed to get to her hands and knees. Next to her, Spunkwater howled his defiance.

"Spunkwater never give up! Spunkwater fight and die!"

The bleb silently obliged the unrepentant manjack. A dozen tendrils enwrapped him and wrung him out like a dishcloth, with a symphony of cracking bones, before hauling the corpse inside.

Pinocchia's limbs felt like water. She couldn't even gain her feet before a large canopy of bleb-flesh dropped on her and dragged her into darkness.

CHAPTER 8

The Blue Fairy's abode. Pinocchia pleads, but the Blue Fairy declines. A surprise brings a change of mind. A real woman at last.

Regaining her senses, Pinocchia found herself held in a lightless cellular vacuole that was dry and not unpleasant. She was reminded of her time in the tin cricket tumulus, and felt reassured. Although she had no idea of who controlled this mountain of dumb flesh or where she was going, she began to relax for the first time in a week. Simply to be freed from the captivity of the Troll Donkeys was heaven enough for her.

Pinocchia estimated that perhaps half an hour passed. She had no real sensation of movement, but had to assume that she and the manjacks were being transported somewhere.

True to her guesses, Pinocchia eventually reached a destination. The vacuole that held her began to migrate through the mass of the bleb, carrying Pinocchia with it. In seconds, it had fused with an organic airlock, letting light and fresh air burst into Pinocchia's chamber.

Pinocchia clambered through the narrow portal and found herself beneath an enormous transparent dome. She stood on a smooth warm ceramic floor.

Pinocchia was at the bottom of the sea. The diamond dome held back an enormous weight of ocean. The bleb clung like a barnacle to a few square yards of the dome at its lower edge. Schools of fishes curved through the waters. Delicate waving fronds trailed upward from their seafloor anchorage.

Pinocchia gazed in awe at the spectacular marine vistas, until a polite cough behind her caused her to turn.

Standing patiently was a fishman: popeyed, all green scales and gills, with jagged fins on his calves and forearms like buckskin frills.

"Adminstrator Kinghorn demands your attendance now."

"Who—who is he?"

"The governor of this bioregion."

Pinocchia was unsure of the exact meaning of this title, but it sounded important. Perhaps this person would be in a position to help her—if he was so inclined.

So Pinocchia asked no other questions, nor made any objections, but just accompanied the fishman further into the dome. She was resolved not to act impulsively nor stubbornly anymore, lest she get herself in further trouble.

Like an inverted fishbowl, the dome held a toy castle within, of human scale. Pinocchia and her guide entered the building, cutting off all view of the sea. Through various corridors hung with paintings and lined with old-fashioned books they marched, until they arrived at a set of double doors.

"Go in," said the fishman.

Pinocchia went shyly in, still naked as she had been on Donkey Island.

The large room was dominated by a rich, floral-figured carpet across which were strewn a wealth of sumptuous pillows. A hookah burbled, and trays of food gave off odors that caused Pinocchia's stomach to rumble.

Several fishmen reclined rather wantonly amongst the pillows, and in their midst was Administrator Kinghorn.

Pinocchia gasped!

"You—you're the Blue Fairy!"

Administrator Kinghorn chuckled, his indigo face manifesting crinkly laugh lines. "Not many people use that name in my presence. You're either utterly innocent, or utterly brash. I wonder which? But, yes, my dear, I am the Blue Fairy."

Standing, Administrator Kinghorn revealed the same proud physique that Pinocchia had seen in her dream: broad shoulders, burly chest, mighty limbs, and a handsome visage. His sole clothing was a tiny black swimsuit that only served to emphasize his sizable genitals.

Pinocchia noticed then a detail absent from her dreams: the Blue Fairy sported tiny wings at his heels.

Pinocchia sought first to express her gratitude. "Blue Fairy—if I may continue to call you by that name—thank you for rescuing me from the Troll Donkeys."

Kinghorn made a dismissive gesture. "Simply doing my job, young lady. If I had not been, ah, distracted by other concerns, I would have dealt with those brigands much earlier. Major damper on the tourist trade they were. But they'll bother no one ever again, as they've all been rendered down to raw nucleotide feedstock."

Pinocchia continued. "If only I could ask for an additional boon,

Blue Fairy. I've come so far and through so much grief to seek your help! I want to ask you to turn me into a real woman."

Administrator Kinghorn laughed, but not in a manner that gave Pinocchia hope. "A real woman? I'm afraid not, my dear. You're runaway property. I've already arranged for you to be returned to the Real-Doll factory for re-tooling."

For a black, broken moment, all words fled from Pinocchia's throat. This was not how she had dreamed her story would end.

"But—but the Talking Cricket said—"

"Ah, yes, the Talking Cricket. One such as this?"

Kinghorn made a gesture, and a nizmo shot out from concealment beneath the pillows. The mechanical bug flew to perch on Pinocchia's shoulder.

"We are sorry, Pinocchia. We only said he had the power to help, not that he absolutely would."

Pinocchia experienced a tumult of emotions: fear, anger, despair, grief. But at last she managed to conquer the disorienting inner storm and summon up fortitude and a bitter pride.

"I want nothing from you, Blue Fairy. Just send me away now."

"In due time. Until then, you may follow the one who led you here. He'll bring you to a private room where you may wash and dress and eat."

Pinocchia swung around and stalked off, nearly blind from captive tears.

At the double doors she stopped and looked back.

The Blue Fairy had returned to his cushions. He had shucked his swimsuit. Two fishmen were sucking his long, thick cock and licking his cobalt balls, while a third straddled Kingston's head and fed the man a length of green penis.

Pinocchia's tears welled out, and she fled.

In the small room assigned her, Pinocchia moved robotically.

She ate some tasteless food first. Then she climbed into the shower.

Talking Cricket left her shoulder to avoid the water, hovering just outside the glassed-in stall.

As the hot water hit Pinocchia's skin, the marvelous sensation began to melt some of the frigid indifference inside her. She wept gently as she soaped herself clean for the first time in over a week.

Her hands reached her groin, and encountered her abnormal clit. Nearly a day without lying had caused it to shrink a bit, but it still loomed like an infantile penis between her fingers. Aroused, her clit demanded relief, and so she brought herself off with vigorous short tugs, twists, and tweakings.

Closing her eyes to shampoo her hair, Pinocchia spent another minute in the shower before shutting off the flow.

When she stepped out, the Blue Fairy was waiting.

Suddenly, Pinocchia was improbably embarrassed. She attempted to cover her breasts and snatch.

"My dear, what's that curious disfiguration you're hiding? The camera lens of a single nizmo on the far side of a steamy glass offers very poor resolution."

"It's—it's nothing," said Pinocchia.

The lie shuddered through her frame to lengthen her clit yet again. The traitorous organ actually poked out between her fingers like a timid kitten's pink nose.

The Blue Fairy gently pulled her hand away, to inspect her mutant genitals. He voiced sotto voce speculations as he did so.

"Uncanny brain chemistry . . . feedback loops . . . enteric system as well as proprioceptors . . . novel configuration of para-neurons . . . might result in Turing-level sapience . . ."

The Blue Fairy straightened and gripped Pinocchia by both hands. "My dear, why didn't you tell me any of this? You're absolutely unique! Those delusions and demands of yours were one thing. I mistook them for mere nonlinear emergent behavior. Totally trivial. But when combined with this somatic phenomenon, they bespeak an utterly unique combination of wetware and software. Orders of magnitude greater than a simple RealDoll. It would be a shame to send you back to the factory. I'm canceling the pickup order right now. Talking Cricket!"

"Done, Administrator."

Pinocchia lost all power to stand, and began to collapse. But the Blue Fairy caught her up in his strong embrace, and carried her to the room's bed. He set her down.

When Pinocchia could speak again, she said, "My vat-flesh—can you change it, so that I won't die so soon?"

"Well, yes, but that might very well destroy the exact properties I wish to study."

Pinocchia sat up, angry. "I'm not a subject of study! I'm a real woman. Everything but my flesh!"

The Blue Fairy pondered Pinocchia's outburst thoughtfully before responding. "You're correct, of course. Pardon me. You've already earned your status. I can only help adjudicate it."

"Oh, thank you! How quickly can you do it?"

"Why, right now. I carry everything I need. My body, you see, is a nanite factory. I customize them internally. To meet your needs, I'll just need a sample of your cells. And I believe I can obtain those most pleasurably for us both."

The Blue Fairy kneeled on the floor alongside the bed. He drew the sitting Pinocchia around so that she sat before him. Then he went down on her phallic clit, tonguing it, suckling it, lapping her juices, murmuring his own enjoyment.

Pinocchia experienced enormous delights, culminating in a transcendent explosion.

The Blue Fairy stood up. His bold cock strained against his suit. Pinocchia pulled down the swatch of fabric, releasing his tool.

"As you surmise, dear, this will administer the nanites to you. But if I could beg your indulgence. My own tastes, you know—"

Pinocchia did not understand, until Kinghorn lifted her bodily and flopped her onto her stomach. He mounted her, his engineered cock discharging large amounts of organic lubricant, and made his gentle approach to her virgin asshole.

Pinocchia had escaped Spunkwater's cock up her cunt, but Kinghorn's large member up her anus felt nearly as split-some. The long minute he took to bury its whole length required bold adjustments and heroic accommodations on her part. But finally she felt his nanite-stuffed balls weigh upon her cunt.

Kinghorn held still until Pinocchia's small residual grunts had segued to a curious cooing. Then he bent forward to whisper, "I've timed ejaculation for ninety seconds. Can you stand that?"

"Please, Blue Fairy—"

"Yes?"

"Take longer than that."

The Blue Fairy grinned. "As you wish."

Kinghorn began to plow Pinocchia's tight ass, and soon she was kneeling and reciprocating with hearty slams against his flesh. He reached around her to play with her clit, and she shrieked. The Blue Fairy's heel-wings fluttered.

Five minutes later, he unleashed deep within her the geyser of nanites that would convert her vat-flesh to a baseline human genetic pedigree.

Spent, the Blue Fairy fell upon Pinocchia, then rolled them over, still conjoined, so that they lay spoon-wise on their sides.

"That is your enfranchisement, dear. What will you do now?"

Feeling the transformative forces surging through her every cell,

Pinocchia thought of Tom Geppi, the sad and lonely man who had first purchased her, for whom she had dared all, for whom she had undergone such trials.

And bumping backwards to reseat the Blue Fairy's undiminished cock up her ass, she knew she could do much better.

Hot, Like Water

Lynne Jamneck

1.

Water

From the Anglo-Saxon and low German root wæter, formerly an abundant substance on earth.

All known forms of life need water. Humans consume what is referred to as "drinking water"—water with qualities complementary to the human body. This natural resource has become scarce with the mounting world population, and its availability is a chief collective and economic concern.

In Dorchester City, the place where I live, there's a club called The Copper Wire. Every weekend there's a small, pitiable group of one-million-credits-a-year-achievers who get their rocks off by gawking at the regular patrons.

Patrons. Yeah, I guess that's as good a word as any.

As the club's name affirms, it's pretty much the folk who keep Dorchester City's cogs turning smoothly who frequent The Wire. Plant workers, like yours truly. Lodge crews. Couple of hard hat girlies from the steel plant, a few rogue deputies and always one or two Indians stocking up on city supplies before they head back into the Wasteland. People who are content with their lives because they don't slither up to the corrupt nature of too much money. That's the irony see: I may have bucket loads of cash, but I have hardly anything worthwhile to spend it on. I don't shimmy for buying people. Fact is—in the city, bodies are major currency. Dead or alive.

I go to The Wire alone. Sometimes I leave the way I came, other times I willingly enslave company to get me through the night.

The women there entice me. I'm not a star-fucker; I like the girlies with their coarse smithy aprons and the smell of gasoline on the soles of their boots.

They know how to fuck.

Unlike the burnished, pig-skin peeled, straight, million-credit-girls who sip their yellow cocktails by the edge of the bar, staring. They flutter their spiderlegged-eyelids at you because they play by the only rules entrenched in their advantaged, unshakable upbringing. Forget that. I don't potty train. One has to have *some* sort of philosophy in life.

But tonight as I sit in a gloomy corner, still wearing my leather-buckled plant uniform and nursing a double-vodka straight, I . . . reluctantly admit that even I want something. Need something, More than just to be casual and callous.

I'd be a rotten liar if I said that watching the two girls three chaotic tables down wasn't turning me on. After all, I'm not dead. Especially not from the waist down.

One of them was the girl with the copper hair; the other was a flash blonde with vicious blue streaks down to her peroxide roots.

I wondered if they saw me watching. I knew they wouldn't care. Quite the opposite.

I was thirsty. Alcohol made my mouth dry.

Copper Girl kissed her friend—the kind of kiss that made you swallow hard and rub sweat from the back of your neck. Their hands moved. Their actions appeared slow beneath the flickering limelights, their hands eventually disappearing into the shadowed curves beneath the table. I ordered another vodka and contemplated inviting them both back to my bunker. My bed was small but we could make it work. We could all take turns.

I've been watching the copper girl. The past few weeks we've been putting ourselves on display for one another. Subtlety above everything else. No one wants to put themselves on the line anymore. We get hurt enough as it is.

I had little interest in the blue-streaked blonde, truth be told. She was another body dressed in so much PVC. But Copper . . . There was something about her. She seemed to prefer her clothing coarser, like the plant workers and the lodge crews. Functionality before anything else.

If anything it was her face that kept me coming back. She was attractive in that certain sense that made me nostalgic. She reminded me of females documented in history books.

I've tried to approach her. Alone, I mean. Why I hold back still, I'm not too sure. Sharing your bed is different than sharing yourself. Something is missing still.

I went home alone. Once locked within the safety of my private space I took a 750ml bottled water from the fridge and placed it on the galley tabletop.

I stripped, peeling myself out of the stiff, creaking, buckle-and-strap-strewn leather. The white cotton body glove came off too, warm from my own heat.

I took the cap off the bottle of Krystal and held it upside down above my head and slowly let the water pour over my naked skin. Jesus, it was *cold*. My nipples were complaining even before the water had run down my shoulders.

I leaned back against the pewter wall, skin covered in gooseflesh, turned on the taps above the sink. And masturbated.

2.

The human body is composed of 75 percent water and 25 percent solid matter. However, there are variations according to sex and age. The body's water supply is responsible for and involved in nearly every bodily process, including digestion, absorption, circulation, and excretion.

I expect—I *guess* it's because I work with it every day. I keep putting my hands in it, through it, touching it and letting myself be touched. It's become such a tactile thing.

Now I know you are going to say that there are people who work with garbage every day but they don't necessarily develop a sexual attraction to it. Suffice to say, I'm not exactly sure how it started. But let me at least start from some sort of reference point.

I work at the Dorchester City water purification plant. I keep it all running smoothly. I'm the Chief Superintendent, see.

Billions of liters of water rush, rumble, flash, and dash through the plant's thousands of pipes every second. The pipes vary in size. While some are as thin as my forearm, others have Arunium casings up to a meter thick in order to withstand the awesome force of the water continuously heaving through. The newer ones reflect their polished novelty with cold vigor, while the older ones down in the plant's bowels are beginning to show the telltale signs of rust, flaking and peeling covertly in the shadows.

The noise—as one might expect—is deafening. I get paid a lot of credits to do a job that some would consider too common or lowly. Not to mention hazardous.

The plant has several security measures in check in case of an emergency. Although, truth be told—if you happen to find yourself in the wrong place at the wrong time . . . One of those corroded tree-trunk pipes finally decide to buckle under the pressure for good, anyone not outside the perimeter of a sealed hull-wall is going to be in deep water. Pardon the pun—I get by on what I can.

I keep telling The Suits they have to replace the elder pipes. They don't listen, of course. The plant was built just shy of a hundred years ago so some degree of degeneration is only normal. Section 7G, for instance. Three of the highway master pipes rattle real bad at the force pumping through them. If you dive down into the submerged levels you can hear the *klang-klang* of the heavy support chains every time the turbines are flushed.

I like to listen to it, though. The chains, the water. I'll even go so far as to take my ear goggles off. I stand with my back pressed to the walls to feel the pressure at the base of my spine.

The Suits don't spend capital as much as they hoard it. They'd much rather kill time until there's an accident. Besides, none of them live in the cities so why should they care? Like I said—I get paid heaps of money to flip the switches.

It's not so much a job as it is a constant, solitary routine. Maybe twenty people in all keep the plant running. Most of it's computerized. Me, I check that the technology behaves and the machinery does their job.

I'm literally enclosed by it every day. It's most of what I hear and see constantly, relentlessly, fourteen hours a day. I see it when I look up, when I turn sideways and when I look down. The pipes run even beneath my industrial-booted-heels, grouped in tight pairs of three, the water moving my feet along. When I go home at night and lie in bed waiting to fall asleep I can still hear it. Inevitably, it's there when I wake up in the morning.

It seems inevitable that I would develop such an obsessive association with the entity that controls the bigger part of my waking days. Shall I be blunt?

Fair enough.

On the morning of my twenty-ninth birthday I realized with some clarity there was nothing in this godforsaken world that turned me on more than water.

Just—water.

3.

Water is considered a purifier in most religions, including Christianity, Islam, Judaism, and Sikhism. Liquid water (H_2O) is often perceived to be relatively average as it is transparent, odorless, flavorless, and ubiquitous. It is the simplest amalgam of the two most common reactive elements in the universe.

A week later the new assistant supervisor finally arrived at the plant.

They found her in Beleria Colony, a technologically overrun village south of the Sacramento desert.

Turns out she didn't bother to answer the digiboard that the suits put in the dailies. So they sent a Representative to the meanest, saddest, baddest, crack-infested hole they could find to get the meanest, maddest, fuck-off-and-die-girl they could find.

Her name was Lex Seven and she could probably hack into the Universe and make it come crashing down.

The Representative—Colby was his name—delivered her uncere-moniously just inside my office door that Monday morning.

Lex Seven. Huh.

Seven of what? Seven things you should never ask her? Was she missing three toes? Three fingers? By the looks of her, possibly the number of times she's managed to wangle herself out of a brig sen-tence? Or the amount of times she could make me come in one night with that body of hers?

Zero, Zero . . . Lust will be the death of you.

Yeah, but what a way to go.

Forget about it. Fraternization between plant workers is strictly forbidden.

In the adjacent Control Room the turbines flushed loudly, rum-bling below my feet, flushing their cargo onward. The sound rushed straight down to my—well, cunt.

I trained my eyes on Lex. "Why aren't you wearing a uniform?"

"Because that asshole Colby didn't give me one."

"It's not the asshole's job to dress you. At least, not that particular one." I chuckled at my own feeble joke. Lex remained unmoved. "He should have taken you to Check-In before bringing you here, though." She held her ground and looked uninterested. "Get dressed," I instructed. "Then come back here for a briefing. And I hope you know how to operate a semi-auto turbine flushtank." The stare-down she offered me in reply told me that she was capable of all that and much more.

I found myself eager to see her in uniform; to hear how her long limbs would make the leather creak and stretch. I wondered about her command over water. Would it bend to her instruction? Would the turbines growl and flush at her command?

I checked the LCD display on the far wall. 9:35 A.M.

4.

The co-existence of the liquid, solid, and gaseous phases of water on earth is perhaps fundamental to the source and progression of life on earth as we know it.

I got pulled into a threesome after all. And just when I was beginning to believe I was over that sort of thing.

Thursday was Retro-DJ night at The Wire. I can't stomach the shit they refer to as music these days. It grates my senses and sets my teeth on edge.

Retro-DJ night was an eclectic amalgamation of classic House from sixty, eighty years ago. Stomping, pungent, driving stuff. Machines and mixing boards having multiple orgasms. It vibrated in between the stirring spaces of your organs and set your Kundalini on fire. It pounced and teased at the coiled serpent at the base of your spine.

Copper Girl was there again. I found out her name was Courtney, but as was the custom, she'd shortened it to Court. Her friend this time was a brunette with a washboard stomach and small shoulders who had the complexion of an innocent and acted the contrary. All shy smiles and modest looks and then she'd say, lips around the tip of her beer bottle "I once let a woman fuck me in front of my boss in her office during break time." You know the type.

Our ménage started at the bar, the two of them curved round me, one on each side. The bulk of my attention naturally drifted to Copper Girl. She looked in my eyes as if she was looking to mine something there. We'd watched for weeks, and now we were actually touching one another.

Soon there was a determined hand on my thigh and a different one on my neck, applying subtle pressure. Drinks I hadn't ordered were passed. Then copper girl was kissing me, open-mouthed and deep while her friend looked on and the music became louder.

It moved to the dance floor, their hips guiding me accordingly from behind and in front correspondingly. The music driving, tribal and downright fucking pagan.

Stage three: the VIP room upstairs. I had money, I had access. There were several people in various stages of euphoria watching us. More drinks going round.

The music up here was somewhat slower, but God, it was unbendable. Before I knew it, Court and her friend were both naked and laughing and I was still dressed, buttoned-up to my throat and breathing shallow. Then someone was kissing me, her tongue moving and hot in my mouth. I was sweating inside my uniform. Hands pulled lightly at my hair and then the weight of the so-called demure brunette on top of me and her mouth muttering 'fuck me' into my neck.

I did. I gave them both what they wanted. A good, hard, semi-anonymous fuck. Shy girl on top and afterward Court beneath me. Different strokes, as they say. But even as I had my fingers inside her I'd already relegated her back to simple Copper Girl status. She was no different after all. Missing that certain . . . something.

By the time I'd satisfied them both I was so turned on that I could probably fuck through first-grade Arunium steel.

Try as I might though, coming was a long way off. I was dehydrated and needed water. But now that the show was over no one seemed to particularly care about my well being. Truth be told, if any one of them had the power to get me off I'd know it. Let's just say I did them the favor.

I closed my eyes and lay back on the couch. I thought of the Plant, the pipes and the water and the swell of it, undulating. The cool off the *dripping-dripping-dripping* when you stood beneath the older ones pipes, the leaky ones that could go without warning. The cool water seeping through my latex-covered fingers when I tested the temperature . . .

"Hey."

I opened my eyes and saw Court's friend, standing there, dressed in her crisp white cotton underwear.

"Looks like you could use some water" she said, indicating a pitcher of clear water in her one hand.

A shock of lust climaxed between my legs and, as she stepped forward to hand me the decanter her footing betrayed her and she tripped. I thought I saw the water congeal mid-air in an amorphous shape before gravity enacted revenge and the cold liquid splashed down on me, trickling down my open collar to find my naked breasts. "Oh, Jesus . . ." I stifled a groan into a tortured whimper and came.

5.

"Empty your mind, be formless. Shapeless, like water. If you put water into a cup, it becomes the cup. You put water into a bottle and it becomes the bottle. You put it in a teapot it becomes the teapot. Now, water can flow or it can crash. Be water my friend."

—Bruce Lee

Lex Seven, it turned out, knew exactly how to handle the turbine flushers.

On the seventh consecutive day she showed up for work I waited for her in the staff locker room. She didn't seem to mind my sidelong glances as she changed from her civs to her uniform. She wore grey unisex cotton boxers underneath instead of a body glove. I wondered where she'd found them. They must have been expensive. Her skin was perfect, body economically muscled. I noticed with a shuddering of pleasure that both her nipples were pierced.

She looked at me as she buckled up, awaiting instructions. I told her the Engine Room needed an inspection and the mainframe could do with a defrag. It was 7:13 A.M. I watched her the whole morning.

At 15:30 Lex came into my office and shut the hatch behind her. As she approached my desk I recalled for some reason that the mossy green of the walls matched several of the tattoos I'd seen on her body in the locker.

Lex sat down on the edge of my glass-top desk. Looked at me.

"I know what you want."

I wasn't sure how to react. "Yes?"

"I do feel though, that you should know something about my body before you decide to do with it what you're not supposed to. Allowed to."

Guideline Six, Reform Seven, Paragraph Eight of the Purification Plant's Personnel Guide & Rulebook: *Fraternization of sexual nature between employees is strictly forbidden.*

• *Side Note:* I once had one of those automaton golems from Steam City South working for me during a union strike who'd taken to studying the Guide & Rulebook on his enforced breaks. I called him Tin Man, but he didn't get it, of course. "Fra-ter-ni-za-tion—what is, explain?" I tried to elucidate him to the meaning of the word and he interrupted me by saying "You mean fucking?" The word had sounded hollow coming from between his clunky metal jaws. Figures he would know a vulgarism like that. Turns out his Animator had taught it to him. Perversely, I couldn't help but wonder why.

I wanted Lex really bad. She made my insides churn. Too many abstracts that made it inevitable. The way she strutted through the corrugated hallways—James Dean. How she cocked her head when she worked the mainframe and she knew I was watching her—my eighth grade teacher in front of her blackboard. Adolescent sex and adjectives.

When she sat in the mess hall, legs far apart and feet planted firmly and smoking an unfiltered cigarillo. Cocky, showing it all off. Was it just me? No one else even seemed to be aware of her.

She made me long to have a dick 24/7. Just in case she strolled into my office and I felt like a slow blowjob at ten in the morning.

There was something else though. An unidentifiable *curiousness* I couldn't quite put my finger on. A pull that went beyond sex and beyond lust and beyond want. Something stronger.

"There's a reason I lived in that desert hellhole," Lex continued, referring to Beleria Colony. I noticed how blue the veins were beneath her skin. She looked at her reflection in the mirror on the wall. "Ever wonder how someone maintains skin like this while living in a 45 degree Celsius environment?"

I waited.

"I'm an experiment. I breathe water. I have no blood."

"Oh." I'd heard about the experiments, the idea of waterbreathers. The Surface became a progressively more hostile place with each passing day. Water was the next frontier. We needed to go down, deep. We needed to go back.

"How did they eventually—I mean, I remember there being all sorts of complications in the initial trials."

Lex shrugged. "Chemicals, cloning, genetic manipulation. Technology is a double-edged sword. And I have no heart. Not like yours, that is. It's a purifier, a machine. It extracts the oxygen from the water in my veins allowing me to breathe." She looked away at the walls. "Almost like this plant."

"Shouldn't you be under surveillance?"

I've been poked and prodded and surveyed for close to ten years. They're done with me. Besides, I'm not quite the perfect model. Not the one The Suits want to show to investors. Not pretty enough by far. And I talk back too much. About the wrong things."

My mouth felt like it was producing too much saliva. "Do you bleed?"

She smiled at the question. "Naturally. I bleed water." Lex slid off the table's edge and walked around to where I sat in the leather high-back chair. She came close and I realized why her presence made my thoughts scramble like a vidscreen tuned to a hacked rate of recurrence. The water, the water . . . She inserted herself between me and the desk and took my head in her hands, her cool palms flat against my temples.

"Would you like me to bleed for you?" She stated the question as if it was the most normal, ordinary, average thing. "I can give you the release I know you want. And I get the added bonus of feeling that I serve some purpose. Even perverts need meaning." She added: "Even freaks need release." Of course, rationally I objected to being called a freak. The part of me that had been fantasizing about doing things to Lex all week though—that part more than *liked* it.

I felt as if a hot and heavy weight was pushing me back into the chair. Lex barely held me, her touch light, her skin cold. Maybe that's why I felt like I was burning up. I was sweating, surely, without doubt. "You think I'm a freak?"

Lex didn't answer. She let go of my face and opened the small pocket on the shoulder of her uniform. Minora still made the best blades. She observed it for a moment and then took the sharp edge to her wrist. Someone walked by outside, their footsteps steadily disappearing down the hall. I swallowed hard. I was turned on but in a way I'd never experienced before. I was terrified of the idea of what it was I contemplated doing.

She was about to cut the thin skin of her wrist when Lex stopped. For a moment I felt disheartened and routed. Then she held the blade out to me with a steady hand.

"You do it. Cut me."

"Okay."

As I brought the blade close Lex shivered. Her reversed wrist held firm. I breathed low, feeling the warmth as I exhaled on my hand.

The blade was sharp. I'd barely touched the skin when a sharp spurt of clear water jettisoned from Lex's blue veins. She gasped—distinctly sexual, lips slightly parted. For a brief moment I was petrified, not knowing what I had just done. Jesus, what if she bled out?

My anticipation turned to a chill and I threw the blade on the floor, away. It skittered out of sight beneath the desk. Lex grabbed my wrist so hard it hurt the skin and settled herself onto my lap. The heat between us was palpable, despite my apprehension. I felt the chi drip from the open wound onto my hand and looked down to see the droplets run down my skin and drop onto the chair.

"Drink" she said, holding the wound to my lips. It looked clean. "Taste it," she mildly instructed as her other hand wavered and then started unbuckling the clasps on the front of my uniform.

The moment I tasted the fluid on the inside my lips sexual excitement veered beneath my skin, back in full force. Dissent and hesitancy gone.

I sucked cautiously, pulling Lex closer. Her hand pulled down the top half of my uniform and snaked those long, cool fingers inside an opening of my body glove to twist my nipples. She strained to get closer to me, obstructed by the chair and the way I leaned over to suck harder at her wrist. She kicked her boots firmly to the floor. I craved her fingers inside me.

We struggled as much with lack of breathing as we did with

performance. This was novel, exhilarating, *hot*. I couldn't get enough of Lex's taste, and holding back was excruciating.

Her mouth was in my neck and suddenly she bit down hard and pulled her hands from my clothes and yanked her wrist away. Her face was flushed. "Fuck, no more. I'm sorry. I need—a bandage. Zero!"

When she yelled my name I came to my senses. "Get off." I stumbled and she got up weakly, leaning back against the desk. I opened one of the bottom desk drawers, grabbed an emergency medical kit and unwrapped a bandage while Lex held the watering wound on her wrist down tightly with two splayed fingers. She looked wan but her eyes betrayed the lust she felt.

"You can have more later" she breathed, barely audible as I wrapped her carefully. I said nothing. I could still taste her in my mouth, crisp and clear. Neither one of us seemed so tough anymore. But we were both contemplating the possibilities.

Once done, I put the kit away and then walked to the opposite end of the room. With a heavy, obnoxious paper holder I smashed the glass console to access the emergency lever for the sprinkler system, and pulled it down hard.

A sharp, cool spray rained down from the roof. Outside in the corridor voices shouted. I stood quiet; letting it soak me and spitting the water dribbling into my mouth to the floor. It tasted cheap. Dirty, even.

I felt Lex behind me, her hands on my hips and let her turn me around. She had the cock to her walk again and the threat was back in her eyes. And she was naked. "You learn fast," she smiled. "Why do you think I'd otherwise consign myself to this hellhole?"

And just like that I was hard for her again.

She took my hand and I went to her, still fully clothed. The water rolled and dripped from us both in thin roads, trailing paths across my leather and the buckles to contrast sharply with Lex's naked skin. On her, the water disappeared beneath her arms and ran trails down her stomach. I noticed the faint suggestion of faded pink vertical lines on her toned flanks and ran my fingers along them slowly. Touching her was like touching an open current of electricity. "Scars," she stated matter of factly. "From the experiments."

I breathed sharply and kissed her hard. It might have been my imagination but her tongue felt liquid as it licked and rolled in my mouth. I was aware of her hands tugging and then pulling at the straps and buckles of my uniform but this time—this time she would listen to *my* commands.

I saw her look at my hands, the blue veins beneath the skin that had popped to the surface as if they were thirsty.

The angular lines of the office and the functionality of the tech against the walls and on the shelves suddenly made me long for something less complicated. But here I was—here she was—and this was what it was.

I steadied Lex against the wall and saw no sign of a shiver as her skin connected with cold wetness. My hand didn't waste time. Surely there would be time for that later. I had three fingers inside her almost immediately because I couldn't ignore the way her hips kept moving desperately against me. Her vulnerability against the wet leather of my uniform was simply too enticing. One of her legs was hooked around my hip and her breasts were mashing against my chest and the promise of a snarl started to tease my lips as she started breathing fast. Slight sounds escaped the back of Lex's throat. She pushed herself into me, trying to ride my water-slicked hand but I held her back, against the wall with my free hand and only had to say "No" one time forcefully before she gave herself over to my mercy.

We fucked.

Sure—it's a vulgarism for a reason.

The Show
M. Christian

Outside, the city was a night sky of square stars: a galaxy of windows,
a constellation of consumers among flashing, pulsing advertisements
—product-placement nebulae.

Smoke was standing, a rectangular sun of a different type, looking
out at the spectacle of nighttime New York. He felt like he should be
sneering, thinking something arrogant—like how he, behind this one
window, wasn't just another sun, but rather a media prank nova ready
to blast the consumer galaxy of NYC with mind-blowing light. Yeah,
something like that. Instead, he was really thinking was how his new
boots—nice though they were—were really killing his feet, that he
only had $17.15 in his checking account . . . and that he was really
worried about Jayne.

"Well, the Master has worked his magic," Truck said from where
he was sprawled in a far corner of the tiny Times Square apartment,

circuit board in his lap, a faint plume of gray smoke rising from the soldering iron in ones hand. "All he needs now is for the talent to do its thing."

Meaning Smoke and Jayne. "Give it a rest, will ya?" Smoke said, still looking out the window at the busy drones of NYC.

"Hey, man, just laying it out, that's all. We've only got a day or so before someone notices my expert hacks. We've really got to do this thing and get the hell out before then."

The apartment was below seedy. Beside the one window, it was just a stained sink under a flaking mirror, a tiny pressboard night stand, a (non-working) wall sconce shaped like a seashell, and the bed. The mattress was way too soft, like a decaying marshmallow, and the piss-colored bedspread smelled of ancient cigarettes and mildew.

The atmosphere wasn't why they were there. "I got it, I got it," Smoke said, running a thin hand through his long dark hair. He sighed. "But I can't force her or anything, man."

"Didn't ask you, too—just stating the facts, is all. Wouldn't want my beautiful work to go to waste, you know."

Running through the interior wall was a special trunk line—part of the Tyrano-Vision screen overlooking Times Square's control system. The circuit board in Truck's lap was patched skullduggerously into it—linking the tiny solid-state camera duct-taped to the wall directly to the eighty-foot monster screen. Their first act of Awareness Terrorism—as they called it—had been to alter some dozen or so billboards throughout Manhattan, turning cigarette ads to GOT CANCER? After that, they'd placed OUT OF DISORDER stickers on hundreds of vending machines all over the island. It was just Smoke, Truck, and Jayne—but they'd made the *Daily News,* the *Times,* and all kinds of local TV stations. Today, though, or better yet tonight, was going to be their coup de grace: a skillful manipulation of corporate propaganda to bring their message to the milling throngs of Times Square—an artistic assault on the plastic culture imposed at dollar-point on the people of New York: Smoke and Jayne, eighty feet tall, fucking on the Tyrano-Vision screen.

A shave and a haircut knock brought Smoke from the window to the scarred and battered door. Jayne stood, looking sheepish and small despite her Army Surplus jacket and black parachute pants, in the hall.

There was just one problem—and it wasn't with Truck's hackwork. "I'm going to check the jumpers on the roof again," he said, carefully putting the circuit board aside. "Let me know if you guys get that romantic spark going." He slipped past Jayne and vanished towards the back stairs.

Jayne stepped in, closing the door behind her. "Just call me frigid," she said with a wry smile, slipping off the glasses and dropping them onto the bed.

Smoke put his arms around her. "Fuck that," he said with a smile. "You do what you want to do—you just don't want to do it. It's cool."

She shook her head. Jayne wasn't a small slip, she was full-bodied and outrageous—or at least normally outrageous. Her face was puckish, her lips and eyes set on Perpetually Amused, and her body language usually broadcasted Fuck With Me If You Dare—but right then she was smaller, drained, and shy. Perpetually Amused seemed more like Sad Self-Deprecation.

Smoke felt something down deep, an ache at seeing the transformation. He liked his wild Jayne, his Jayne who liked to fuck on the L line, so liked to walk around his scummy little West Side apartment, proudly nude. He liked to hear her mumble when they made out, telling him in explicit detail what she wanted to do, was going to do to him, with him. It was only because of Outrageous Jayne that the Times Square prank was even considered—and she'd seemed all for it. In fact, she seemed more than all for it for weeks, until, that is the day before, when Outrageous Jayne, the Jayne who liked to flash her plump tits at passing tour buses, had come down with a severe case of . . . shyness?

"It's just . . . I don't know," Jayne said, pushing herself back into Smoke's thin arms. "I'm just nervous, that's all—and it freaks me out."

"Doing it?" Doing it in front of a thousand strangers. "Or being nervous?"

"Both, I guess," she said, turning carefully around until her lips were just about even with Smoke's. "It's weird—and I don't like it."

Smoke didn't say anything—instead he just bent down and kissed her. Jayne was wearing her favorite lipstick, Urban Decay, and the familiar heavy slickness of her lips on his made Smoke's breathing start to come fast and quick.

"Whatever turns you on," Smoke said, slowly drawing his lips across hers, "or doesn't is cool with me. Okay, babe?"

"Yeah . . ." she said, her voice sad and heavy. She put her face down onto Smoke's chest. His FUCK THE FUCKERS T-shirt was barely clean but that was good, because Jayne could relax into its comfortable smell, sagging just a bit in his arms. "I know. But I really wanted to, you know? I've been thinking of nothing else for the last few days. Up here," she said, pulling an arm free to tap her forehead, "It really gets me going. The idea of all those people watching us, getting turned on while we do it . . . oh, man, but something gets caught down here," she shifted her finger down between her plump breasts, "it gets stuck somehow, gets all mixed up. I don't know what to do."

"You do whatever you want to do, babe. Don't worry about Truck or me—fuck, what's more important? Screwing with the people out there or doing what you want to do? We can fuck with them anytime—it's you that's really important."

"Thanks," she said in a sweet little voice, a little girl's tones from the young woman's full mouth. She kissed him again, from gentle to a slow, hot, dance of firm tongues. "I want to—I'm just scared," she said, breaking the kiss long enough to say it.

"Yeah, I know." Smoke knew he should have been all caring and shit, but his body wasn't listening. A hard cock wasn't really 'caring'—but it didn't seem to care: in his battered, threadbare jeans his dick felt like another arm, one that throbbed towards Jayne. "It would have been fun, wouldn't it?"

"Oh, yeah," Jayne said, running a finger around where his nipples made small tents in his T-shirt. "All those people down there, looking up at us. I'm such a freak—but it really gets me going."

Smoke returned the gesture, opening her jacket and circling her nipples with his finger tips, but Jayne responded with greater gusto—the tents that appeared on her own T-shirt were five times larger, and much more sensitive: she arched her back against Smoke's methodical circles, and her eyes slightly glazed over. "Me, too."

"I've been thinking about it a lot," Jayne said as Smoke pushed her jacket off her shoulders. It fell to the ugly yellow carpet with a heavy fabric impact. "How about we start by just standing there, up on the screen, just the two of us . . . naked. Oh—"

The thought—but also Smoke lifting her T-shirt up and placing a single, firm kiss to her left nipple—made her voice fade, trail off. But her voice and words returned as he gave the same treatment to her right. "You'd be hard. Oh, yeah, hard like you are now, right? Fucking hard: cock all big and pretty. Bobbing up and down just a bit, maybe even a little bit of come at the tip. Just the way I like it." As she spoke, Jayne rubbed her hand down the front of Smoke's jeans, playing with the fat bulge, tracing the outline of his hard cock. "Just the two of us, eighty feet high, naked—hard and . . ."

"Wet?" Smoke said, lifting her shirt up and off, as it finally passed over her head he leaned forward and kissed her, long and firmly.

"Very," Outrageous Jayne said, smiling. "Very wet. I wish I could be like those porno girls. You know, with pussy juice dripping down my legs. But—well, what the fuck, why not? Okay, there we are, standing there, eighty feet tall, your cock all nice and really fucking hard, and me, pussy juice making all thighs all wet and shiny. . . ."

She stopped as Smoke pulled off his own shirt, then bent forward to kiss, then suck, at her firmly erect nipples. Her breasts were full, plump—white, but not pale—and they jiggled slightly as Smoke worked his lips around the so-soft skin and directly on the brown nipples.

As he broke the kiss, the suck, she continued: "Yeah, eighty feet tall. People would look up and stare at us, look at us, up there—very hard and wet. They'd stare, stare at us. Maybe a cab would crash, the guy not looking where he was going. Guys would get all hard, their cocks tight in their pants. Some chicks would get wet, and their nipples really hard. But some would he all shocked and shit, and try not to look—but you know they would, 'cause their cocks and cunts would be all hard and wet, too."

Shoes, pants on the floor. Then Smoke, too. Like in her story, she was wet—though her juice didn't paint her thighs, at least not yet—and he was very, very hard. "Then we'd start to kiss, and touch each other. You'd grab my tits—oh, yeah—" her voice quavered as Smoke did just that "—and I'd wrap my hand around your cock, and slowly jerk you off."

A little bead of pre-come had dotted the head of Smoke's cock, and Jayne spread it over the tip, the head, and the shaft. There wasn't a lot, but there was enough to make him slippery enough. Smiling down at the dick in her hand, she smiled, eyes dancing over all the details of him. "—and they'd be so hard, so wet down there, watching us. Maybe a guy would start to jerk off: taking his little weenie out of his pants and beating off looking up at us on that big fucking screen. Maybe some chick would grab her tits, pulling at her nipples." Jayne did the same, smiling wickedly at Smoke.

Smoke smiled back, feeling his heart hammering in his chest. Reaching out, he softly petted her shaven mons, enjoying—as he always enjoyed—the soft pebble of her most recent shave. Without a word, Jayne spread her legs, allowing two of his fingers to go between and up, parting her lips.

"Then I'd suck your cock. I'd get down on my eighty-feet tall knees and take your dick in my mouth and start to suck you off—and all those people down there, they'd all watch and they'd all start to moan. Maybe a couple of them, some freaks like us, or maybe some straights who just couldn't take it any more would start to do it—sucking and fucking like us."

Like in her narrative, Jayne lowered herself to the dirty carpet. Kneeling, facing Smoke's long cock, she stroked it a few more times. Then, smiling, she kissed the tip—tasting salt and bitter pre-come. "Maybe a couple of dykes, too, would get down there on the street. Skirts all pulled up, panties pushed aside, they'd eat each other's pussies—chowing down on sweet muff in the middle of Time Square. Nasty little fag boys, too: they'd get down on and start sucking cock, then swallowing come as they all watched me take you in my mouth, down my throat."

Then she put actions to words—carefully opening her mouth and easing Smoke's cock into her mouth and then, inch by inch, down her throat. It was a familiar game for both of them, so Smoke knew to spread his legs and push his cock down just a bit and Jayne knew to tilt her head just so.

Time stretched out, and world shrank. Smoke knew he should say something to keep the game going, but his vocabulary drained out of him, whole classifications of words with each inch of his cock down Jayne's throat. Still, he loved Jayne, and so he tried his best. "Yeah, oh yeah, they'd watch us. They'd watch us fuck and suck each other. The guys would be real hard, the women all fucking wet.

They'd do it with us. Fuck and such each other as we did on the big picture. Oh—"

They'd been together long enough, had done it enough, that Jayne knew when Smoke was coming close to . . . coming . . . so she pulled away, smiling up at the joy on his face. "Let me," she said, stroking him a few times, "I think I'm better at this, babe." She lost herself in Smoke's cock for a minute. "Yeah, we'd fuck for them. We'd make their days, their weeks, their years—they'd talk about us forever, how they'd seen us up there on that big screen. We'd be in their dreams. They'd fantasize about us—they'd jerk off to us, fuck people but think about us . . . for years."

As Jayne stroked him, she reached her hand around to his firm little ass and carefully hunted for his asshole. Ringing it with a fingertip, she continued. "We'd fuck our ways into their heads, stud. We'd screw our ways into the dreams. How would it feel to fuck five hundred people? Have all those cocks, all those cunts out there wanting you?"

Jayne licked her finger then returned to Smoke's asshole. In. In, and Smoke arched his back, hissing harshly. Inside, Jayne positioned herself: cock in front of her eyes, finger deep inside his asshole, fingers stroking plump cunt lips—and then pushing inside her self, hissing as she went.

"They look at us, they'd want us—all of them. We'd be sex to them, we'd be New York to them. Guys would jerk off thinking of us, shooting off to what we'd done. Girls would stroke their nasty little pussies and scream out loud while dreaming of doing us." As the words came, Jayne stroked herself, and finger-fucked Smoke—staring at the gleaming, bobbing tip of his cock.

Above, Smoke moaned, low and deep, begging with vowels for her lips again.

"We'd fuck for them, babe—we'd fuck for them eighty feet tall."

Then she leaned forward and quickly, surely, eased his straining cock into her mouth and then down her throat again.

One, he came, moaning loudly—the sound thunderous in the small room; two—a minute later as Jayne swallowed spoonful after spoonful of hot, heavy semen, she followed. Two, their orgasms blurred their vision, clipped their muscle control. Slowly, they sank to the carpeting: Jayne sprawled on her back, breaking hard, Smoke next to her, cock still hard but none of his muscles working right. They lay there for a long time—minutes stretching into what felt like hours, the world slowly returning to them.

Finally, a word between them: "Sorry," Jayne said, shame making her words slow and heavy. "I'm sorry," she didn't need to say more, because Smoke knew it was that she couldn't bring flesh into reality. He stroked her thigh, mumbled something supportive.

More minutes—or maybe more hours, who could say? The door quickly opened and Truck stood there, red-rimmed eyes staring. With the door open, the sound of car horns and cheers from somewhere close by.

"Fuck!" Truck said, his frantic vibe falling away to deep laughter. "Fuck! The line was live—I just figured it out. Just listen to those assholes out there!"

Smoke and Jayne did, their bodies tense with shock where they lay on the floor. One, Jayne, her body shaking; two, Smoke, snorting and then howling into the ugly carpeting. Then, together, they laughed.

Truck helped them up—no stranger to seeing the two of them naked—and into their clothes. When they could finally stand after their giggles and laughter, they climbed back into their clothes. "The least you fucks can do is come up on the roof and take a bow," Truck said, beaming.

So they did: they climbed the rickety iron steps and made their way among cheap TV antennas and ventilator hoods until they stood at the edge. Below them, chaos. Below them, thousands of people. Below them, sirens and blue and red flashing lights.

They held hands and, stiffly at first, but then with assurance, pride, they took their bows to the thunderous cheers of New York and Times Square.

More Than the Sum of His Parts

Joe Haldeman

21 August 2058

They say I am to keep a detailed record of my feelings, my perceptions, as I grow accustomed to the new parts. To that end, they gave
me an apparatus that blind people use for writing, like a tablet with
guide wires. It is somewhat awkward. But a recorder would be useless, since I will not have a mouth for some time, and I can't type
blind with only one hand.

Woke up free from pain. Interesting. Surprising to find that it has
only been five days since the accident. For the record, I am, or was,
Dr. Wilson Cheetham, Senior Engineer (Quality Control) for U.S.
Steel's Skyfac station, a high-orbit facility that produces foamsteel and
vapor deposition materials for use in the cislunar community. But if
you are reading this, you must know all that.

Five days ago I was inspecting the aluminum deposition facility and had a bad accident. There was a glitch in my jetseat controls, and I flew suddenly straight into the wide beam of charged aluminum vapor. Very hot. They turned it off in a second, but there was still plenty of time to breach the suit and thoroughly roast three quarters of my body.

Apparently there was a rescue bubble right there. I was unconscious, of course. They tell me that my heart stopped with the shock, but they managed to save me. My left leg and arm are gone, as is my face. I have no lower jaw, nose, or external ears. I can hear after a fashion, though, and will have eyes in a week or so. They claim they will craft for me testicles and a penis.

I must be pumped full of mood drugs. I feel too calm. If I were myself, whatever fraction of myself is left, perhaps I would resist the insult of being turned into a sexless half-machine.

Ah well. This will be a machine that can turn itself off.

22 August 2058
For many days there was only sleep or pain. This was in the weightless ward at Mercy. They stripped the dead skin off me bit by bit. There are limits to anesthesia, unfortunately. I tried to scream but found I had no vocal cords. They finally decided not to try to salvage the arm and leg, which saved some pain.

When I was able to listen, they explained that U.S. Steel valued my services so much that they were willing to underwrite a state-of-the-art cyborg transformation. Half the cost will be absorbed by Interface Biotech on the moon. Everybody will deduct me from their taxes.

This, then, is the catalog. First, new arm and leg. That's fairly standard. (I once worked with a woman who had two cyborg arms. It took weeks before I could look at her without feeling pity and revulsion.) Then they will attempt to build me a working jaw and mouth, which has been done only rarely and imperfectly, and rebuild the trachea, vocal cords, esophagus. I will be able to speak and drink, though except for certain soft foods, I won't eat in a normal way; salivary glands are beyond their art. No mucous membranes of any kind. A drastic cure for my chronic sinusitis.

Surprisingly, to me at least, the reconstruction of a penis is a fairly straightforward procedure, for which they've had lots of practice. Men are forever sticking them into places where they don't belong. They are particularly excited about my case because of the challenge of restoring sensation as well as function. The prostate is intact, and they seem confident that they can hook up the complicated plumbing involved in ejaculation. Restoring the ability to urinate is trivially easy, they say.

(The biotechnician in charge of the urogenital phase of the project talked at me for more than an hour, going into unnecessarily grisly detail. It seems that this kind of replacement was done occasionally even before they had any kind of mechanical substitute, by sawing off a short rib and transplanting it, covering it with a skin graft from elsewhere on the body. The recipient thus was blessed with a permanent erection, unfortunately rather strange looking and short on sensation. My own prosthesis will look very much like the real, shall we say, thing, and new developments in tractor-field mechanics and bionic interfacing should give it realistic response patterns.)

I don't know how to feel about all this. I wish they would leave my blood chemistry alone, so I could have some honest grief or horror, whatever. Instead of this placid waiting.

4 September 2058

Out cold for thirteen days and I wake up with eyes. The arm and leg are in place but not powered up yet. I wonder what the eyes look like. (They won't give me a mirror until I have a face.) They feel like wet glass.

Very fancy eyes. I have a box with two dials that I can use to override the "default mode"—that is, the ability to see only normally. One of them gives me conscious control over pupil dilation, so I can see in almost total darkness or, if for some reason I wanted to, look directly at the sun without discomfort. The other changes the frequency response, so I can see either in the infrared or the ultraviolet. This hospital room looks pretty much the same in ultraviolet, but in infrared it takes on a whole new aspect. Most of the room's illumination then comes from bright bars on the walls, radiant heating. My real arm shows a pulsing tracery of arteries and veins. The other is of course not visible except by reflection and is dark blue.

(Later) Strange I didn't realize I was on the moon. I thought it was a low-gravity ward in Mercy. While I was sleeping they sent me down to Biotech. Should have figured that out.

5 September 2058
They turned on the "social" arm and leg and began patterning exercises. I am told to think of a certain movement and do its mirror image with my right arm or leg while attempting to execute it with my left. The trainer helps the cyborg unit along, which generates something like pain, though actually it doesn't resemble any real muscular ache. Maybe it's the way circuits feel when they're overloaded.

By the end of the session I was able to make a fist without help, though there is hardly enough grip to hold a pencil. I can't raise the leg yet, but can make the toes move.

They removed some of the bandages today, from shoulder to hip, and the test-tube skin looks much more real than I had prepared myself for. Hairless and somewhat glossy, but the color match is perfect. In infrared it looks quite different, more uniform in color than the "real" side. I suppose that's because it hasn't aged forty years.

While putting me through my paces, the technician waxed rhapsodic about how good this arm is going to be—this set of arms, actually. I'm exercising with the "social" one, which looks much more convincing than the ones my coworker displayed ten years ago. (No doubt more a matter of money than advancing technology.) The "working" arm, which I haven't seen yet, will be all metal, capable of being worn on the outside of a spacesuit. Besides having the two arms, I'll be able to interface with various waldos, tailored to specific functions.

I am fortunately more ambidextrous than the average person. I broke my right wrist in the second grade and kept re-breaking it through the third, and so learned to write with both hands. All my life I have been able to print more clearly with the left.

They claim to be cutting down on my medication. If that's the truth, I seem to be adjusting fairly well. Then again, I have nothing in my past experience to use as a basis for comparison. Perhaps this calmness is only a mask for hysteria.

6 September 2058

Today I was able to tie a simple knot. I can lightly sketch out the letters of the alphabet. A large and childish scrawl but recognizably my own.

I've begun walking after a fashion, supporting myself between parallel bars. (The lack of hand strength is a neural problem, not a muscular one; when rigid, the arm and leg are as strong as metal crutches.) As I practice, it's amusing to watch the reactions of people who walk into the room, people who aren't paid to mask their horror at being studied by two cold lenses embedded in a swath of bandages formed over a shape that is not a head.

Tomorrow they start building my face. I will be essentially unconscious for more than a week. The limb patterning will continue as I sleep, they say.

14 September 2058

When I was a child my mother, always careful to have me do "normal" things, dressed me in a costume each Halloween and escorted me around the high-rise, so I could beg for candy I did not want and money I did not need. On one occasion I had to wear the mask of a child star then popular on the cube, a tightly fitting plastic affair that covered the entire head, squeezing my pudgy features into something more in line with some Platonic ideal of childish beauty. That was my last Halloween. I embarrassed her.

This face is like that. It is undeniably my face, but the skin is taut and unresponsive. Any attempt at expression produces a grimace.

I have almost normal grip in the hand now, though it is still clumsy. As they hoped, the sensory feedback from the fingertips and palms seems to be more finely tuned than in my "good" hand. Tracing my new forefinger across my right wrist, I can sense the individual pores, and there is a marked temperature gradient as I pass over tendon or vein. And yet the hand and arm will eventually be capable of superhuman strength.

Touching my new face I do not feel pores. They have improved on nature in the business of heat exchange.

22 September 2058

Another week of sleep while they installed the new plumbing. When the anesthetic wore off I felt a definite *something*, not pain, but neither was it the normal somatic heft of genitalia. Everything was bedded in gauze and bandage, though, and catheterized, so it would feel strange even to a normal person.

(Later) An aide came in and gingerly snipped away the bandages. He blushed; I don't think fondling was in his job description. When the catheter came out there was a small sting of pain and relief.

It's not much of a copy. To reconstruct the face, they could consult hundreds of pictures and cubes, but it had never occurred to me that one day it might be useful to have a gallery of pictures of my private parts in various stages of repose. The technicians had approached the problem by bringing me a stack of photos culled from urological texts and pornography, and having me sort through them as to "closeness of fit."

It was not a task for which I was well trained, by experience or disposition. Strange as it may seem in this age of unfettered hedonism, I haven't seen another man naked, let alone rampant, since leaving high school, twenty-five years ago. (I was stationed on Farside for eighteen months and never went near a sex bar, preferring an audience of one. Even if I had to hire her, as was usually the case.)

So this one is rather longer and thicker than the predecessor— would all men consciously exaggerate?—and has only approximately the same aspect when erect. A young man's rakish angle.

Distasteful but necessary to write about the matter of masturbation. At first it didn't work. With my right hand, it felt like holding another man, which I have never had any desire to do. With my new hand, though, the process proceeded in the normal way, though I must admit to a voyeuristic aspect. The sensations were extremely acute. Ejaculation more forceful than I can remember from youth.

It makes me wonder. In a book I recently read, about brain chemistry, the author made a major point of the notion that it's a mistake to completely equate "mind" with "brain." The brain, he said, is in a way only the thickest and most complex segment of the nervous system; it coordinates our consciousness, but the actual mind suffuses through the body in a network of ganglia. In fact, he used sexuality as an example. When a man ruefully observes that his penis has a mind of its own, he is stating part of a larger truth.

But I in fact do have actual brains imbedded in my new parts: the biochips that process sensory data coming in and action commands going back. Are these brains part of my consciousness the way the rest of my nervous system is? The masturbation experience indicates they might be in business for themselves.

This is premature speculation, so to speak. We'll see how it feels when I move into a more complex environment, where I'm not so self-absorbed.

23 September 2058

During the night something evidently clicked. I woke up this morning with full strength in my cyborg limbs. One rail of the bed was twisted out of shape where I must have unconsciously gripped it. I bent it back quite easily.

Some obscure impulse makes me want to keep this talent secret for the time being. The technicians thought I would be able to exert three or four times the normal person's grip; this is obviously much more than that.

But why keep it a secret? I don't know. Eventually they will read this diary and I will stand exposed. There's no harm in that, though; this is supposed to be a record of my psychological adjustment or maladjustment. Let *them* tell me why I've done it.

(Later) The techs were astonished, ecstatic. I demonstrated a pull of 90 kilograms. I know if I'd actually given it a good yank, I could have pulled the stress machine out of the wall. I'll give them 110 tomorrow and inch my way up to 125.

Obviously I must be careful with force vectors. If I put too much stress on the normal parts of my body, I could do permanent injury. With my metal fist I could certainly punch a hole through an airlock door, but it would probably tear the prosthesis out of its socket. Newton's laws still apply.

Other laws will have to be rewritten.

24 September 2058

I got to work out with three waldos today. A fantastic experience!

The first one was a disembodied hand and arm attached to a stand, the setup they use to train normal people in the use of waldos. The difference is that I don't need a waldo sleeve to imperfectly transmit my wishes to the mechanical double. I can plug into it directly.

I've been using waldos in my work ever since graduate school, but it was never anything like this. Inside the waldo sleeve you get a clumsy kind of feedback from striated pressor field generators embedded in the plastic. With my setup the feedback is exactly the kind a normal person feels when he touches an object, but much more sensitive. The first time they asked me to pick up an egg, I tossed it up and caught it (no great feat of coordination in lunar gravity, admittedly, but I could have done it as easily in earth-normal).

The next waldo was a large earthmover that Western Mining uses over at Grimaldi Station. That was interesting, not only because of its size but because of the slight communications lag. Grimaldi is only a few dozens of kilometers away, but there aren't enough unused data channels between here and there for me to use the land-line to communicate with the earthmover hand. I had to relay via comsat, so there was about a tenth-second delay between the thought and the action. It was a fine feeling of power, but a little confusing: I would cup my hand and scoop downward, and then a split-second too late would feel the resistance of the regolith. And then casually hold in my palm several tons of rock and dirt. People stood around watching; with a flick of my wrist I could have buried them. Instead I dutifully dumped it on the belt to the converter.

But the waldo that most fascinated me was the micro. It had been in use for only a few months; I had heard of it, but hadn't had a chance to see it in action. It is a fully articulated hand barely a tenth of a millimeter long. I used it in conjunction with a low-power scanning electron microscope, moving around on the surface of a microcircuit. At that magnification it looked like a hand on a long stick wandering through the corridors of a building, whose walls varied from rough stucco to brushed metal to blistered gray paint, all laced over with thick cables of gold. When necessary, I could bring in another hand, manipulated by my right from inside a waldo sleeve, to help with simple carpenter and machinist tasks that, in the real world, translated into fundamental changes in the quantum-electrodynamic properties of the circuit.

This was the real power: not crushing metal tubes or lifting tons of rock, but pushing electrons around to do my bidding. My first doctorate was in electrical engineering; in a sudden epiphany I realize that I am the first *actual* electrical engineer in history.

After two hours they made me stop; said I was showing signs of strain. They put me in a wheelchair, and I did fall asleep on the way back to my room. Dreaming dreams of microcosmic and infinite power.

25 September 2058
The metal arm. I expected it to feel fundamentally different from the "social" one, but of course it doesn't, most of the time. Circuits are circuits. The difference comes under conditions of extreme exertion: the soft hand gives me signals like pain if I come close to the level of stress that would harm the fleshlike material. With the metal hand I can rip off a chunk of steel plate a centimeter thick and feel nothing beyond "muscular" strain. If I had two of them I could work marvels.

The mechanical leg is not so gifted. It has governors to restrict its strength and range of motion to that of a normal leg, which is reasonable. Even a normal person finds himself brushing the ceiling occasionally in lunar gravity. I could stand up and find myself with a concussion, or worse.

I like the metal arm, though. When I'm stronger (hah!) they say they'll let me go outside and try it with a spacesuit. Throw something over the horizon.

Starting today, I'm easing back into a semblance of normal life. I'll be staying at Biotech for another six or eight weeks, but I'm patched into my Skyfac office and have started cleaning out the backlog of paperwork. Two hours in the morning and two in the afternoon. It's diverting, but I have to admit my heart isn't really in it. Rather be playing with the micro. (Have booked three hours on it tomorrow.)

26 September 2058

They threaded an optical fiber through the micro's little finger, so I can watch its progress on a screen without being limited to the field of an electron microscope. The picture is fuzzy while the waldo is in motion, but if I hold it still for a few seconds, the computer assist builds up quite a sharp image. I used it to roam all over my right arm and hand, which was fascinating. Hairs a tangle of stiff black stalks, the pores small damp craters. And everywhere the evidence of the skin's slow death; translucent sheafs of desquamated cells.

I've taken to wearing the metal arm rather than the social one. People's stares don't bother me. The metal one will be more useful in my actual work, and I want to get as much practice as possible. There is also an undeniable feeling of power.

27 September 2058

Today I went outside. It was clumsy getting around at first. For the past eleven years I've used a suit only in zero-G, so all my reflexes are wrong. Still, not much serious can go wrong at a sixth of a G.

It was exhilarating but at the same time frustrating, since I couldn't reveal all my strength. I did almost overdo it once, starting to tip over a large boulder. Before it tipped, I realized that my left boot had crunched through about ten centimeters of regolith, in reaction to the amount of force I was applying. So I backed off and discreetly shuffled my foot to fill in the telltale hole.

I could indeed throw a rock over the horizon. With a sling, I might be able to put one into orbit. Rent myself out as a lunar launching facility.

(Later) Most interesting. A pretty nurse who has been on this project since the beginning came into my room after dinner and proposed the obvious experiment. It was wildly successful.

Although my new body starts out with the normal pattern of excitation-plateau-orgasm, the resemblance stops there. I have no refractory period; the process of erection is completely under conscious control. This could make me the most popular man on the moon.

The artificial skin of the penis is as sensitive to tactile differentiation as that of the cyborg fingers: suddenly I know more about a woman's internal topography than any man who ever lived—more than any *woman!*

I think tomorrow I'll take a trip to Farside.

28 September 2058

Farside has nine sex bars. I read the guidebook descriptions, and then asked a few locals for recommendations, and wound up going to a place cleverly called the Juice Bar.

In fact, the name was not just an expression of coy eroticism. They served nothing but fruit and juices there, most of them fantastically expensive earth imports. I spent a day's pay on a glass of pear nectar and sought out the most attractive woman in the room.

That in itself was a mistake. I was not physically attractive even before the accident, and the mechanics have faithfully restored my coarse features and slight paunch. I was rebuffed.

So I went to the opposite extreme and looked for the plainest woman. That would be a better test anyway: before the accident I always demanded, and paid for, physical perfection. If I could duplicate the performance of last night with a woman to whom I was not sexually attracted—and do it in public, with no pressure from having gone without—then my independence from the autonomic nervous system would be proven beyond doubt.

Second mistake. I was never good at small talk, and when I located my paragon of plainness I began talking about the accident and the singular talent that had resulted from it. She suddenly remembered an appointment elsewhere.

I was not so open with the next woman, also plain. She asked whether there was something wrong with my face, and I told her half of the truth. She was sweetly sympathetic, motherly, which did not endear her to me. It did make her a good subject for the experiment. We left the socializing section of the bar and went back to the so-called "love room."

There was an acrid quality to the air that I suppose was compounded of incense and sweat, but of course my dry nose was not capable of identifying actual smells. For the first time, I was grateful for that disability; the place probably had the aroma of a well-used locker room. Plus pheromones.

Under the muted lights, red and blue as well as white, more than a dozen couples were engaged more or less actively in various aspects of amorous behavior. A few were frankly staring at others, but most were either absorbed with their own affairs or furtive in their voyeurism. Most of them were on the floor, which was a warm soft mat, but some were using tables and chairs in fairly ingenious ways.

Several of the permutations would no doubt have been impossible or dangerous in earth's gravity.

We undressed and she complimented me on my evident spryness. A nearby spectator made a jealous observation. Her own body was rather flaccid, doughy, and under previous circumstances I doubt that I would have been able to maintain enthusiasm. There was no problem, however; in fact, I rather enjoyed it. She required very little foreplay, and I was soon repeating the odd sensation of hypersensitized exploration. Gynecological spelunking.

She was quite voluble in her pleasure, and although she lasted less than an hour, we did attract a certain amount of attention. When she, panting, regretfully declined further exercise, a woman who had been watching, a rather attractive young blonde, offered to share her various openings. I obliged her for a while; although the well was dry the pump handle was unaffected.

During that performance I became aware that the pleasure involved was not a sexual one in any normal sense. Sensual, yes, in the way that a fine meal is a sensual experience, but with a remote subtlety that I find difficult to describe. Perhaps there is a relation to epicurism that is more than metaphorical. Since I can no longer taste food, a large area of my brain is available for the evaluation of other experience. It may be that the brain is reorganizing itself in order to take fullest advantage of my new abilities.

By the time the blonde's energy began to flag, several other women had taken an interest in my satyriasis. I resisted the temptation to find out what the organ's limit was, if indeed a limit exists. My back ached and the right knee was protesting. So I threw the mental switch and deflated. I left with a minimum of socializing. (The first woman insisted on buying me something at the bar. I opted for a banana.)

29 September 2058

Now that I have eyes and both hands, there's no reason to scratch this diary out with a pen. So I'm entering it into the computer. But I'm keeping two versions.

I recopied everything up to this point and then went back and edited the version that I will show to Biotech. It's very polite, and will remain so. For instance, it does not contain the following:

After writing last night's entry, I found myself still full of energy, and so I decided to put into action a plan that has been forming in my mind.

About two in the morning I went downstairs and broke into the waldo lab. The entrance is protected by a five-digit combination lock, but of course that was no obstacle. My hypersensitive fingers could feel the tumblers rattling into place.

I got the micro-waldo set up and then detached my leg. I guided the waldo through the leg's circuitry and easily disabled the governors. The whole operation took less than twenty minutes.

I did have to use a certain amount of care walking, at first. There was a tendency to rise into the air or to limpingly overcompensate. It was under control by the time I got back to my room. So once more they proved to have been mistaken as to the limits of my abilities. Testing the strength of the leg, with a halfhearted kick I put a deep dent in the metal wall at the rear of my closet. I'll have to wait until I can be outside, alone, to see what full force can do.

A comparison kick with my flesh leg left no dent, but did hurt my great toe.

30 September 2058

It occurs to me I feel better about my body than I have in the past twenty years. Who wouldn't? Literally eternal youth in these new limbs and organs; if a part shows signs of wear, it can simply be replaced.

I was angry at the Biotech evaluation board this morning. When I simply inquired as to the practicality of replacing the right arm and leg as well, all but one were horrified. One was amused. I will remember him.

I think the fools are going to order me to leave Nearside in a day or two and go back to Mercy for psychiatric "help." I will leave when I want to, on my own terms.

1 October 2058

This is being voice-recorded at the Environmental Control Center at Nearside. It is 10:32; they have less that ninety minutes to accede to my demands. Let me backtrack.

After writing last night's entry I felt a sudden excess of sexual desire. I took the shuttle to Farside and went back to the Juice Bar.

The plain woman from the previous visit was waiting, hoping that I would show up. She was delighted when I suggested that we save money (and whatever residue of modesty we had left) by keeping ourselves to one another, back at my room.

I didn't mean to murder her. That was not in my mind at all. But I suppose in my passion, or abandon, I carelessly propped my strong leg against the wall and then thrust with too much strength. At any rate there was a snap and a tearing sound. She gave a small cry and the lower half of my body was suddenly awash in blood. I had snapped her spine and evidently at the same time caused considerable internal damage. She must have lost consciousness very quickly, though her heart did not stop beating for nearly a minute.

Disposing of the body was no great problem, conceptually. In the laundry room, I found a bag large enough to hold her comfortably. Then I went back to the room and put her and the sheet she had besmirched into the bag.

Getting her to the recycler would have been a problem if it had been a normal hour. She looked like nothing so much as a body in a laundry bag. Fortunately, the corridor was deserted.

The lock on the recycler room was child's play. The furnace door was a problem, though; it was easy to unlock but its effective diameter was only twenty-five centimeters.

So I had to disassemble her. To save cleaning up, I did the job inside the laundry bag, which was clumsy, and it made it difficult to see the fascinating process.

I was so absorbed in watching that I didn't hear the door slide open. But the man who walked in made a slight gurgling sound, which somehow I did hear over the cracking of bones. I stepped over to him and killed him with one kick.

At this point I have to admit to a lapse in judgment. I relocked the door and went back to the chore at hand. After the woman was completely recycled, I repeated the process with the man—which was, incidentally, much easier. The female's layer of subcutaneous fat made disassembly of the torso a more slippery business.

It really was wasted time (though I did spend part of the time thinking out the final touches of the plan I am now engaged upon). I might as well have left both bodies there on the floor. I had kicked the man with great force—enough to throw me to the ground in reaction and badly bruise my right hip—and had split him open from crotch to heart. This made a bad enough mess, even if he hadn't compounded the problem by striking the ceiling. I would never be able to clean that up, and it's not the sort of thing that would escape notice for long.

At any rate, it was only twenty minutes wasted, and I gained more time than that by disabling the recycler room lock. I cleaned up, then changed clothes, stopped by the waldo lab for a few minutes, and then took the slide walk to the Environmental Control Center.

There was only one young man on duty at the ECC at that hour.

I exchanged a few pleasantries with him and then punched him in the heart, softly enough not to make a mess. I put his body where it wouldn't distract me and then attended to the problem of the "door."

There's no actual door on the ECC, but there is an emergency wall that slides into place if there's a drop in pressure. I typed up a test program simulating an emergency and the wall obeyed. Then I walked over and twisted a few flanges around. Nobody would be able to get into the center with anything short of a cutting torch.

Sitting was uncomfortable on the bruised hip, but I managed to ease into the console and spend an hour or so studying logic and wiring diagrams. Then I popped off an access plate and moved the micro-waldo down the corridors of electronic thought. The intercom began buzzing incessantly, but I didn't let it interfere with my concentration.

Nearside is protected from a meteorite strike or (far more likely) structural failure by a series of 128 bulkheads that, like the emergency wall here, can slide into place and isolate any area where there's a pressure drop. It's done automatically, of course, but can also be controlled from here.

What I did, in essence, was to tell each bulkhead it was under repair, and should not close under any circumstance. Then I moved the waldo over to the circuits that controlled the city's eight airlocks. With some rather elegant microsurgery, I transferred control of all eight solely to the pressure switch I now hold in my left hand.

It is a negative-pressure button, a dead-man switch taken from a power saw. So long as I hold it down, the inner doors of the airlocks will remain locked. If I let go, they will all iris open. The outer doors are already open, as are the ones that connect the airlock chambers to the suiting-up rooms. No one will be able to make it to a spacesuit in time. Within thirty seconds, every corridor will be a vacuum. People behind airtight doors may choose between slow asphyxiation and explosive decompression.

My initial plan had been to wire the dead-man switch to my pulse, which would free my good hand and allow me to sleep. That will have to wait. The wiring completed, I turned on the intercom and announced that I would speak to the coordinator, and no one else.

When I finally got to talk to him, I told him what I had done and invited him to verify it. That didn't take long. Then I presented my demands:

Surgery to replace the rest of my limbs, of course. The surgery would have to be done while I was conscious (a heartbeat dead-man switch could be subverted by a heart machine) and it would have to be done here, so that I could be assured nobody fooled with my circuit changes.

The doctors were called in, and they objected that such profound surgery couldn't be done under local anesthetic. I knew they were lying, of course; amputation was a fairly routine procedure even before anesthetics were invented. Yes, but I would faint, they said. I told them that I would not, and at any rate I was willing to take the chance and no one else had any choice in the matter.

(I have not yet mentioned that the ultimate totality of my plan involves replacing all my internal organs as well as my limbs—or at least those organs whose failure could cause untimely death. I will be a true cyborg then, a human brain in an "artificial" body, with the prospect of thousands of years of life. With a few decades—or centuries!—of research, I could even do something about the brain's shortcomings. I would wind up interfaced to EarthNet, with all of human knowledge at my disposal, and with my faculties for logic and memory no longer fettered by the slow pace of electrochemical synapse.)

A psychiatrist, talking from earth, tried to convince me of the error of my ways. He said that the dreadful trauma had "obviously" unhinged me, and the cyborg augmentation, far from effecting a cure, had made my mental derangement worse. He demonstrated, at least to his own satisfaction, that my behavior followed some classic pattern or madness. All this had been taken into consideration, he said, and if I were to give myself up, I would be forgiven my crimes and manumitted into the loving arms of the psychiatric establishment.

I did take time to explain the fundamental errors in his way of thinking. He felt I had quite literally lost my identity by losing my face and genitalia, and that I was at bottom a "good" person whose essential humanity had been perverted by physical and existential estrangement. Totally wrong. By his terms, what I actually *am* is an "evil" person whose true nature was revealed to him by the lucky accident that released him from existential propinquity with the common herd.

And "evil" is the accurate word, not maladjusted or amoral or even criminal. I am as evil by human standards as a human is evil by the standards of an animal raised for food, and the analogy is accurate. I will sacrifice humans not only for my survival but for comfort, curiosity, or entertainment. I will allow to live anyone who doesn't bother me, and reward generously those who help,

Now they have only forty minutes. They know I am

—end of recording—

25 September 2058
Excerpt from Summary Report

I am Dr. Henry Janovski, head of the surgical team that worked on the ill-fated cyborg augmentation of Dr. Wilson Cheetham.

We were fortunate that Dr. Cheetham's insanity did interfere with his normally painstaking, precise nature. If he had spent more time in preparation, I have no doubt that he would have put us in a very difficult fix.

He should have realized that the protecting wall that shut him off from the rest of Nearside was made of steel, an excellent conductor of electricity. If he had insulated himself behind a good dielectric, he could have escaped his fate.

Cheetham's waldo was a marvelous instrument, but basically was only a pseudo-intelligent servomechnism that obeyed well-defined radio-frequency commands. All we had to do was override the signals that were coming from his own nervous system.

We hooked a powerful amplifier up to the steel wall, making it in effect a huge radio transmitter. To generate the signal we wanted amplified, I had a technician put on a waldo sleeve that was holding a box similar to Cheethm's dead-man switch. We wired the hand closed, turned up the power, and had the technician strike himself in the chin as hard as he could.

The technician struck himself so hard he blacked out for a few seconds. Cheetham's resonant action, perhaps a hundred times more powerful, drove the bones of his chin up through the top of his skull.

Fortunately, the expensive arm itself was not damaged. It is not evil or insane by itself, of course. Which I shall prove.

The experiments will continue, though of course we will be more selective as to the subjects. It seems in retrospect that we should not use as subjects people who have gone through the kind of trauma Cheetham suffered. We must use willing volunteers. Such as myself.

I am not young, and weakness and an occasional tremor in my hands limit the amount of surgery I can do—much less than my knowledge would allow or my nature desire. My failing left arm I shall have replaced with Cheetham's mechanical marvel, and I will go through the training similar to his—but for the good of humanity, not for ill.

What miracles I will perform with the knife!

Acknowledgments

Thanks to Rachel Silber, for listening to me whine about deadlines and proposing a lovely solution, and to Rob Hill and Kelly J. Cooper for moral support when my brain felt like it was leaking from my eyes. To my agent, Lori Perkins, for never forgetting about this project, and to John Oakes, for "getting it." And to corwin, for being far more than a self-proclaimed "writer support system."

Some of the stories in this book previously appeared elsewhere:

"That Which Does Not Kill Us" by Scott Westerfeld previously appeared in the zine Say . . . Aren't You Dead? and Agog! in Australia.

"The Show" by M. Christian first appeared in The Bachelor Machine (Green Candy Press, 2003).

"More Than the Sum of His Parts" by Joe Haldeman first appeared in Playboy, May 1985.

"Softly, with A Big Stick" by Gavin J. Grant previously appeared in Singularity.

About the Contributors

Steve Berman's work often blends the erotic with the strange. Three times nominated for the Gaylactic Spectrum Award, he has sold queer and weird stories to *Best Gay Erotica 2005*, *Men of Mystery*, and *Skin & Ink*, as well as to the less sordid anthology *The Faery Reel*. More of his stories can be found in his collections, *Trysts* and *Second Thoughts*. Ironically, on the day his story was accepted for this book, news broke of the first facial transplant. Steve plans on hiring a cheap and tawdry lawyer from his native New Jersey to pursue a legal claim against all surgeons involved.

Beth Bernobich's short fiction has appeared, or will appear, in a number of publications, large and small, including *Asimov's Science Fiction*, *Clean Sheets*, *Strange Horizons*, and *The Mammoth Book of Best New Erotica* (vols. 1 and 4). Her obsessions include coffee, curry, and writing about men and women without shirts. She is currently working on a fantasy novel that includes magic, sex, and pirates.

G. Bonhomme is a thorny rose.
G. Bonhomme dreams of a world where all men are sisters.
G. Bonhomme disbelieves in heavier-than-air flight.
G. Bonhomme watches it snow.
G. Bonhomme hopes you are not too totally abandoned.

John Bowker: Though his house does contain a suspicious amount of *Godzilla* memorabilia, John Bowker's interest in the king of monsters is strictly platonic. A graduate of the 2003 Odyssey Writers Workshop, his fiction and food writing have appeared in several magazines including *On Spec, Other,* and *Flashquake.* He lives and writes outside of Boston, Massachusetts.

M. Christian is the author of *The Bachelor Machine* (Green Candy Press, 2003), editor of numerous anthologies (*Speaking Parts, Dirty Words, The Wildest Ones,* among others) and the author of the novel Running Dry (Alyson Publications, January 2006). Keep tabs on him and his many projects at www.mchristian.com.

Paul Di Filippo's work has been described by Bruce Sterling as "ambitious . . . and weirdly visionary." He is the author of *Ciphers, The Steampunk Trilogy,* and *Ribofunk,* and his work has appeared in just about every science fiction magazine there is.

Gavin J. Grant has been published in *Scifiction, Strange Horizons,* and *Monkeybicycle,* among others. He runs Small Beer Press and co-edits (with Kelly Link) the fantasy half of *The Year's Best Fantasy & Horror*

(St. Martin's Press) and *Lady Churchill's Rosebud Wristlet*, a bi-annual zine. He lives in an old farmhouse in Northampton, Massachusetts.

Joe Haldeman sold his first story in 1969, while he was still in the army, post-Vietnam, and has been a constant writer ever since, with a little time off for teaching. He's written about two dozen novels and five collections of short stories and poetry, and appears in about twenty languages, including Klingon, which he suspects will generate letters he won't want to answer. Since 1983, he and his wife Gay have spent the fall semester in Cambridge, Massachusetts, teaching at MIT. He is an associate professor (adjunct) in the Department of Writing and Humanistic Studies. His novels *The Forever War* and *Forever Peace* won both the Nebula and Hugo Awards; *Forever Peace* also won the John W. Campbell Award, the first such "triple crown" since Pohl's *Gateway*, twenty-two years earlier. He's won several other Nebulas and Hugos, and three times the Rhysling Award for science fiction poetry, as well as the World Fantasy Award. His novel *Camouflage* won the James Tiptree Award for gender exploration. His latest novel is *Old Twentieth*.

He also paints and plays guitar, both as a devoted amateur, and bicycles whenever the weather allows. He and his wife recently bicycled across America, 3,050 miles, from Florida to California. When he can, he seeks out dark skies for his 12-inch telescope.

Lynne Jamneck is the author of the Samantha Skellar Mystery series as well as several decidedly naughty stories, featured in a host of erotic anthologies. Her fiction has been featured in speculative markets such as *H. P. Lovecraft's Magazine of Horror* and upcoming anthologies *Spicy Slipstream Stories*, edited by Jay Lake and Nick Mamatas and *So Fey: Queer Faery Fictions*, edited by Steve Berman. A transplanted South African, Lynne currently lives in New Zealand with her partner Heidi. Check for updates on Lynne's blog here: http://publishedwork1lynne.blogspot.com/

Shariann Lewitt is the author of ten novels and forty short stories, almost all hard science fiction. When not writing she makes fused glass and teaches at MIT.

Sarah Micklem is the author of a fantasy novel *Firethorn* that was included in lists of the Best Science Fiction and Fantasy of 2004 by both Borders and Amazon. She has published short stories in *Tri-Quarterly* and *Lady Churchill's Rosebud Wristlet*. She lives in New York and Indiana, where she is working on a sequel to *Firethorn,* teaching fiction, and doing occasional freelance graphic design. The portrait of the book collector is real. Micklem saw the painting in a museum, promptly forgot all the important details, and couldn't track it down again. www.firethorn.info

Elspeth Potter's erotica has appeared in *Best Lesbian Erotica 2001–2004, Best Women's Erotica 2002* and *2005, Best of Best Women's Erotica, Tough Girls*, and the forthcoming *Mammoth Book of Best New Erotica Vol. 5*. She is a member of the Science Fiction and Fantasy Writers of America. The idea for "Poppet" came from the possibility that Paleolithic "Venus" figurines were actually Stone Age porn and from a separate conversation about science fictional ways to compensate for physical handicaps.

Jennifer Stevenson didn't intend to become, like, a sex writer. It's just that everything they're paying her for is the stuff about sex. Look for her 2004 Small Beer Press release *Trash Sex Magic*, about white trash sex magicians, and in November 2006, the first book of her new Del Rey series, *The Brass Bed*, about a con artist, a reluctant incubus, and a fraud investigator for the Chicago Department of Consumer Services. She's also proud of her story for Circlet Press's *Sextopia*, "Something for Everyone," about using Jewish sex magic to power commercial airlines between Mercury and Saturn. www.jennifer-stevenson.com

Cecilia Tan is a writer, editor, and publisher. She founded Circlet Press, Inc. in 1992 to publish work that combined science fiction with erotica. Through Circlet she has edited over forty anthologies of sf/f, while also publishing her own erotic science fiction in such varied places as *Ms. Magazine, Penthouse, Asimov's,* and *Nerve,* not to mention *Best American Erotica* and oodles of other anthologies. www.ceciliatan.com

Scott Westerfeld is best known for his *Midnighters* and *Uglies* young adult series. His latest novel is *Peeps,* a tale of vampires and parasites. He splits his time between New York and Sydney.